The Town with No Roads

Joe Siple

Black Rose Writing | Texas

The final approval for this literary material is granted by the author.

Third printing

This is a work of fiction. Names, characters, businesses, places, events and incidents are either the products of the author's imagination or used in a fictitious manner. Any resemblance to actual persons, living or dead, or actual events is purely coincidental.

ISBN: 978-1-68433-170-3
PUBLISHED BY BLACK ROSE WRITING
www.blackrosewriting.com

Printed in the United States of America
Suggested Retail Price (SRP) $18.95

The Town with No Roads is printed in Palatino Linotype

For my daughters, Maya and Lily.
Living examples of Loving Kindness.

The Town with No Roads

Day One

Jamison

Everyone has a story to tell.

That truth has bound humanity together for ages. From the caveman who discovered fire to the toddler who fell off the Monkey Bars, every person who has lived could say those magical words: "Guess what happened?"

And that was where Jamison Hightower fit in. He told people's stories.

Some people said his stories didn't matter. Actually, most people said his stories didn't matter. They thought the important part of the news was at the top of the show. The latest cheaters on Wall Street or the murder on the corner of 7th and Fairfax. Or even the weather—as if the chance of rain was somehow more important than stories of humanity.

They mocked his assignments. Called them "fluff" and "kickers." Half the time Chance Browner intentionally went over his allotted four minutes just so he could point out yet again that people care more about the Twins-Yankees game than about Mrs. Hutchinson's fund raiser over at St. Francis Elementary.

"People thank me every day for cutting into your time," Browner had said last week. "No one cares what you have to say."

And it was probably true. But it didn't change the fact that someone needed to say it. At least that's the way Jamison Hightower saw things.

Which was why he stood in three inches of mud in front of Farmer Holliday's 80-acres of corn and soybeans, trying to ignore the raindrop that dripped from his NBC baseball hat and wove its way down his neck, tickling like crazy. Because Farmer Holliday—which was exactly how he had introduced himself, Jamison had no idea of his first name—

looked like he had just won the lottery. Eyes smiling between weathered cheeks and furry eyebrows. Burly chest stuck out proudly.

And the truth was, Jamison loved him for it. If hosting a small-market television reporter in his corn field for a piece of "fluff" was going to be the story he told his grandchildren on his deathbed, well, God bless him. Tell away, Farmer Holliday.

"We're live in one minute."

It was J.D.'s voice from behind the camera. A routine, although unnecessary, warning. Jamison had Master Control piped into his earpiece and J.D. obviously knew when they'd be on camera. But J.D. liked to see the reaction from the little crowds that gathered every time they did a live-shot. Not that Jamison could blame him. Based on the murmur of excitement that rippled through the gathering, they could have been watching Tom Brokaw.

Jamison knew this much—he was no Tom Brokaw.

"Twenty seconds," J.D. said.

"I think I'm going to faint." Farmer Holliday put one of his giant paws against his granite stomach and groaned.

Jamison rested his hand on Farmer Holliday's shoulder. It was thick and rippled beneath his sweaty tee-shirt. The shoulder of a man who tossed bales of hay like most people toss the newspaper onto the breakfast table. "Don't worry," Jamison said. "I'll take care of everything, I promise."

"Nope," Farmer Holliday said. "Ain't going to faint. About to puke."

Normally, that would be on the short list of things Jamison would address. But just then J.D. pointed to him and the red light on the camera started flashing. There wasn't much Jamison could do but hope the man next to him had a stomach as strong as his deltoid.

"I'm Jamison Hightower, live in rural Olmsted County, where the farmland behind me may look ordinary, but inside grows a kernel of wonder. Actually, make that 157 kernels. Because one ear of corn in Farmer Holliday's 80 acres has grown with bright—some might even say neon—orange kernels."

Jamison pictured Chance Browner in the sports office, incredulous.

This was why he couldn't have an extra two minutes for his sportscast? Well, yes. Jamison never said everyone's story would be worthy of the Silver Screen, just that they deserved to be told.

Jamison put his hand on Farmer Holliday's back and pulled him close, then gave him a quick wink, as if the farmer's nerves were a little secret between the two of them. "Farmer Holliday joins me now, and sir, when did you discover this unprecedented ear of corn?"

Farmer Holliday stood there, wide-eyed and looking like his vomit prediction was about to come true. If something were to come out of his mouth, Jamison was pretty sure it wasn't going to be words. It wasn't uncommon. Jamison had been there before. The time for open-ended questions had passed.

"I mean to say, did you just discover it recently?"

Jamison was relieved for the big farmer when he blinked and mumbled, "Yes."

Jamison had been doing the same job for nine years—since he graduated from J-school—so he knew from experience that he should count his blessings to have gotten that much out of him. Time to wrap it up.

"Amazing," Jamison said, and then turned back to the camera, nonverbally dismissing Farmer Holliday—although the big man continued to stand there, his eyes bulging like aliens were conducting experiments on his brain. Jamison looked back into the camera, hoping J.D. was smart enough to zoom in until he was the only one on-screen.

"Farmer Holliday says he has no plans for the piece of corn, but if the National Academy of Science wants to purchase it for research, or Green Giant wants to buy the rights for advertising, Farmer Holliday says he is 'all ears.'"

Jamison fought a cringe. No one was going to confuse that with Tom Brokaw.

He gave his signature move—the one he had done since his very first live-shot as a twenty-two year-old newbie. A bounce of his left eyebrow, followed by a quick wink. Kind of ridiculous, he realized. But it had become a calling card, of sorts.

"Reporting live, I'm Jamison Hightower, KTRP News."

Behind the camera, J.D. held up his hand for everyone to remain still. "And we're clear," he said a moment later. The small, elderly crowd immediately swarmed Farmer Holliday. They slapped his back and shook his hand. Farmer Holliday basked in his newfound fame. On a job well done.

An old lady with a walker picked her way through the mud. Her slickers were soaked and the wind whipped a few strands of white hair into her eyes. She set the legs of the walker three inches deep into the mud and took his elbow with bony fingers. "You're a powerful man, Jamison Hightower," she said.

Jamison followed her gaze to Farmer Holliday, whose chest was sticking out, rocky shoulders set back, and Jamison realized this was why he did his job.

"When are you coming back, sonny?" the old woman asked. "I got a raspberry patch over yonder that's taking over my pumpkins. Now there's a story for your newspaper station."

"Well ma'am, I'd love to come back," Jamison said. "But I'm not sure my boss will let me."

"Oh? Why not?"

He leaned in conspiratorially and water gushed from the brim of his cap. "Just between you and me, he's a bit of an idiot."

The woman roared a laugh and wandered off, but then Jamison noticed J.D. press his hands against his earphones and lunge toward switches in the live-truck. Jamison thought back on his last words and kicked himself for being so stupid. He knew what was coming before he even heard the words.

"Jamison," J.D. said, stifling a laugh. "You're not going to believe it, man. Your mike was still live."

•   •   •   •   •

To get on a boss' bad side, it turned out all you had to do was this: Gather a group of, say, two hundred-thousand people, from all socio-economic classes, all professions, several ethnicities. Then, in a strong, clear voice that every one of them can hear, call your boss an idiot.

Then chuckle a little bit, just to really rub it in.

Needless to say, Jamison's boss, Thomas Harris III, wasn't exactly pleased. Then again, he was never pleased with Jamison, which was why he sent him out on the most worthless stories. If Harris ever discovered Jamison didn't consider it punishment, he'd surely stop. Make him cover a high profile murder investigation or something.

But Harris was really upset about the "idiot" fiasco. As soon as Jamison had returned to the station, Harris' temples had begun throbbing and he got warmed up by firing J.D. on the spot. Somehow, Jamison had been able to talk him down from that. After all, Jamison had said, technical problems happen. It wasn't J.D.'s fault Jamison had made a bad decision.

So Harris had turned his fury to Jamison. *You're fired!* had surely been on the tip of his tongue when he had stopped suddenly. A blank expression had covered his face for a moment, as if remembering something. Then he had banished Jamison to a small town on the fringe of the market, where he'd been trying, unsuccessfully, to sell advertising for months. Some silly story about a girl receiving messages from her comatose father. Typical fluff.

Jamison couldn't wait.

He was so happy to still have a job it didn't matter that it was a rainy Saturday…and he had to take his own car…and he wouldn't have a photographer. He was all over this assignment.

His '86 Chevy Nova didn't roll down the road as much as it hydroplaned if there was the faintest sheen of mist. New tires didn't make a lick of difference. It was as if it had been engineered by the 1980 Miracle on Ice team. Rust dimmed the headlights and there was a dime-sized hole in the floor by the gas pedal—with each puddle he hit, everything below his waist was soaked with Round-Up infused rainwater.

But through streaks on the driver's-side window, the sun shimmered on the horizon, igniting the sky in red, purple and orange. Jamison wondered how someone ten miles away could be enjoying such a dazzling view while he was rained on inside his car.

He skidded by corn fields, each row marked by little signs. Garst.

Monsanto. Syngenta. Soon he reached a plunge leading to a valley and suddenly, everything changed. It was like moving from one news story to the next, where the entire scene shifted to a new city, or country, or even a new world, all in the milli-second it took to flash from one screen to another.

There was a little town below. A row of thatched-roof shops faded into neighborhoods of modest cottages. A river meandered through and ended in a waterfall, which splashed into a lake twice the size of the entire town.

But from Jamison's eagle-eye view, one thing was noticeably absent. He couldn't see a single road of any kind in the entire town of Sparkling Pond. As he approached, the highway made an abrupt curve and swung him away from the town, so he pulled his right-side tires onto the grassy shoulder, threw the bobsled-car into park, and went to explore.

In the middle of a footpath at the edge of town stood a statue of a man in a fisherman's hat, carrying a bucket of trout, which spouted water from their mouths into a pool below. An inscription read, *Hank Lyons welcomes you to Sparkling Pond.*

And then Jamison heard a sound that melted his heart without even knowing exactly what it was or where it originated. Sniffling. Not cold-symptom sniffles, but crying sniffles. He wandered around to the back side of the fountain and there, wiping a tear from her perfectly rounded cheek, was a girl, maybe eight years-old. Jamison couldn't help but wonder what made her story such a sad one.

He tried to approach softly, making just enough noise for her to hear his footsteps, but not so much that he scared her. Still, she startled when he got within a few steps.

Jamison understood perfectly well that he had a complex of sorts, where he thought he could solve everyone's problems if they just poured their soul out to him. If they shared all of their story with him. He knew that wasn't how it worked—spill your secrets to a stranger and your problems were solved. But he didn't feel like a stranger to this girl. He felt like another human being with problems of his own and a free ear for listening. Nothing more, nothing less.

"Want to play hide-and-seek?" the girl asked, swiping at a tear.

It took Jamison a second to get over the surprise of this girl he'd never met speaking to him, but in that second he realized that yes, actually, he did want to play hide-and-seek. In fact, he wanted to play hide-and-seek more than just about any other thing. The kid looked like she could use a little distraction.

"Cover your eyes and count to ten," she said. "Ten-*Mississippi*. Tanner Miller counts to ten-Maine, but that's cheating."

"Ten-Mississippi by twos, got it."

Her eyes bulged like she'd never heard of such treason. "Kidding!" Jamison said. "Ten-Mississippi by ones."

"And no peeking."

Now she had him pegged for a cheater—someone she had to keep a close eye on. Jamison did cover his eyes, he didn't peek, and strangely, the world immediately came to life. Birds he hadn't known were there chirped from nearby trees, singing a duet with the fountain. Rose pollen seemed inches from his nose. Even the rough marble of the bench that circled the statue felt more real. More solid. As if losing his sense of sight made him see the world more clearly.

It reminded him of a story he'd once done on a blind man who'd learned to run marathons with the assistance of his ears and in some cases even his nose, but without the help of a guide. The man had been so touched by the news coverage, he'd asked Jamison to "watch" the story with him. Jamison would never forget the ear-to-ear grin as the man heard things on the video that Jamison surely would never catch.

"Eight-Mississippi, nine-Mississippi, ten-Mississippi. Ready or not, here I come," Jamison yelled out. He hoped that was what kids yelled when they reached ten-Mississippi. There had been a serious lack of hide-and-seek in his own childhood.

They were in a wide-open area in which the only possible place to be hidden from plain sight was the other side of the fountain. Kind of anticlimactic, actually. By five-Mississippi Jamison had been looking forward to scouring hidden nooks and crannies.

He wandered to the other side of the fountain but she wasn't there. He ran around the fountain because the only thing she could have been doing was sliding along the circular bench, keeping the statue as a curtain between them. But unless that little girl was the fastest third-grader in Minnesota, she wasn't pulling the run-around-in-circles trick.

Jamison was seriously stumped—and actually becoming a bit worried. There was nowhere else she could have gone. An answer came as a gasp for breath and a quick splash. Jamison went to the edge of the fountain and peered down into the shimmering surface.

Sure enough, the girl was gliding in a pool that quadrupled in size beneath the statue. She stretched her arms over her head, cut through the water like a dolphin, and pulled herself forward in a breaststroke. She was like a mermaid under the ripples, drifting easily, her hair flowing behind her in wisps. Then she popped to the surface and shook droplets from her hair.

"Are you sure you didn't peek?" she asked.

"Who do I look like, Tanner Miller?"

She looked at him skeptically for a moment, then hopped out of the fountain. It made Jamison feel good that she seemed to have forgotten whatever was making her cry.

"What's your name?" she asked.

Jamison hesitated, because that was a more difficult question than she realized. She flashed a crooked smile, like he was either crazy or just plain stupid.

"Sorry," she said. "I didn't mean to confuse you." The tone of her sarcasm was a bit off, as if she was still trying to figure out how it worked. But to Jamison, it just made her sound even sweeter.

"I forgive you," he said. "But ease up on the tough questions, okay?" After she hopped out of the fountain, he extended his hand and she took it, pulling her shoulders back as if to look very formal. "I've figured it out. My name is Jamison and it's a pleasure to meet you." And suddenly, unexpectedly, he was having a conversation with an eight-year-old girl. Apparently, there's a first time for everything.

"What are you doing here?" she asked.

"I'm here to do a story for the news."

"Well that's interesting, don't you think?"

"I suppose so. Actually, I'm pretty lucky. I do stories like this all the time."

She snapped her fingers and cringed. "Rats for you. After all, variety is the mac-and-cheese of life."

Jamison tried not to laugh out loud, but the kid seemed to think she was thirty years-old, and yet..."Mac-and-cheese?"

Her face scrunched up like the fact that he wasn't smart enough to understand was physically painful for her. "Well yeah. I'm a kid. I literally hate spices."

He tried to figure out if it was a joke, and she took his silence as more proof of his ignorance.

"Get this Jamison," she said, trying a different track. "Two fish swim into a concrete wall. Then one turns to the other and says, 'Dam!'" She slapped her knee, doubled over, and belly-laughed. "You thought I swore, didn't you?"

"I have to admit, I was about to go tell your mom." Jamison remembered why he was there and a thought hit him. "Hey, is your name Aspen?"

Without a word, she began skipping through lush, green grass toward town. "Hey, wait!" Jamison said. "Where are you going?"

But she was already gone. In P.E. class, she probably ran the mile in a skip, and left all the boys in the dust. Jamison didn't have a prayer. But he jogged through the grassy walkways, where roads and sidewalks should have been, and tried to keep her in sight.

•   •   •   •   •

It turned out Jamison's difficulty finding a road wasn't his fault. The further he walked, the more obvious it became—the town had no roads. Not a main drag or a side street. Blacktop, gravel, dirt. Nothing. Well, nothing but wide expanses of plush grass and colorful wildflowers that extended all the way to the town square—which was packed with a surprising number of people for a town so small. Where a main road should have been, the river gurgled gently to the lake.

Jamison took his eye off the girl for a moment and spun a circle, feeling like Julie Andrews on a mountaintop. Which wasn't a comparison he would make in front of Chance Browner at the TV station. But he couldn't believe it. No cars? No trucks? No exhaust? He had stumbled upon paradise, two hours away from where he had spent his entire life.

Since he was trying to keep up with the fastest skipper this side of the continental divide, Jamison forced himself past the tempting scent of open-flame rotisserie chicken at The Bent Spoon and the heavy perfume emanating from Auntie Anne's Antiques and Collectibles. He couldn't help but peek into Rad Collie's Dangling Cliff Adventures, where a long-haired man with a graying beard was gesturing with his entire body toward an uncomfortable looking customer.

"So we cut the top-rope and free-climbed it. Epic, dude. Utterly epic."

Jamison left the voice behind because he had just spotted the girl, heading toward the lake. He jogged past small cottages grouped into little neighborhoods and caught a glimpse of a group of kids playing "Duck-Duck-Gray Duck" under a cloud of shrieks and giggles.

He finally caught up with the girl at the lake's edge, wiped a stream of sweat from his brow, and looked at the girl next to him as if she were super-human. She wasn't even breathing heard. Did she have no idea how fast she'd been skipping?

"Oh, I know," she said, grabbing his hand. "Follow me."

And off they went again, Jamison and the Skipping Queen.

Aspen

Aspen's hair flowed behind her as she wound through the hallways of Sparkling Pond Hospital on the WEB Train. She pushed a button by her knees and the train eased to a stop at the nurses' station, where Tammy Wellington looked up from her computer.

"Had enough riding for one day?" Tammy said with a knowing smile.

"Never," Aspen said. "But…things to do, people to see, right?"

"See you tomorrow. And don't worry." Tammy shot both hands up and stopped Aspen before she could ask. "We won't wake him without you."

"Thanks," Aspen said. She had been told as much during the daily 5pm Physician's Team Meeting but still, you could never be too careful. Aspen pushed another button by her knees and the train slid forward. She waved as the train rounded a corner and sped off.

It was no exaggeration to say she couldn't get enough of the train. Of all the hospital's wonderful features, surely it was the best. A comfortable, wheelchair-accessible train that took patients and visitors anywhere in the building. The hospital's few elevators sat mostly unused, except for the rare emergency when a nurse rushed a stretcher to the upper floors. But the WEB Train—short for Well-Being Through Rides and Interactive Navigation—was constantly full, emitting puffs of music of the passenger's choosing in place of smoke.

Aspen hopped off at the main entrance and an elderly woman, apparently seeing the train for the first time, tentatively reached for the hand rail. She stared at the small step for a moment before her foot slowly inched upward, barely creating space between her shoe sole and the ground.

Aspen tried to convince herself she hadn't seen. She took several steps away from the train, then cursed under her breath and ran back to the WEB.

"Excuse me," Aspen said. "Would you like a hand? I've been telling the hospital for years they made these steps far too high." It was a blatant lie, but the woman's face relaxed into a smile. She leaned against Aspen with a surprising amount of weight and lifted her foot ever so slowly, the heel of her shoes barely clearing the top of the step.

Aspen made sure the woman was safely aboard, then turned to leave while she had the chance. "I never have gotten used to being old," the woman said. It was the kind of care-free voice that suggested she was preparing for a long conversation.

"Well," Aspen said, giving in, "I hope I look as good as you when I'm sixty."

The woman's face lit up as she said, "Sixty? I'll be eighty-seven next week!"

"Is that right? I guess you just proved my point then, didn't you?"

The woman's posture straightened, her chin lifted, and her eyes gleamed behind off-center contact lenses. Aspen really needed to get going—or get back to her father's bedside, one or the other—but she forced herself to sit next to the woman. "Who's your favorite singer, ma'am?" she asked.

"Maxene Andrews. Who else?"

"The Andrews Sisters," Aspen said as she scrolled through the "A's." She selected "Don't Sit Under the Apple Tree" and the woman slapped her hands together in delight. Aspen was about to hop off when she noticed the woman staring blankly at the touch-screen consul. "You just choose the floor you want and press it with your finger," Aspen explained.

"Well, I want the third floor, but I'm not sure if I understand how…"

"No problem." Aspen made selection for her and said, "That should get you there. Have a great day."

"Oh, you're a dear," the woman said. The Andrews Sisters began crooning from the boxcar as the train puffed smokelessly away. A crackly voice joined the Sisters drifting from the train, "*I wrote my mother, I wrote my father…*"

A familiar pit in Aspen's stomach scolded her for not staying by her father's bed. But at least he had Rufus with him. She knew it was crazy, but it was reassuring to know the old dog would be there while she was gone. *Slobber,* June 2, age 27. That had been her journal entry on her father's fourth day in the hospital.

She gave the growing crowd at the town square a wide berth and headed for the cemetery. She needed some peace before dealing with the crowds again. But at the gates of the cemetery, she saw Little Holly Torrey skipping toward her, holding the hand of a man Aspen had never seen before. She strode to meet them, the man's embarrassed grin becoming clear around his square jaw.

Jamison

This, Jamison realized, was a sure-fire way to feel uncomfortable: Hold hands with a young girl you've just met while an attractive woman—who likely knows the girl, and knows that you *don't* know the girl—asks unanswerable questions with her beautiful, fern-colored eyes. But what was he supposed to do when the kid grabbed his hand and clutched it like long, lost treasure?

"Hey kiddo," the woman said, leaning to the girl's level and ignoring Jamison's presence. "Do your DeDe and Papa know where you are?" When the girl shook her head the woman said, "Better go find them, okay?"

"But I want to play with my new friend," the girl said. "We literally just met." She squeezed Jamison's hand and he was surprised to realize the awkwardness was gone, replaced by a fondness for his new "friend."

The woman was obviously flustered, and Jamison couldn't blame her. If the situation was reversed, he wasn't sure if he'd call the cops or ask if he could play too. Jamison took a knee so he was level with the girl's eyes, then set a hand on her shoulder.

"How about this," he said. "Before I leave town, we'll go back to that fountain and play another round of hide-and-seek, okay? This time, I hide."

Her lower lip stuck out and Jamison could swear her bottom eyelids drooped. And Jamison thought she had skipping skills. The kid had better puppy-dog-eyes than a basset hound.

Finally, she nodded her head reluctantly and skipped in the direction of the cottages. Good thing, too, Jamison thought. After a few seconds of that look, he was about to start begging her to play hide-and-seek with him right away.

"Cute kid," he said to the woman, who was still giving him a sideways glance. As if seeing him through her peripheral vision would give her an advantage if he attacked.

"She lost her parents a few years back and her grandparents have been raising her ever since. Although the whole town looks after her. It takes a village, right?"

Jamison watched the girl disappear into the shadows and suddenly wished he was still holding her hand. "Sounds like it would be hard for her."

"She's a pretty resilient kid."

"Her name doesn't happen to be Aspen, does it?"

The woman's green eyes flashed. "No, it's Holly. Why do you ask?"

"Well, I'm supposed to find a little girl named Aspen who has some pretty crazy ideas, and that kid seemed to fit the bill."

"Fit the bill?"

"You know. A little starry-eyed. Maybe a bit gullible."

"Interesting," the woman said. The perfect symmetry of her eyes squinted and her brow furrowed. "You're not from a small town, are you?"

"Not really. Why?"

"Because in a small town, everybody knows everybody. So while saying something like that about a little kid might fly off into the ether of a big city, around here, it makes the rounds until some gossipy old lady decides she should make a big deal out of it. Pretty soon you have an all-out scandal on your hands."

"But you're not a gossipy old lady, are you?"

"Nope," she said. "Just your average Sparkling Pond twenty-something." She reached out her hand to shake his. "It's nice to meet you. I'm Aspen Collins."

Jamison smacked his forehead, which hurt more than he had thought it would and made him wince. But fortunately, the woman was laughing at him. Beautiful, sweet bubbles of laughter. Or maybe that was unfortunate. Jamison was a bit of a mess at the moment, he realized.

"Come on," Aspen said. "I'll buy you a cup of coffee."

•   •   •   •   •

Coffee shops were some of Jamison's favorite places in the world. Not for the coffee, although he had acquired the taste. But given the turbulence of his childhood, it was the steadiness, the sense of community, the smell. It didn't matter if he had been to a Starbucks or the local "ma and pop" shop, his clothes smelled the same when he left. That mix of espresso and roasted coffee beans that followed him the rest of the day, saying to everyone he passed by, "Yes, I was at a coffee shop today. I read a book or talked to a friend or listened to a man with his guitar. It has been a good day."

Sparkling Pond had only one coffee shop—the aptly named Squinting Café. With a southern exposure, walls made mostly of glass, and a sharp glare off the lake, patrons either donned sunglasses or squinted so they looked like they were just in a fist-fight, their eyes swollen half-shut.

The owner apparently had a thing for the sun because everywhere Jamison looked was a replica—from the art on the walls to the names of the drinks, even an enormous, yellow play-dough ball—created by the town's kids and cooked in a kiln, according to a small label.

"What's that all about?" Jamison asked Aspen as they passed a hospital chair with a man sprawled in it, as if awaiting surgery.

"The Vitamin D Recliner," Aspen said. "For $10 an hour, you can lay back, open the window, and bask in the sun until you're crispy red. No coffee purchase necessary."

Jamison noticed a placard next to the chair. Under the title of the State Health Department was a message--

This feature has been deemed illegal due to the encouragement of excess exposure to ultraviolet rays without the presence of readily available, high SPF sunblock. Violators will be prosecuted.

--But in addition to the middle-aged man lounging in the recliner, a three-person line snaked behind the chair.

And then there was the music. Deafening rock and roll that might be expected in an old-time record shop. The volume increased as they approached the counter.

"What can I get you, darling?" yelled a woman with a badge that read "Crystal Lux—Owner." Her hair went to her waist and varied from green to purple, depending on how the sunlight touched it. But Jamison was pretty certain its natural color was gray.

"What do you recommend?" Jamison yelled back.

"What's that, sweetie? It's a little loud in here. The Grateful Dead is playing 'High Time'. Day two, act five, fourth song. They only played five, you know."

Being a journalist, Jamison liked to think he had a decent handle how conversations go. But the woman's words went so far over his head, it might as well have been Swahili.

Aspen tiptoed near his ear, setting flight to a swarm of butterflies in his stomach. She yelled, "She's talking about Woodstock. I think she's part encyclopedia."

"Aspen Collins?" Crystal said. "What are you doing out in the land of the living?"

Aspen kneaded at the hem of her dress and studied the fabric. "I probably shouldn't be."

"What's that, sweetie? Can't hear you. The music's too loud."

Jamison realized from Aspen's continued fidgeting that there was a story there. Life was pretty straight-forward, he'd found. Any time questions started to seem cryptic and answers didn't make much sense, there was definitely a story worth discovering that would explain it all.

Like the twenty year-old man from Lanesboro whose story Jamison had covered two years before. The man hadn't spoken a word for ten full years. Speculation about the reason for his silence ranged from severe depression to post-traumatic stress to a mysterious and unexplained physical ailment. Jamison had arrived on the ten year anniversary to tell the story and everyone was shocked when, in the middle of the live-shot, the man's watch alarm went off and he explained—as if he'd never taken a break from speaking—that he was simply winning a bet with his younger brother, who had "double-dog dared" him to shut up for a decade. He then strode into the small audience, collected his ten dollars from his brother, and walked away. Talking to himself the whole time.

But the middle of a deafening café wasn't the place to learn more about Aspen's story, and Aspen was back to being obsessed with the hem of her dress, so Jamison tried to bail her out. "She was just telling me I should try the Campfire Roast," he said. "Actually, make that two."

"Coming right up. Oooh," Crystal said in a brief moment of peace between songs. "Turn on your Lovelight is next."

Crystal handed them each a mug-full of coffee and bounced away, nodding her head as if Jimmy Hendricks was hammering out a guitar solo in her mind. Aspen made a bee-line for a corner booth without any nearby speakers, and Jamison followed, appreciating the relative quiet.

"So," Aspen said. She sipped her drink, then folded her hands. "You know me, but I'm out of the loop here. What's your name?"

Jamison chuckled. "You're kidding, right?" As soon as he said it, he knew it had come out wrong. He might as well have said, *I'm kind of a big deal.*

"About what?" she asked.

"About who I am." Inside, Jamison screamed at himself not to, but he couldn't help it. He eyebrow-bounce-and-winked her. "Jamison Hightower. KTRP-TV."

Aspen looked at him like she was trying to decide if he was joking or pathetic. Even Jamison knew it had to be one of the two. Who does that anyway? Certainly not him. Not anymore.

The truth, he had to admit, was that he used to be a cocky, egotistical twenty-two year-old who found that when he did his eyebrow-bounce-and-wink, girls swooned, viewers cheered, and everyone saw him as a star. But somewhere along the line, he had realized the cockiness was a mask and the bounce-and-wink wasn't him. Now he was like an old rock star who'd matured beyond the music of his early years and yet, every time he toured, the fans wanted the old stuff. They demanded his youth, even though he couldn't even recognize it.

Apparently, Aspen wasn't one of the fans demanding his old hits. The edges of her shoulders dipped and she said, "Oh. Well, it' nice to meet you."

Her tone left no doubt about her disappointment. Jamison realized it was time to change the subject. He pointed to the faded notebook with the frayed cover that was sandwiched under her hand like she was afraid the wind would blow it away. "What do you have there?"

Aspen's fingertips turned white around the edges of the notebook, but she cracked an embarrassed half-smile. "Nothing. Just my daily word journal."

"What's a word journal?"

Jamison tried not to stare at her exposed collarbone when she gave a little shrug. "I figured if I had a real journal, I wouldn't stick with it. So every day, I just write one word or phrase—whatever best explains that day. If I open to any page and read it, it takes me right back to that day, to the moment I wrote it."

"How long have you kept it?"

Aspen seemed to count in her mind. "Since April 13th, when I was five."

"Wait, you know the exact day? What happened?"

"My parents bought me a dog. I wanted to remember the day forever, so I started my word journal."

"So let me guess, the first word in there is 'dog'."

She seemed to consider it for a moment, then slid the notebook across the table and looked away.

Jamison opened to the first page and read the first word, written in child-like scrawl. *Joy.* He scanned the page, reading more simple words. *Popsicle. Fishing. Sunshine.* He flipped a thick chunk of pages and the words had a new feel. *Self-conscious. Cute. Basketball.* Several pages later, *aromatherapy, medicine,* and *integral.* When he leafed toward the end, the last several pages were covered with only a few words, repeated. *Wake up. Wake! Please, wake up.*

"Those get a little personal," she said, covering the pages with her hand and sliding the journal back to her side of the table.

Jamison shuffled in his seat, having a hard time finding a comfortable position. He had to force his eyes off of Aspen before he started giving off the creepy vibe. "I have to admit, this is the most unique town I've ever visited," he said, turning his gaze out the window. "How have I never heard of it?"

Aspen reached back and tightened her pony tail with a quick tug. Her eyes reflected a touch of turquoise in the fading sunlight. "I guess secrecy is in our history. The way I heard it, the town was founded by walleye fishermen who used to float the river. One day, a family a beavers started building a dam downstream. The fishermen had to make a decision—stop the beavers because they didn't know how a dam would affect the fishing, or live and let live.

"I guess these guys were kind of crunchy. Granola before Granola was cool, you know? So they decided they'd let the beavers be beavers and see what happened. Turns out the dam created the perfect spawning grounds for walleye. It started as a pond—hence the town's name—but the beavers kept working and water kept backing up until the entire lake was formed."

"And the whole town with no roads thing?" Jamison asked.

"Same fishermen, lounging at their fishing hole, they say. I happen to think it's the best idea in the world."

"So there really are no roads anywhere in town? No cars at all?"

"Well, that's what we like to say." Aspen draped her elbow over the back of her chair and sipped her coffee. "Truth is, if you walk about a quarter mile out of town, kind of northeast through the neighborhoods, you come to a big parking lot."

She motioned out the window with her coffee mug, but Jamison could only see darkening forest. "Almost everyone in town has a car there," she said. "Stores get supplies delivered there and cart them into town. It's a bumpy drive, but it meets up with County Road 7. You just have to go about a mile through corn fields. But enough of that. If you're from a TV station and you've been looking for me, my guess is you're not here to talk about the town."

"Busted," Jamison said. "So what *is* the story with your dad? I hear he sent you something, but he's in a coma?"

He had tried to keep his tone neutral, but apparently it hadn't worked. "You don't believe it," Aspen said.

Jamison shrugged it off. "I guess it just sounds like a tall tale."

"Look, I know this whole thing is ridiculous. I may live in a place completely cut off from the rest of the world, but I haven't always been here. I went to college, and to medical school. I know this isn't possible. But that doesn't change the fact that what's happening here is a miracle."

And there it was. She used the word. The one word that can take all credibility and flush it right down the toilet. *Miracle.* Jamison wanted to tell her she needed to wake up, but he actually did have to do a live-shot on this story the next day at noon. So instead he said, "You and your dad are pretty close, I take it?"

She stared like she wasn't done scolding him, but then her attack-pose relaxed.

"What can I say? I have the perfect father."

"Perfect?" Jamison said.

"Yeah, perfect. I seriously can't remember him ever doing anything wrong."

The opening chords of a new Grateful Dead song covered Jamison's discomfort. Hearing something like that, it was hard not to compare his own father. Or lack thereof. "Where did it happen?" he said. "The, ah, miracle I mean."

"The playground in the town square."

"Why there?"

"My dad used to take me there after church when my mom ran errands. It was our one-on-one time."

"Who do you think put it there?"

"What do you mean?"

Jamison struggled for something tactful to say, but came up empty.

"Oh, I see," Aspen said. "You hear me say a miracle is happening and you immediately assume I'm a back-woods hick so ignorant she'll believe anything."

"That's not what I meant. I mean it wasn't supposed to come off like—"

"You made it perfectly clear what you meant."

Crystal Lux appeared at the table, without a trace of tension radar, and slapped a napkin down right in front of Jamison. "Can I have your autograph? I'm a huge fan." She blushed and Jamison was afraid he knew what was coming. "And the eyebrow thing?" she added.

Yep. That was it.

He scribbled his name quickly just to get it over with, and hoped it didn't come off as arrogant. Then, feeling as stuck as he could possibly be, he tried to shield his face from Aspen while he did a quick bounce-

and-wink toward Crystal. Crystal squealed and swayed back toward the cash register.

Aspen stood and ironed her dress with her hands. "Again, it was a pleasure to meet you. I'm sorry I wasn't more helpful."

Just as she extended her hand for a final farewell, an enormous explosion of shouts burst through the open café windows. Aspen's eyes flicked to the town square, where the noise had originated.

"Oh my gosh," she said. "It's happened again." She looked straight at Jamison, and just before she darted out the door, she said, "It's another miracle."

Aspen

Aspen sprinted from the café and headed straight for the town square. Another miracle! She had expected her father to speak to her again, but part of her could hardly believe it was really happening.

The possibilities of what word she would put in her journal were endless. *Elation. Hope. Alive.*

When she reached the playground, a woman in a tee-shirt that read "Team God" was waiting for her. Aspen had never seen her before, which meant she surely wasn't from town. The woman held a stuffed animal and an envelope in front of her, as if offering communion. Aspen reached for them gently, cradling the stuffed animal in her arms and treating the envelope like an ancient piece of parchment.

She studied the stuffed animal—a gray duck with a bright orange beak and bright orange feet. She waited for some sense of recognition to sweep over her, but nothing came. She searched her mind for meaning, but there was none.

Her confusion made her even more anxious to read the letter. Surely, it would explain everything. She eased the envelope open, removed a piece of paper, and unfolded it.

What she saw only increased the cloudiness in her mind. Instead of her father's familiar handwriting there were giant letters, scrawled in crayon, covering the entire page.

This is sacrilegious.

When Aspen looked up from the note, the woman who had given it to her was staring at her. Her words came out thin, through a small, bitter smile.

"Only God can work miracles," the woman said. Then she lifted her chin and spoke loud enough for everyone in the town square to hear. "And God doesn't work through ghosts."

A mass of people behind her, all wearing Team God shirts, began to chant something low and ominous that sounded like it belonged at a ceremony of sacrifice. Aspen shuttered when she realized she was their lamb.

She wanted to scream at them. To demand to know why they would be so cruel. Why they thought they knew how God would choose to work. But in the end, no matter how hard she tried not to give them the satisfaction, she broke down and wept in front of them.

When she turned to go home, things got even worse. At the edge of the playground, the reporter, Jamison, was watching the entire thing. She hated the way he looked at her. The crinkle between his eyebrows. The slight tilt of his head. She suddenly knew what word she would put in her journal—*pity.*

She threw the stuffed duck and the letter to the ground, ran past Jamison without looking at him, and didn't stop running until she was safely in her own home.

• • • • •

Sparkling Pond was no stranger to the occasional stray cat. Growing up, Aspen remembered a different one showing up every few months. They were all the same. Different colors and sizes, but she could see the ribs poking out of each one, the mangy fur that wouldn't stay down no matter how hard they licked it.

Her parents had told her to ignore them, they would leave as soon as they realized there was no food. Aspen didn't listen—couldn't listen. One cat in particular, with tabby stripes and wide, pleading eyes—was too cute to ignore. So she snuck it into her room, where she secretly fed it, cleaned up after it, and tried to love it.

Over the course of two days, it destroyed her room. She was left with slashed curtains, carpets smelling of cat urine, and scratch marks up and down her arms. In the end, she couldn't wait to let it return to the woods outside town, where it, too, would be happier.

Her dad explained that stray cats don't make good house pets. They're wild animals, despite their lovable appearance. They came around for one thing, and it wasn't a little girl's love. As soon as they satiated their appetite, they would move on, coming back only for more table scraps. Certainly not for your affection.

Aspen always owned a cat or two when she was young. Rufus seemed to enjoy taking them in and acting like an enormous father. But the cats always came from the humane society, saved from a lifetime in a cage. They seemed to understand that the relationship was reciprocal. Love was received, and it was given. Rescue cats made wonderful pets.

The strays, Aspen would ignore. Sooner or later, they all went away.

The Ghost

Humans have free will. I've always known that. And I'm not in the business of forcing Aspen to live a certain way or make specific decisions. But running out on Jamison wasn't in the plan.

Apparently this situation I'm in isn't all that different from real life. Unexpected things happen. Things that threaten to change everything that follows. When faced with those obstacles, we have to find another way to achieve our goals.

So that's what I'll do. I'll find another way. I didn't put in all this effort just to quit. Aspen deserves more than that.

Jamison

Jamison had a secret that only a handful of people knew.

It was about his name. Jamison Hightower. Impressive, he knew that much. If you took the name of some expensive whiskey and mixed it with the most grandiose sounding word you could think of and bellowed it from the hilltops, *Jamison Hightower* is what would come out.

When someone in Master Control made the C.G. of his name that showed up on the TV screen every time he was on-air, it was in all capital letters—JAMISON HIGHTOWER. It wasn't like that for anyone else at the station. He had tried, unsuccessfully, to discover if someone accidentally hit the Caps Lock key, or if it was supposed to be some sort of ironic insult. "Jamison Hightower joins us now for a story about a waterskiing squirrel." Maybe it was an invitation to point and laugh. Either way, it felt like a lot to live up to.

One viewer had told him it sounded like he should be the starting power-forward for the Timberwolves. After a backboard-shattering dunk, an amplified voice would shake everyone's eardrums with a bellowed, "JAM-I-SON HIGH-TOWERRRRR." The sound waves would shake the seats, rattling his name through fans' skulls.

Jamison Hightower. It was intimidating. It was inspiring. It was larger-than-life.

It also wasn't him.

He felt like such a fraud. As if he should begin every introduction with a preemptive apology for false advertising. Like he should explain that if he were to attempt ten lay-ups, he'd probably make four. That he wasn't who they thought he was.

And that was why it hurt so badly when he was walking through the dark path leading away from Sparkling Pond and back to his car and he heard the sweetest, most vulnerable voice he could imagine struggling through tears to call him by a name that wasn't even his.

"Jamison," the little girl said.

She was in the same spot as the first time he'd found her, and again she was crying into her sleeve. But she didn't jump at a chance to play hide-and-seek this time. Instead, her sniffles turned into an all-out bawl when Jamison sat next to her. Next thing he knew, he had snot all over his shirt, ringing in his ears from the volume of her cries, and a girl he wouldn't mind adopting wrapped tightly around his neck.

"What's wrong?" he asked.

"Astwa," was what her reply sounded like. But after a moment, she realized he couldn't understand what she had said, and repeated more clearly, "Baxter."

"Who's Baxter?"

"My Weimaraner," she said.

"Your…whine…I don't think I know what that is."

She laughed, doubling the amount of snot on his shirt. Apparently, his stupidity could lighten even the saddest of moods. "It's a kind of dog, silly. Baxter was one. But he died. Why does everyone I love die?"

Talk about walking into a situation he wasn't ready for. The poor kid already lost her parents, then her dog died, and she was crying on his shoulder, asking him why? Jamison would have given ten years of his life to come up with an adequate answer, but the truth was, he had nothing. The world could be cruel and unfair to the most deserving of people. The most deserving of kids. And no one knew why. And that was one thing about life he would never understand. But that wasn't what she needed to hear.

"I'm so sorry…" He knew Aspen had mentioned her name, but he couldn't quite conjure it.

"Holly," she said. Jamison realized the kid had more intuition than he gave her credit for. Maybe that was part of growing up fast, part of dealing with grown-ups who didn't know how to break bad news. She'd learned to read people's meaning without words. No wonder Holly thought she was thirty years-old. She'd had to act like it for far too long.

"Can I ask you something, Jamison?"

After her last question, Jamison was afraid to say yes. But not nearly as afraid as causing her any undue pain. "Of course," he said. "Anything."

"Am I bad?"

"You? You're a great person. Why would you think you're bad?"

She wouldn't look at Jamison when she answered. "Because I wish

Aspen's dog Rufus would have died instead of Baxter. Rufus is so much older and Baxter was just a puppy." Her head tilted to the side, as if the weight of her guilt was too heavy to bear. "But that's a bad thing to think, because Rufus is a nice dog, too."

Jamison took her hands and clasped them in his. For a moment, he forgot about whether it was appropriate to be holding hands with a kid he barely knew and just focused on what the girl next to him needed at that very moment. "That doesn't make you bad, Holly. Wanting your puppy to be alive makes you good. It shows your capacity to love. And even though I only met you today, I can tell you're one of the sweetest, kindest, most caring people I've ever met. And I've met a lot of people."

The greatest thing about what he just said to her, Jamison realized, is that he hadn't told a single lie. She rested her head on his shoulder and squeezed his hand. "Are you going away?"

"No," he said. "Not tonight. I'm staying with Claire Lyons tonight. Do you know her?"

His ignorance was the cause of yet another giggle. "Everyone knows Ms. Lyons. I hope you're not on a diet."

Some chirping crickets reminded Jamison it was getting late and he needed to be up early to figure out how to cover a story when the subject of the story wouldn't talk to him. "Shouldn't you be getting home?" he asked. "I hope no one's worried about you."

"Yeah," Holly said. "See you, Jamison." She popped up from the bench and started walking back toward town. After a few strides, the walk turned into a slight bounce, and then a full-on skip. For the moment, her tears over Baxter already seemed a distant memory.

The Ghost

I have a power, or an ability, I never used to have. But I haven't been given absolute knowledge. I don't know if what I'm doing will accomplish my goal. I can't even be sure it won't end up making things a lot worse.

But after having seen what I just saw, I know this much—my concerns were unfounded. Jamison Hightower was definitely the right choice.

Jamison

As if navigating through a town without roads wasn't difficult enough, the tire tracks in the cornfield leading to the parking lot were impossible to find. On Jamison's fourth pass, he finally saw some faint ruts and bounced along them, squishing into his soaked driver's seat with each bump.

Finally, he parked in an open field of matted grass and hauled his camera bag and tripod through fragrant clover to the log cabin belonging to Claire Lyons. She had sounded pretty old on the phone and sure enough, all the lights were out even though the ten o'clock news wouldn't even start for another hour.

So she didn't watch the news, meaning she wouldn't know who he was. A good thing to remember, after his earlier encounter with Aspen.

Jamison tiptoed through the unlocked front door and saw a note written in loopy penmanship on a faded yellow notepad.

Jamison Hightower,
Help yourself to anything in the fridge or cupboards. Your room is upstairs, first door on the right. Breakfast at 7am. Be hungry.
Claire

Upstairs in the bedroom, he realized he had no idea what came next. There was all this excitement over what was happening in the town square, and Harris delayed firing him so he could cover the story. But he didn't have a story to cover because Aspen wouldn't talk to him.

And he felt like he was missing something. Like there was more happening than what the townsfolk knew.

You'd have to be an idiot to believe any human being is capable of perfection. Not a single mistake his entire life. Jamison didn't know much about Aspen Collins, but he did know this—she was no idiot. Yet she had said her father was perfect. He'd never done anything wrong. Which left only one possibility.

Aspen Collins was hiding something.

Day Two

Jamison

As a gentle breeze fluttered the wispy, transparent curtain of the bedroom window, Jamison awoke thinking not of his looming live-shot or even of Aspen Collins, but of Holly. How unfair it was that such an innocent girl could lose her parents while she was so young, and then her puppy while *it* was so young. And how strong that little kid must be.

On his way down the stairs, the scent of coffee, bacon, and sugary pastries made him imagine childhood breakfasts. Dad straightening his tie on the way through the kitchen, kissing mom and sneaking a butt-tap just before she flips a pancake. Little sister giggling because she caught them. Happiness. Security. Love.

It was an invented memory—there was nothing real about it. He certainly never experienced anything like that. But someday, he thought, maybe he would be one of those parents in his imagination.

"Good morning," he said as he entered the kitchen.

A tiny white-haired lady was stooped over the stove. Her loose-fitting night gown glittered with crescent moons and swayed as she whisked and mixed. She waddled and shuffled as she turned, and she was already smiling, her eyes twinkling like the sun's reflection off the lake.

"Jamison Hightower," she said in a surprisingly strong voice. "Have a seat, have a seat. What a wonderful name, Jamison Hightower. It sounds like you could be royalty."

"Actually, ma'am, it's James Smith," Jamison said. "But the promotions department at my employer decided that sounded a bit too plain. Not glamorous enough for TV. So, now I'm Jamison Hightower." He wasn't sure why he said it. He didn't admit that to anyone. But he had a feeling this old lady wasn't going to be disappointed that he wasn't capable of any backboard-shattering dunks. Sure enough, she moved on without a second thought.

"Have you ever had bacon in your crepes?"

"Bacon in my crepes?"

"Oh, you haven't lived until you've had bacon in your crepes. A bit of a specialty, really."

She waddled back to the stove, where a bowl of batter waited. Her slow, deliberate movements became smooth as she poured a small amount of batter on a heated frying pan. Suddenly, she was swaying gracefully, twirling two spatulas like batons and dancing lightly while trimming the edges of the pastry.

"Some people say you shouldn't worry about the edges of a crepe. Nonsense. Aesthetics are half of being a chef. I learned that from a cooking class I took in 1988 at the senior center. Are crepes and chocolate croissants enough for you, or should I put on some sausage patties, too?" She shuffled back to the freezer without waiting for an answer.

Jamison was well aware that he didn't have a lot of role models growing up, but he knew enough not to sit on his butt while an elderly lady waited on him. "Let me help you with that," he said.

"Sit," she ordered, and it was no request. He sat. "And call me Claire." She removed two sausage patties from the freezer and began frying them on a skillet.

"This is quite a spread," Jamison said. "Where did you learn to cook?"

"Most of my life, I could only cook fish," Claire said. "That's all we ate, back in the Depression."

"You lived through that?"

"Close enough. Nourished only by the walleye of Sparkling Pond. Quenched only by its pure waters. Boiled of course, since St. Paul is upriver. By the time we had any money, I would've sooner eaten the lake's mud than its fish. And when my kids came along, I had plenty of opportunity to practice my cooking."

"How many kids do you have?"

"Seven!" Then, as if hit by a memory, her posture sank. "Six, now.

Lost Charlie to the lake when he was twelve. Sometimes I still forget he's gone."

"I'm sorry." After an appropriate pause, Jamison continued. "That's a lot of children. Your husband didn't mind having so many kids?"

"Oh, he didn't even know what was causing them 'til after the fourth one. Besides, George would've done anything for me. He was a great man." She gazed out her window. "The lake took him, too."

Claire delivered a plateful of food and Jamison decided it was quite possibly the best thing he'd ever tasted. "You could be a chef," he said between mouthfuls.

Claire's eyes twinkled and her stretchy skin pulled into a smile. "Someday, Jamison Hightower, someday. That's been my dream for thirty years now."

"Thirty years? Why haven't you done it? Yours would be the hottest place in town, with food like this."

"Oh, I just like to cook. Preferably French food. I don't know anything about starting a business. Rent, prices, hiring help. I guess I'm just too old for all that."

"Well you're depriving the whole town of immeasurable pleasure."

Claire hummed something that sounded like Carla Bruni and shuffled to the coffee pot.

"You're here to do a story for the television set, I hear," she said. She topped off Jamison's coffee and reloaded his plate. He had no idea how he was going to eat it all, but he would certainly give it his best shot.

"That's right. For KTRP out of Rock Prairie."

"Oooh, how exciting. Pity about those reporters from RISK-TV, isn't it? How do they rationalize sending more people over there, anyway? It's like sending them into certain death."

It seemed Jamison couldn't go anywhere without someone asking about the controversial news outlet, with controversial tactics. As far as Jamison could tell, the station's business plan was to make a name for itself by setting a record for the number of its reporters killed in the field. Two deaths in Syria in the past week had put the number at eight for the year. And it showed no signs of slowing down. Ratings were ratings, after all.

"I guess they rationalize it because the reporters go willingly," Jamison said. "Hoping to make a name for themselves, probably."

"Well, I think it's terrible, and that's a fact."

Jamison nodded, but didn't tell her his own little secret—that he'd been contacted by the station just last week with an offer to take the place of the latest casualty. He didn't say anything to Claire, but something told him he didn't have to. Claire's penetrating stare suggested she could read his discomfort like a book.

"Claire, do you know Aspen Collins?" he asked.

Claire paused before answering, a wordless articulation of her understanding that he was changing the subject. "Sure," she finally said. "Everyone knows Aspen. She's a sweetheart among sweethearts, that girl. Pretty, too. Reminds me of me in that way."

"Must be hard for her to be the second most beautiful woman in town," Jamison said. He wiped a bit of chocolate off the corner of his mouth and enjoyed Claire's giggle. "When I was talking to Aspen yesterday, I got the impression she was hiding something."

"Oh? How's that?"

"I don't know. Just a feeling, I guess. Is there some kind of secret I'm not supposed to know?"

Claire waddled back toward the stove. "You certainly are a reporter, aren't you? Simple curiosity is fine, but you should know that intruding into other people's lives can have consequences."

Jamison wanted to ask what consequences she was talking about, and for whom? Instead, he went with a safer question. "Do you believe her father's sending her messages?"

Claire gazed out her window in the direction of the mass of people gathered. "It seems the entire town believes it. Have you been out to the square? You would think Josephine Baker herself was back to dance the Charleston."

"Yes, but do you believe it?"

Claire looked thoughtful for a moment, as if the question had never occurred to her. "If something is happening, I suppose it doesn't much matter if I believe it or not."

Aspen

Aspen couldn't remember when she and Claire had become friends. It could have happened when Aspen's parents invited Claire along for a day of fishing and Claire had taught Aspen how to hook a worm. *Slimy,* August 29, age 10. Or maybe it was when Aspen was in high school and Claire caught her sneaking out of the house with her boyfriend but never told on her. *Relief,* March 19th, age 18.

Now that she thought about it, it was possible they had been friends her whole life. But Aspen hadn't begun showing up for morning coffee until after her mother had died. A day when no single word would suffice. *Soul torn to shreds,* May 10th, age 24.

When Claire had heard the news, she had delivered dinner at the doorstep every night for two weeks. She would ring the doorbell, then waddle away, trying not to be seen.

When Aspen had grieved long enough, she sought Claire out to thank her for the meals. Over a cup of coffee, Aspen had learned more about her mother than she had ever known. That she had been skydiving twice. That she had spent two years in Ethiopia with the Peace Corps. And that she loved dandelions because the layers reminded her of the honey comb at Aspen's great-grandfather's farm.

Three years later, two things remained unchanged — Aspen still had morning coffee with Claire at least once a week, and Claire still denied ever leaving food on her doorstep.

Today was like many others in that Aspen awoke early and went to the hospital to see her father. Then to the cemetery to pick weeds from beneath her mother's cherry tree. At eight o'clock, she dropped by Claire's house for a cup of coffee. What made the day different was the man sitting across from Claire at the dining room table.

There was no reason to be happy to see him and Aspen tried to ignore the feeling, wondering why it was there in the first place. When he saw her, he rushed to sip the last of his coffee before patting Claire's hand. "Thanks so much for breakfast," he said. "If you'll excuse me, I need to make a phone call."

Jamison acted like she had Ebola as he passed. He pursed his lips and practically slid up against the wall on the way by. Had she really been so rude? Aspen watched him climb the stairs and told herself it was for the best. She poured a cup of coffee and sat across from Claire.

"I didn't realize he was staying here," she said, and immediately wished she had spoken of something else.

"You don't approve?" Claire said.

"It doesn't matter to me. It's not my business."

"I thought he was here to do a story about you and your father."

"He thought so, too."

"Well?" Claire said.

"Well what? Why would I want someone to do a story about it? Especially him."

"You have something against Jamison?"

"Have you spent any time with him? Mr. Hightower has quite an ego on him. And apparently no one in town is going to do anything about it. Did you know Crystal Lux asked him for his autograph?"

"And that offends you?"

"It doesn't offend me. It just seems ridiculous. Why is he special just because he's on TV?"

"You're being pretty hard on him, don't you think? What has he done to earn your scorn?"

Aspen squirmed in the chair. She hadn't thought about what he had done. "He just seems arrogant. Expecting everyone to know him. Signing autographs all over town. His stupid eyebrow thing."

"Do you want to know what I think?"

"I think I already know. He flashed his beautiful smile at you and now you've fallen head over heels and think he's the dreamiest boy since Elvis Presley."

Claire bounced as she chuckled, sloshing the coffee in her mug. "I think he reminds me of someone."

"Who? Rad Collie?"

"Rad Collie? Heavens, no. I was thinking he reminds me of your father."

A drop of coffee squirted from the side of Aspen's mouth. She swallowed, took a napkin from the centerpiece, and patted her chin slowly. "Please tell me you're kidding."

"Well, not your father as you know him, I suppose. But no one is born exactly who he turns out to be. People are shaped by their experiences. You of all people know that. Your father has become a humble, forgiving person. A truly great man. But has he been perfect every second of his life?"

Aspen knew the answer to that. She stared at her coffee. *Weak*, July 5th, Age 9.

"I'm not saying Jamison's a polished piece of pottery," Claire said. "But away from the crowds, behind the eyebrow thing you speak of, I think he's a good egg."

Aspen couldn't think of what to say. Claire was messing with her thoughts, confusing what had been so clear. "Were you the one that called him here?"

"Oh, heavens no," Claire said. "What would I do that for? The only television I watch is Lawrence Welk reruns." She patted Aspen's hand and winked at her. "But maybe I would have, if I had known how cute he is."

"See," Aspen said. "That's what's so ridiculous. He does his little eyebrow thing and everyone falls all over themselves."

"I've never known you to be so quick to judge."

"I'm not judging him."

"No? What do you call it?"

"Nothing. I just think he's arrogant."

Claire tipped her mug for longer than she could possibly have been drinking. Then she pushed up from her seat and wiped the counter clean. She started to speak, sighed deeply, and wiped the counter again.

Aspen was well aware of her own short temper. Fiery, is what her father called it. But in their occasional verbal sparring, Claire had a different name for it—amusing. Which would explain her smothered grin as she pretended to clean the kitchen. But Aspen wasn't in the mood for her games today.

"If you have something to say, just say it."

"I'm just wondering why you don't like Jamison. The real reason, that is."

Aspen felt the fire inside her die down. It was useless to argue with Claire when she knew Aspen better than Aspen knew herself. So finally, she told the truth.

"Because he doesn't believe me."

Jamison

J.D., the cameraman, catapulted the live-truck over the precipice and dropped into the valley, where Jamison was pacing in front of the Hank Lyons fountain because he had no idea what he was going to say in his live-shot. He didn't know anything more than when he arrived, and it felt like he was the only one not in on the secret. The only thing he knew for sure is if he didn't come through with a story that was either surprising or interesting or inspiring, or...*something*, this would be his last day as a news reporter.

As if his thoughts had been read like a book, his cell phone rang. The Caller ID said *RISK-TV, New York, NY*. Jamison perched his thumb on the Reject button and tried his hardest to tap it. Instead, he found himself tapping the green circle and saying, "Jamison Hightower speaking."

"Mr. Hightower. This is Marlon Anderson, General Manager at RISK-TV. How are you?"

"About to do a live-shot," Jamison said. "And I already told your News Director, I'm not interested in your offer."

"The terms aren't to your liking?" the silky voice said into his phone.

"The terms were fine. But I don't have a death wish."

"Our reporters have the courage to enter dangerous situations in the name of telling important stories. And I think you have that courage, that desire, too."

"Oh? And what makes you think that?" Jamison said, annoyed that he hadn't hung up yet.

"Because you answered my call."

Jamison shook his head, swore under his breath, and ended the call. He didn't want to think about the offer from RISK-TV. The truth was it scared him. Not the offer itself, or the intense conflict he would be entering, or even the high likelihood of being killed. What scared him was his thinly veiled desire to accept the job.

For the time being, he forced the thought from his mind and looked around to regain his bearings. The mass of people in the town square continued to grow. A few entrepreneurs had even set up stands right in the middle of the playground. Kids flashed them dirty looks as they detoured around the giant cardboard signs.

Miracle in Sparkling Pond Tee-Shirts—BOGO

Guess The Time Of The Next Miracle, Win A Free Teddy Bear From Cuddly Cal's

A tug on Jamison's sleeve was accompanied by his new favorite voice. "Hi Jamison," Holly said. "Whatcha doing?"

"Good question," Jamison said. Holly looked at him with that *You're really not that smart, are you?* look, so he clarified. "I have to be on TV in a few minutes, and I'm not ready because I don't know what's going on here."

"I do. I'm the one who found the princess and letter."

Jamison took a knee so his eyes were directly at her level. "Do you want to be on TV?"

Ten minutes later, Jamison was standing in front of the camera, relying on an eight-year-old girl to bail him out of the jam he was in. As usual, a small crowd had gathered, having migrated from the town square to see what was going on. J.D. did his "live in one minute" thing and Holly's eyes widened just like Farmer Holliday's had.

"Jamison?"

She sounded like a kid having second thoughts about a rollercoaster. But she was already strapped in. Jamison grabbed her hand and held it, but he resisted the urge to give it a comforting squeeze. He didn't want to make it seem like there was anything to brace for. She grabbed his hand with both of hers and leaned into his side. Jamison was so worried about Holly and busy kicking himself for putting her in this position that he almost missed his cue from the anchors back at the station.

"Jamison Hightower joins us now from, uh, Sparking Pond?" It was John Hammerstein's voice, all disdain and mockery. "Always covering the big story, eh Jamison?"

Jamison had no avenue for retaliation, nor did he have any interest in playing juvenile games. "That's right, John, I'm here in Sparkling Pond. A sleepy, peaceful town snuggled in the corner of the state. But recently, someone or something the town now calls The Ghost has given one woman reason to hope for the impossible.

"I have with me eight year-old Holly Torrey, who discovered a small princess figurine and a note, written to a woman named Aspen Collins. And Holly, who were these things from?"

"The Ghost," Holly said with complete confidence. All nerves were gone and Jamison knew right away, this kid was going to steal the show. "It was a princess figurine that her puppy had chewed up—that's how she knew it was hers. Her daddy sent it to her."

"I thought you said it was The Ghost?"

"Her daddy is The Ghost. His name is Pike, like the fish. He's in a coma over there in the hospital."

"And why did he send her the princess figurine?"

"Because he wanted to remind her..." Holly's voice trailed off and she scratched her chin. Then, as if reciting a memorized line, she said, "...that her beauty extends beyond how she looks. Because she went on a date and the boy didn't ask her out again, so she thought she was looking old." She leaned in slightly, as if what she was about to say was between just the two of them. "I didn't tell her, but she is old. Almost thirty, I think."

"Do you know why that princess figurine would remind her that her beauty extends beyond the way she looks?"

"Because her daddy took all her princess toys away when she was a little girl. He thought it would teach her that lesson or something. He explains it all in the note."

Jamison was so proud of her he almost gave her a hug, but instead he turned to the camera. "A father, commonly referred to here as The Ghost, is in a coma. But he sent his daughter a reminder from her childhood, and a note. If it's real, this truly is one of the most astonishing gestures of fatherly love you'll ever be likely to find."

"Reporting live from Sparkling Pond, I'm Jamison Hightower."

He bounce-and-winked the camera, J.D. gave the all-clear, and then Jamison wrapped Holly in a hug. "You were great," he said.

"Thanks," Holly said. "You were pretty good too. But next time, I think I should hold the microphone."

Cornelius

Two thousand miles away, in his Los Angeles apartment, Cornelius Brown, PhD. logged onto his computer and browsed the latest headlines. Nothing caught his eye, so he went deeper and deeper, until he was swimming through headlines like "What Your Horoscope Means" and "50 Stocks To Buy In September." He was about to slam his laptop shut when something caught his eye. A long shot, but he hadn't found work in weeks and was starting to get desperate. He clicked the link and grainy video from some small-market newscast popped up.

He watched the two-minute clip, then sat back in his chair. *Her daddy is The Ghost.* It was just what Cornelius was looking for. He tossed his laptop into a backpack and headed toward his garage. He had a lot of packing to do, and he had to get to Sparkling Pond as quickly as possible.

The Ghost

I made the news. It's not unexpected. Bring a reporter to town and it's the natural progression. But I've never been completely comfortable with this aspect of the plan. It seems risky.

This miracle, confined to Sparkling Pond, is beautiful. But open the gates to the rest of the world and suddenly things can change. Open the gates to the rest of the world, and you might not be able to control what comes through.

Jamison

Holly ran off to tell her grandparents about her television debut, J.D. packed up and left for his next assignment, and Jamison sat next to the fountain where he first met Holly, thinking it was time for him to move on as well. His phone rang. It was Harris.

"I guess I've seen worse from you," was his greeting.

"Thanks," Jamison said. He hated having to be so deferential to his boss, but when he considered his only alternative was RISK-TV and "certain death" as Claire put it, he didn't see much choice.

There was a long pause and Jamison got the feeling Harris didn't like having to say whatever he was going to say next. "You're staying," he finally blurted out. "We're getting quite a bit of online action out of this story, so I want you to dig deeper."

Jamison's thoughts immediately turned to Aspen. True, she wouldn't give him the time of day, but just knowing they were in the same town gave him goose bumps.

"Listen closely," Harris said. "I'd rather pull you out and put someone better in there, but our contact in Sparkling Pond says they want you. For the life of me, I can't figure out why, but it looks like you're going to have to see this through. So we're going to do daily live-shots for the noon show. And Hightower? I don't want your usual crap. It's sweeps month and to jump into second place we need hard news, got it? I need you to transition from a fluff-covering nobody to a real reporter. This is your big opportunity. But if you screw it up, there won't be another. Do we understand each other?"

Let me see, Jamison thought. *I'm a nobody, he doesn't want me on the story, and if I screw up I'm headed to Syria for RISK-TV.* "We do," Jamison said. "We understand each other perfectly."

Cornelius

Cornelius Brown, PhD. had made a career out of hunting ghosts. It was all about the search for helium.

After graduating from MIT, he'd spent two years studying quantum mechanics. As hard as he tried to grasp the concepts, it always sounded like magic. And yet, it was science. It made his old college roommate's claims that his side of the room was haunted seem more plausible, and Cornelius began to search for ways to discover the supposed ghosts.

Most ghost catchers were fixated on the electro-magnetic field. They were convinced that the presence of paranormal beings could be detected by any disturbance in the EMF. But they didn't consider that ghosts aren't the only things that disrupt the EMF—any electromagnetic wave of the same wavelength would do that.

But helium, now that's how you detect ghosts. Emit a blast of condensed helium into the suspected area and if there is a ghost there, the helium won't dissipate—it will disappear. Ghosts, it turns out, love to consume helium.

The search for ghosts had always driven Cornelius' work. And it had begun well. His first five jobs had revealed the presence of paranormal beings and he found himself in high demand. The Discovery Channel even featured him as part of a documentary. But when he was unable to find ghosts at his next two jobs, he was suddenly out of work. As it turned out, people didn't like to be told their house wasn't haunted. What they really wanted was validation.

Cornelius sipped his coffee and slapped his cheeks to stay awake. He had packed the big rig full of gear and was half way between Denver and the Nebraska border. By morning, he would cross into Minnesota and arrive in Sparkling Pond, where the townsfolk had already decided there was a ghost.

Cornelius wasn't a fraud. He wasn't a sellout. But after his last two experiences, he certainly hoped the townsfolk were right.

Jamison

Jamison was heading back to Claire's house, still unsure of how to give Harris the "hard news" he so craved, when he realized he was being followed. The skipping queen was back, bouncing her way toward him, and Jamison was pretty certain he had an admirer.

"Hey Jamison, are you looking for Aspen?"

Jamison wondered if he had a little match-maker on his hands, and actually, he kind of hoped he did.

"She's in the cemetery, like usual," Holly said. "She's literally always there. Or at the hospital. I think it's because her mommy's dead and her daddy's a ghost."

"I see." Jamison realized he couldn't rely on a little kid the entire time. At some point, if he hoped to keep his job, he was going to have to try again with Aspen. "Can you show me the way to the cemetery?" he asked Holly.

Holly struck the same pose Farmer Holliday had, shoulders back and chest stuck out proudly. "You mean I can come with?"

"Of course. All friends are welcome."

Her face turned bright red and her mouth dropped open. "You mean we're really friends?"

After all we've already been through, Jamison thought, *how could she even wonder?* "I guess I don't know," he said. "Let's see. Do you think I'm nice?"

"I sure do." Her pigtails bounced as she nodded hard.

"And I think you're nice. Do you want to be my friend?"

Another hard nod. "I sure do."

"And I want to be your friend. Will you be nice to me?"

She giggled this time—a "yes" in Jamison's book. "And I'll be nice to you. So there it is. We meet every one of the requirements as devised by the International Council of Friendship. If we shake on it, we're officially friends. Agreed?"

The firmness of her shake told Jamison she was serious about this. "Agreed."

She took off and skipped a few feet away, did a somersault, then ran back and grabbed Jamison's hand again. "Ella Roberts can do perfect cartwheels, but I've never taken gymnastics because my parents are dead. So I do somersaults because Ms. Alamosa says I should focus on my strengths."

She led Jamison toward the cemetery, but they had to pass through the town square to get there. The peaceful town began to feel more like a circus and Holly looked at people as though she didn't recognize a single one. On one side of the merry-go-round were a dozen or so people wearing white tee-shirts that said "Team God," but they weren't alone anymore. Across from them, wearing scowls and looking ready to fight, were the same number of people in black tee-shirts that read "Team Ghost." There was excitement and tension, like a hockey fight. Everyone wanted to watch, but underneath it all, danger lurked.

Jamison pulled Holly closer and escorted her through the mob, then she led him toward a hillside full of blooming flowers, bushes, and trees. They passed under a wrought-iron gate that said "Sparkling Pond Cemetery." The array of colors was one of the most beautiful things Jamison had ever seen. Until he saw Aspen in a yellow sundress, under a cherry tree at the hilltop.

Suddenly the flowers had been seriously outshined.

Aspen

Atop the hill, Aspen brushed her hand along the plush grass, searching for any rogue dandelion, any creeping strand of crabgrass. This place was the source of more words in her journal than any other over the past three years. *Concurrent. Blooming. Crutch.*

She focused on the task of pulling weeds—the only thing that seemed to take her mind off the live-shot she had seen on TV. Jamison Hightower, looking like a proud big brother to Holly. It reminded her of Claire's unusual concern about her relationships, and the advice to give Jamison a chance.

And then he was there, in the most intimate of places for her, with Holly Torrey skipping happily by his side.

"Guess what, Aspen?" Holly said. "Jamison and I are friends."

Aspen thought about her first meeting with Jamison. She thought about Claire's impression of him. She didn't want to give him a chance, but then Holly had come along and forced her hand. The little girl's obvious love for Jamison made disliking him impossible. A guy who could be so sweet with a kid like Holly couldn't be all bad. Jamison was looking at the flowers that covered the cemetery, but they seemed to confuse him somehow.

"What's wrong?" Aspen asked.

Jamison looked startled, as if he hadn't expected her to speak to him. "Where are all the headstones?"

Aspen reached for a begonia petal near her feet, bursting with fiery red and yellow. "There aren't any."

"It's a cemetery, but there aren't any headstones?"

"No one in Sparkling Pond has been buried for generations," she said. "Instead, they're cremated. Then their family takes their ashes out here, mixes them with soil and compost, and plants something. Something beautiful that will grow and live on."

Jamison crinkled his nose. "That's kind of weird."

"To me, it seems weird to walk on a thin layer of grass and dirt that hides hundreds of boxed up, decaying bodies. Now that gives me the creeps. But nothing here is dead. It's all completely alive."

Aspen eased onto the springy turf, cradled her journal under her arm, and sat, leaning back against the thin trunk of the cherry tree. Holly plopped down next to her and found a ladybug to play with. Jamison came near, but seemed unsure if he was invited to join.

"My mother," Aspen said. She nodded to the branches of the cherry tree above. "My dad and I planted this tree a few weeks after her funeral. Having it here has been a great comfort. It's like she's still around, you know?"

Jamison shoved his hands into his pockets. "When your father passes—whenever that may be—do you know what you're going to plant for him? With...him..."

Aspen felt her smile curl at the edges as she tried unsuccessfully to contain it. "He always said he wanted to be thistles at the base of mom's cherry tree. You know, to keep all the other men away from it. Actually, the way he said it was, 'That way I can give them a good, hard poke in the butt cheek.'"

Holly covered her mouth, but couldn't contain her giggles. "You said 'butt.'" Repeating the word brought on another round of laughter.

"I don't think he was serious," Aspen continued. "So I've decided I'll plant eupatorium."

"What's that?"

"'Boneset' is what a lot of people call it, because a long time ago, it was used to set broken bones."

"Why do you think it's right for your father?" Jamison asked.

"I love that it has so many medical uses. Dengue Fever, arthritis, migraines, even malaria. It's helped countless people over the years. And it's supposed to represent regeneration. His disease is destroying his body, but after he passes he won't be confined by the physical world anymore."

"About your father," Jamison said. "And about what's going on here. I'm sorry for what I said yesterday."

Aspen waved it off. "It's fine. I was just being crabby. A friend helped me see that. Actually..." She flipped open the frayed pages of her journal and removed a folded letter. "I thought it might be nice to show you this."

Jamison stared at it like he was afraid to touch it. Holly tapped his shoulder. "You should read it, Jamison. It's pretty."

When he finally took it, Aspen leaned closer to read over his shoulder.

Dear Aspen,

It's been twenty-two years since I took your princesses away from you. I know it must have seemed cruel. I hope that time, experience, and perspective might allow me some redemption in your eyes. I hope this letter might provide some understanding.

The value our society puts on external appearances is not new. That people could be judged based on something they have so little control over is a flaw that has existed for generations. What good is goodness, what value do brilliance or compassion or empathy have if all of those qualities can be overlooked because of an ugly face?

You are beautiful, as I'm sure society has told you. And I'm proud of that, despite myself. But I didn't want you to be trapped by that beauty. I didn't want it to be what defined you. Beauty as part of an identity can be wonderful. Beauty **as** *an identity is smothering.*

When I saw you playing with princesses, it was more than play. It became a culture in every sense of the word. And in a culture, the whole has enormous influence over the actions, thoughts, and even feelings of the individual.

But we didn't have to buy into it.

Maybe it's the fact that I'm a man. I wanted to fix things. To do something big and sweeping and productive. So I took many of your things away from you.

I didn't want to make you sad. I wasn't trying to hurt you or get back at you for anything. I simply wanted to be the best father I could be.

I hope you know now that everything I've ever done, since the day you were born, has been because I love you. Even to this day, as I lie in a coma, what I do, I do for you.

Always,
Daddy.

Jamison

When Jamison finished the letter, his mind was too full of thoughts to articulate any of them. Mostly, he wondered what it must be like to be so loved by a parent. But he shook that off and focused on the last line of the note. *Even to this day, as I lie in a coma...*

"And you think this is his writing?" he said.

"I'm sure of it," Aspen said.

Jamison stared at the note for a while, trying to figure out a rational explanation for how someone in a coma could write a letter mentioning his coma. It was beyond impossible. "We should verify that," he said.

"You don't believe her, do you?"

Jamison startled at the sound of Holly's voice. Her ladybug had flown away and she was staring at him as if the entire conversation had intrigued her. "Why do you say that?"

"Because you're an adult. Adults always think they know everything."

"They're usually right, don't you think?" Jamison said.

"Chaaa." It took him a moment to realize it was a rebuke. "I learned in school that for thousands of years, adults thought the world was flat. And they thought if someone was sick, you should drain a bunch of their blood or drill a hole in their head to let spirits out. And they thought you could change metal into gold, that witches were taking over the world...adults have believed a bunch of stupid stuff. But don't worry, I'll still be your friend."

"Well I'm certainly happy about that," Jamison said.

"Hey Jamison, do you think we could plant Baxter together?"

Jamison could think of very few requests he would deny Holly, and he was about to agree wholeheartedly when Aspen chimed in. "Holly, you know the cemetery is just for people. That's the rule."

Holly gave them her champion pouter face. "But it's no fair. Baxter was nicer than lots of people I've met. He should get to be in the cemetery and the mean people shouldn't."

Jamison had a hard time arguing with her logic. So even when Aspen said, "Sorry kiddo. I don't make the rules," he was already scheming ways to get that dog's ashes planted.

Holly stood abruptly and started down the hill. "This is literally the most boring thing ever," she said over her shoulder. "I'm going to get something to eat."

Jamison smiled and watched as she skipped away, then he absentmindedly flipped the letter over. There, on the back side, bottom right corner, in barely legible scribble, something was written.

"What's this?" he said. He tilted the paper slightly to make it easier to read. There were three words, obviously meant for Aspen.

"Oh my God," she said. "Jamison. Oh my God."

The Ghost

Jamison just flipped the note over and found the instructions, so I can rest a little easier now. It's easy for the people of Sparkling Pond to assume The Ghost can make anything happen that he wants. Unfortunately, that's not how it works.

Chance and luck are still big factors in this game I'm playing. And you never know when an unexpected turn of events might derail everything.

But for now, I can't go on any longer without a nap. I may be a ghost, but I still need my rest.

Jamison

Aspen leaned over Jamison's shoulder, pressing softly against his back. He doubted she had any idea how hard it was making it for him to focus. Or maybe she did. He had never really understood women.

"Oh my God," she said again.

"Same handwriting, it looks like, right? Tiny, though."

"What's it say?" Aspen craned her neck to match the slanted scribble.

Jamison squinted and read, "*Canoe the Mississippi.* Probably some sort of instruction, huh? Like he meant for you to do it."

Aspen stood up and brushed some grass off her dress. "I can't. He wouldn't have written that."

It was about the last thing Jamison expected. "Why not? You can't swim or something?"

"No, it's just…"

"Just what? If this note actually is from your father, then he left you a hidden instruction. What are you afraid of?"

Aspen was quiet for several moments before her short breaths became a long sigh. "Take your pick," she finally said.

"Alright, let's go with reason number one."

Aspen's eyes darted to the sun, sliding toward the horizon. "Something like that would take several hours. I need to get back to the hospital by five o'clock for a meeting."

Jamison glanced at his watch. "It's two o'clock now. That's plenty of time."

"What if something goes wrong? What if the car broke down or the canoe sprung a leak? This meeting is really important to me."

"Alright. We'll just do it tomorrow."

Aspen shook her head. "I can't tomorrow either."

"Okay, well how about the next day?"

She shook her head again and if before Jamison simply didn't understand women, now he felt like he was studying trigonometry. "There's a meeting every day?"

Aspen nodded.

"So what, you never go anywhere for more than a few hours?"

It was a joke, of course, but Aspen shook her head. "If they wake him, and I'm not there…"

Jamison took her shoulders as gently as he could, hoping she would listen to reason. "We can get you back for the meeting, Aspen. Five o'clock is still three hours away. If we only go a mile upriver we could walk back if something goes wrong."

She nodded kind of sideways like she understood the logic, so Jamison couldn't figure out why she was still hesitant. "Have you ever done it before? With your father, maybe?"

"No," Aspen said. "Never. It's not something I would do."

"Why not?"

"Reason number two."

"Which is…"

Aspen's glare was full of challenge. "I'm afraid of moving water."

The conversation felt too serious so Jamison tried to lighten the mood. "What, like, coming out of the faucet?"

"Very funny. I mean like raging rivers and giant oceans. Small lakes are good. But when the water moves, I'm out."

"Why?"

"Have you ever been at the mercy of the power of moving water?"

"Not that I recall."

Aspen stared into space for several moments. Jamison waved his hand in front of her eyes and they flicked back to him. "I have," she said.

"Then conquer your fear. Meet the world head first."

Aspen rolled her eyes. "My gosh, you're persistent. If I go, will it at least shut you up for a while?"

"I promise. I'm already shutting up. In fact, I'm already shut up."

Aspen chewed the insides of her cheeks like the decision was physically painful for her. "Only because my father seems to want that for some reason. And we absolutely must be back to the hospital by five o'clock."

Jamison knew he was supposed to be there for work, but he couldn't control the butterflies in his stomach. "Let's go canoe the Mississippi," he said.

Aspen nudged him with an elbow and Jamison was amazed at how far they had come since the Squinting Café. "Shut up," she said.

They were the most beautiful words he had ever heard.

Claire

Claire Lyons knew she had lived a charmed life. Sure, her family's slow recovery from the Depression had been a challenge and losing a son and husband to the hand of fate had brought a pain that had momentarily paralyzed her. But she had six healthy, loving children, fond memories of a seventh child and a husband, and had been blessed to spend her life in the most enchanted place she knew. Obviously, not everywhere was as beautiful as Sparkling Pond.

Still, she wasn't prepared for the peeling paint and crumbling foundations of the homes in the North Minneapolis neighborhood she walked now. She used her foot to slide an empty McDonald's bag off the cracked sidewalk and weaved through the maze of crinkled beer cans, plastic grocery bags, and broken glass. She looked at the scrap of paper in her hand again and matched the address to the number on the house in front of her. She hoped the person she talked to at the television station had given her the right information.

George would disapprove if he was still alive. He had always scolded her for meddling in other people's business. *Mind your own, and head on home* he would say when she mentioned that the neighbors had caught more than their limit on the lake or that she didn't agree with the school board's decision to do away with uniforms. If he was here, she would have been on the receiving end of a very audible throat-clearing—the farthest extent of his anger.

Claire climbed the sagging, wooden steps in front, careful not to touch the railing, which slanted away from the door and bounced lightly with the breeze. It wasn't gossip she was after, she reminded herself. She had seen how Jamison looked at Aspen and was looking out for the people she loved, the best way she knew how. Surely, George would understand.

She tapped the door, careful not to get splinters in her knuckles, and it opened immediately. The eyes that scrutinized her weren't hostile, but they squinted as if emerging from a dark cave. As the woman's eyes adjusted to the light, Claire recognized Jamison in the roundness of the irises and the flecks of gold in the pupils.

"Mrs. Smith?" Claire said.

"That's right." The woman's voice was as unused as her eyes.

"My name is Claire Lyons. Forgive me for the intrusion, but I was hoping I might take a few moments of your time. I'd like to talk about your son, James."

"Well, apparently I'm Ms. Popular these days."

"Excuse me?"

"Someone beat you to it. Came asking about James, wondering what he's like."

The words came out harsh, but the woman's eyes were misty. "And what did you tell them?" Claire asked.

"That he left me when he was sixteen. Among other things." After a long sigh the woman said, "Would you like to come in?"

The door creaked open and she disappeared into the darkness. Claire followed, leaving the door open behind her. She found a light switch and flipped it on, bathing the room in a harsh light. Instead of the broken, littered scene she expected, Claire couldn't find a speck of dirt in the entire room. It looked like it had just been vacuumed, dusted, and polished within the hour. But rather than providing a feeling of comfort, the cleanliness seemed sterile. The room smelled antiseptic.

"It's Caroline, right?" Claire said.

"Yes, ma'am. Please, sit," Caroline said, and motioned to a couch that had lost most of its stuffing.

Claire sat and studied the woman's long hair, streaked with more gray than black. Caroline's hands shook, but her eyes were clearing. "Thank you," Claire said. "I see where Jamison gets his good manners."

Caroline attempted a smile—a small flicker at the edges of her lips. Claire wondered how long it had been since she'd smiled with real joy.

"I didn't realize Jamison ran away. That must have been hard."

Caroline draped her hair to the front of her shoulders and stroked it on both sides. "Not as hard as the fact that I haven't talked to him in fourteen years."

"Oh, I didn't realize..." Claire couldn't think of what it was she didn't realize. What kind of disagreement ends up with a mother and son not talking for fourteen years? "If I may be so bold, why?"

Caroline focused on separating a gray hair and yanking it out. "My history, I suppose. My mistakes."

Claire nodded as if that explained everything but gave Caroline plenty of silence.

"I got pregnant when I was sixteen," Caroline finally said. She yanked another strand of gray hair and continued speaking, as if to her hair. "I had already been introduced to meth by then. You've never known need or addiction until you've tried meth."

Her eyes seemed to bulge, as if a demon was about to surface. But a moment later, she took a deep breath and seemed to regain control. "James never saw me high, but he saw me once when I was needing a fix. The panic, the desperation, the need. I can't imagine how scary that must have been for him."

"When was this?" Claire asked.

Caroline yanked another gray hair, this time several black strands came with it. "James was in high school. A couple weeks later he ran away and hasn't returned any of my calls since."

Claire kneaded the hem of her shirt. Making a mistake doesn't make someone a bad person. Good people, with good hearts, make mistakes. Claire had seen it first-hand plenty of times. But few paid as high a prince as this woman.

For the first time, Caroline met her eyes and leaned forward. "You want to know what he's like. Well, the James I know is very sensitive. It makes him very sweet, very loving. But also very vulnerable. It's why, when he saw me craving a fix all those years ago…"

Her voice trailed off and Claire shifted on the couch. Springs poked at the loose muscles of her hamstrings. Caroline's eyes were back on her hair, which she stroked furiously. "I'm afraid I don't understand," Claire said.

"After he saw me strung out, James changed," Caroline said. She shrugged, but Claire could see the emptiness of the gesture. "His behavior worsened. He was always young and impulsive, but now he had no father and a mother addicted to drugs."

"How do you mean? What changed?"

"He began taking risks, and not small ones. I hoped he was just a teenage adrenaline junkie, but I knew that wasn't the case. It was like, he wouldn't kill himself, but he was hoping one of his stunts might do the job for him. When they didn't, he went further."

"Further?"

"First he went to the bluffs to catch rattlesnakes. He'd never touched a snake in his life. He was terrified of them. And there he was, taunting them to strike. He said he was testing his reflexes. When that didn't work, he went hang gliding without even taking any lessons or anything. I grounded him for two weeks for that. But the very next day, he topped them all."

Claire wasn't sure she wanted to hear the answer to her question, but she asked it anyway. "What topped them all?"

"The jump." When Claire didn't speak, Caroline heaved a deep sigh and continued. "There's a swimming pool in town, just a few blocks down the road. A couple of the buildings nearby are very close to it. There's always been a story around town about a kid who jumped from the roof of the tallest building and landed in the pool. It's just an urban legend. I don't think it's true. Just something kids make up to scare themselves."

"Did the child survive?" Claire asked. "In the legend, I mean."

Caroline's eyes held unique sadness as she shook her head. "No."

"And James…"

"He jumped. Landed in the deep end, thank God, but hit his arm first. Broke it in three places. I was furious. When we walked out of the hospital I swore he would never leave the house again. Obviously I didn't mean it. I was just so mad. How could he put himself at such risk?

"When I pulled into the driveway, he said he wasn't going to be told what to do by a druggie. He got out of the car, walked away from the house, and never stopped walking." Caroline broke down in earnest now. "I haven't seen him since. Other than on the news.

"I've been clean since that day. Fourteen years, now. I guess it just took his leaving to make me do it." Caroline's eyes flashed to Claire again, an urgency behind them now. "Will you see him again?"

"Yes. He's staying with me for the time being."

Caroline was at her side in a flash. She knelt in front of Claire, still kneading her hair. "Watch over him, please? Don't let anything bad happen to him?"

Claire thought about her own children—the ones alive and the one she lost. She thought about Jamison as the impulsive teenager Caroline had described, and the Jamison she knew now. And she thought of his reaction when they talked about the reporters at RISK-TV willingly shipping off to certain death.

She loosened Caroline's fingers and slid her hair behind her shoulders. "I'll do my best, sweetie."

Aspen

Aspen and Jamison stood next to the rushing river, her father's canoe at their shins.

She wondered why her father wanted her to canoe the Mississippi River when he knew better than anyone about her fear of moving water. Knowing her father, there had to be some purpose. Some universal truth he was trying to bring to life for her. What that might be, she couldn't fathom. *Intriguing* was in the running for word of the day.

She swallowed, grabbed a paddle from inside the canoe, and pushed the craft to the water's edge. She hadn't come here for nothing. "Hop in. I'll push off and steer from the back."

She took a deep breath and leaned into the canoe. When the front of the boat hit the current, it spun down river. Aspen hopped in, stuck her paddle deep into the water, and strained to hold it in place.

But the river was strong. It pulled them into the middle and shot them forward. Aspen barely heard Jamison's elated howl, focusing instead on controlling the canoe. A flush of panic gave Aspen the strength to stab a quick back-paddle and steer them into an eddy, where they spun a slow circle outside the reach of the current's power.

"See, that's what I was talking about," Aspen said. *Confirmation.*

"It's awesome." Jamison acted like he didn't even hear her.

"You seriously want to keep going?"

"Definitely. Your dad's orders, right?"

Aspen scowled. "Okay. But if we die in this river, I'm not going to be happy with you."

She steered the canoe back into the current and they were again launched down river. She was more prepared this time. The river was still strong, but she was more able to handle it.

"Enjoying yourself?" Jamison said over the rush of water.

Aspen's senses were heightened, but death didn't seem to be imminent. She relaxed her grip on the paddle slightly. "Yes, actually," she said. "I used to spend a lot of time on the river. Before…"

Several seconds passed before Jamison said, "Before what?"

She wasn't sure how to answer. It felt stupid to say that it terrified her because she had learned she couldn't reason with it. Couldn't negotiate. That moving water is like a good friend who inexplicably turns against you. *Old Yeller* maybe.

Except there's no gun powerful enough to euthanize this rabid dog.

"Before I realized how powerful water is when it moves," she said.

There was more to it, of course. A lot more. But it wasn't something she wanted to share with Jamison. Or anyone else. Not now. Not ever.

Before Jamison could question her again, her body when rigid. She squeezed her paddle, as if it were a magic broomstick that could fly her to safety. "Capsize Drop," she said.

"What?" Jamison's head snapped around to see what she was talking about.

"It's called 'Capsize Drop,'" Aspen said. "It's supposed to be bigger than the waterfall in Sparkling Pond."

"And you knew about this?"

"I've heard about it." Aspen raised her voice over the increasing roar of water. "But I'd forgotten. Blocked it out, maybe. I never even knew if it was real. I've never been to this stretch."

"Looks real to me!" Jamison shouted over the roaring water.

As the current funneled the canoe to the top of the plunge and the river took total control, Aspen felt a moment of dread she hadn't experienced since she was a kid. Since the horrible day that changed everything.

She forced her mind to focus, dragged her paddle, and fought as hard as she could. She leaned into the paddle with all her weight and her triceps burned, but it didn't affect the boat's speed or direction in the least.

And then her stomach dropped out from under her.

Although it couldn't have been more than a couple seconds, the time in which they were airborne felt infinite. As if they were in slow motion.

But as soon as the tip of the boat smashed against the water below, the world jumped into fast forward. The next thing Aspen knew, she was underwater. The current yanked at her arms and legs, spinning her through a washing machine of waves. Panic consumed her. The water would never release her. She imagined the S.S. Edmond Fitzgerald at the bottom of Lake Superior. *Shipwreck.*

But then she broke through the surface and started drifting, as if the river had decided she tasted sour and spit her back up. She gulped oxygen and realized that, as quickly as it had started, it had finished. She was safe. Looking back at it, she hadn't ever been in real danger, despite her panic. But her hands still shook.

The canoe eased by with Jamison clutched to the outside of it. He shook his head, his grin crinkling at the sides.

"Your dad's insane," he said.

Aspen tried to calm herself. She was here, twenty-seven years-old, alive, with a guy named Jamison Hightower. A reporter, who would surely ask questions she didn't want to answer if he noticed she was too affected by the ride.

She kicked toward him and pulled at the water until she could grab the side of the boat. She didn't want Jamison asking questions, so to cover the reason she was so frazzled—as if plummeting over Capsize Drop wasn't enough—Aspen took a couple deep breaths and focused on another thing that had been bothering her.

Jamison didn't understand her. Her motivations, her history, the reasons behind her decisions. He didn't know any of it. Some of it would have to stay hidden. But not all of it. Maybe it was time to start letting Jamison know her better. At least a little.

"Come with me," she said.

Jamison looked all around, searching for their destination.

"I mean the meeting," Aspen said. "At the hospital. I want you to see why I can't miss it. Why it's so important to me. I'll ask at tonight's meeting if it's okay with the doctors and tomorrow, you should come."

Aspen thought she saw a spark in his eyes. "Alright," he said. Then his cheeks turned an adorable shade of pink. "Thanks for the invite."

Aspen wasn't sure she was actually ready to bring him along. It was entirely possible she'd just been trying to distract him from asking personal questions. But it was too late now.

At least it had helped her decide on a word for the day—*vulnerable.*

Cornelius

The sun dropped quickly in Cornelius' rear-view mirror as he crossed the Minnesota border. By the time he reached Sparkling Pond, the day was nearing an end. A quick Google search of the town had revealed that no roads led through it. Certainly an oddity, but in his line of work, Cornelius had run across stranger things.

He eased the 18-wheeler onto the shoulder of the small highway and put the first piece of equipment—the Atmospheric Density Tester—onto a dolly. As he rolled it past a fountain and toward the massive gathering of people near the center of town, he noticed the double-takes that followed wherever he went with his bulky, futuristic equipment. But one double-take turned into an all-out stare. The woman rushed over and took his hand off the dolly in her excitement to shake it. The dolly tumbled over and the Atmospheric Density Tester crashed to the ground.

"I'm so sorry, I'm so sorry. You're Cornelius Brown! My name's Crystal. Crystal Lux. And I love you!"

After the documentary that had aired on the Discovery Channel, Cornelius had wondered if people might recognize him. But it hadn't happened. Not once. Not even at the West Coast Regional Paranormal Conference, where he had been keynote speaker.

"Ah, thank you," Cornelius said.

"Oh my gosh! You brought the Atmospheric Density Tester. Can I help you with it?"

"Yes, of course, thank you."

Crystal squealed and helped replace the equipment onto the dolly. Together, they continued to the town square, where hundreds of people prepared for the long night ahead by drinking coffee and staring at the merry-go-round.

"Make way! Make way!" Crystal shouted, creating a path through the sea of people. "The Ghost Hunter, Cornelius Brown, PhD., is coming through!"

The scene was unlike anything Cornelius had seen. He usually worked alone in a musty basement or a cramped attic, but here he was surrounded by people of all kinds, now clamoring for a look at him. Crystal Lux continued her proclamations as dozens of people in Team Ghost shirts talked excitedly. Those on the other side of the merry-go-round pointed threateningly.

"Sensitive equipment coming through!" Crystal shouted. "You want proof that a ghost is here? Here's your man. The best ghost hunter in the world. Make way! Make way!"

Cornelius set the Atmospheric Density Tester facing straight at the playground toy everyone seemed fixated on and turned his attention to the woman shouting his praises at the top of her lungs. Her flowing hair shimmered in an array of colors, like a waterfall cascading down her back. Her face was contorted from shouting and her eyes were bug-like with excitement, as if they might pop out of her head at any moment.

The tingling in Cornelius' chest reminded him of when a blast of helium would disappear. Excitement would shoot through his body—adrenaline prickling his senses. But in this case, he hadn't yet found a ghost. He had found something else entirely.

As the last of the sun's rays dropped below the horizon, framing Crystal's form in a heavenly glow, Cornelius Brown, PhD. had found love.

Day Three

Jamison

"Jamison, look who's here!"

Jamison was weaving his way through the mass of people who had camped out near the town square—the crowd had swelled well beyond the playground's boundaries—when Crystal Lux bounced up to him and presented her prize. A man ten years younger than her, with wire-rimmed glasses and a floppy comb-over. He had the look of a person who had spent most of his life bent over a book or a microscope and was staring at Crystal like she was the first woman he'd ever encountered. "It's Cornelius Brown, PhD.," Crystal said, which turned the guy's cheeks red. "He's here to find The Ghost."

"It's a pleasure to meet you," Jamison said, shaking his hand.

"Enough socializing, honey," Crystal said to Cornelius. "We have important work to do today. See you later, Jamison."

Crystal escorted Cornelius toward a huge array of machinery that would have made NASA jealous. Jamison made a mental note to find that guy for the day's live-shot. Maybe some professional input would impress Harris.

Jamison neared the river and saw a sign that read "Collins' Carrots and More" at the edge of the Sparkling Pond Farmer's Market. But when he got there, Aspen was nowhere to be found.

"Hee-Haw," a crackly voice said.

An old man wearing a cowboy hat, leather pants, and boots with spurs saddled up to Jamison. The man's hat was drooping and he kept tapping it with his index finger so it wouldn't block his vision. "Sir," Jamison said with a nod.

"She ain't here, sonny. Went to the john, I do believe."

"Oh. Okay." Jamison stood there awkwardly while the cowboy

grinned between lasso-shaped arches of tobacco spit. "So, she'll be back soon?"

"I'm back already," Aspen said. She appeared from behind an enormous oak tree, with an armful of potatoes, still dirty from the field. "And I wasn't in 'the john,' but thanks for that, William."

The cowboy cackled and wandered away aimlessly. Aspen sat in a chair next to a large bucket of river water and began scrubbing fresh dirt from the potatoes. Jamison felt like Cornelius Brown PhD., the way he couldn't stop staring.

"That guy seems pretty interesting," he said to cover his gawking.

"That's William. 'Crazy Willie' is how he's known around town."

"Well that's flattering."

"I know. But I don't think people mean crazy-insane. More like crazy-brave. I've heard William was pretty wild in his younger days. Pulled some pretty crazy stunts. So, Crazy Willie."

"But you didn't call him that," Jamison said.

"No." Aspen put the clean potatoes in a pile on the table, right between the green onions and the spaghetti squash. "It's insulting, if you ask me. Besides, that would be like calling an uncle who's a little quirky Crazy Uncle Whatever."

"He's your uncle?"

"Might as well be. He's always been around."

"Crazy Willie?"

Aspen's eyes flashed, which was enough to make Jamison feel sufficiently scolded. "William," she said. "And yes, he and my dad were friends back in high school. One day, they were trying to impress a couple of girls, so they charged over a wooden fence and into a pasture where there was a full-grown bull grazing. William ran right up to it and hopped on its back. Started howling, pretending he was swinging a lasso over his head, the whole nine yards.

"Unfortunately, the bull bucked him off. It trampled him pretty badly before my dad was able to get to him. My dad pulled him out from under the bull, heaved him over his shoulder, and sprinted out of the pasture with the bull at his heels the whole way."

"Wow," Jamison said. The town was full of stories he didn't know whether to believe.

"Exactly. When my dad used to tell it, he'd get this misty glaze over his eyes at the end, like he never did figure out how he was able to toss a teenage boy over his shoulder and outrun an angry bull. And, of course, there was the fence. The other people there swear my dad jumped over it—a four foot fence, with William still draped over his shoulder." Aspen stared at the horizon. "Sounds impossible to me. But everyone who was there tells the same story."

"And William? It changed him?"

"Never been the same since," Aspen said. "He had some head trauma. I guess it was pretty scary for a while. He came through, but they say that's when he became a bit more eccentric."

"Eccentric?"

"Quirky. Like, he's terrified of cows. PTSD, I guess. That's a good thing to remember when you're near him. Don't mention cows. Not even steaks or ground beef. It kind of freaks him out."

Crazy Willie strode back to his stand, his spurs clinking with every step. His strut still made him look formidable, but he kept poking the floppy brim out of his eyes, like a second-grader in a store-bought Halloween costume three sizes too big.

William sat on an overturned bucket at his display stand and waited. He was a painter, Jamison realized. And a good one. Every canvas was covered with cowboys in full glory, with William's signature in the bottom corner. Cowboys atop bucking broncos, lassoing a stray calf, or just the grizzled face of a weather-hardened man. There were even a few paintings of bulls with enormous horns. Apparently, William's fear didn't extend to the canvas.

Jamison was studying the paintings while Aspen went to Crazy Willie's stand and spoke briefly with him. Then she jogged back and said, "I told William you won't be in town long and he said he would handle things at my booth for a while so we can do something together."

"Do something together?" Jamison tried not to swallow, then he swallowed.

"Yeah, I was thinking we could go for a run. I could show you more of the town and we could get some exercise at the same time. It's been forever since I've been out running. Probably over a week now. Do you like to run?"

Before Jamison could say no, they were walking toward her house, where he was supposed to borrow a pair of her father's running shoes. As they passed near the town square, a small group of men worked with a pulley system, lifting giant spotlights. They heaved the final array of lights into place, making the playground look like a football stadium, with all the lights pointed directly at the merry-go-round.

"Do you think anything else will appear?" Jamison asked.

Aspen shaded her eyes from the sun so she could look up at the lights. "I don't know. But if it does, we'll know right away. Ever since the false alarm, they always have someone on watch making sure no one plants something there again and then calls it a miracle. This whole thing has brought the crazies out of hiding."

They were almost to Aspen's house when she stopped and cursed under her breath.

"What's wrong?" Jamison asked.

"My running shoes." Aspen's shoulders slouched and her chin dropped to her chest. "I just remembered. The whole front of the right shoe blew out on me last time I went for a distance run. It's been so long, I'd forgotten about it. But with my dad in the hospital…Actually, if I'm not going to be working, I should really go see him."

What Jamison initially thought was fatigue, he now recognized as sadness. It changed her eyes—still a deep emerald but less vibrant. A big part of him wanted to discourage her from going to the hospital again. For his sake, obviously. Spending time with her was addicting. But for hers as well. It seemed wrong to give up so much of her life. But that was the thing—it was her life, not his.

"Then go be with him," Jamison said. "I'll take a rain check."

Her smile barely moved her lips, and then she said the most unexpected thing. "Maybe this is something you should see, too."

Cornelius

When all his equipment was set up and turned on, the man Cornelius would come to think of as "the stranger" slipped a folded piece of paper into his hand and disappeared. Cornelius managed to find a moment of privacy from Crystal by pretending he was adjusting the levels on the Helium Emitter. He unfolded the crinkled paper.

Hank Lyons Fountain. Five minutes.

Cornelius had no idea who the man was, what he wanted from him, or why it had to be so secretive. But he had dealt with eccentric people before. It came with the territory for ghost hunters. So he told Crystal he needed something from his truck, asked if she would protect his equipment while he was gone, and made his way to the only fountain he had seen in town.

When he arrived, he heard a voice, hidden on the other side of the fountain. "Stop right there."

Cornelius stopped. It wasn't often a disembodied voice spoke to him, despite his profession. "What do you want?" Cornelius said.

"Do you believe in ghosts, Dr. Brown?" the voice said above the tinkling of the fountain.

Cornelius looked around. The area was deserted. Everyone was at the town square. He knew he should proclaim his absolute certainty in the supernatural, but something about the voice seemed safe. "I'm not sure," Cornelius said.

There was a long pause. "Do you *not* believe in ghosts?"

"I think it's possible they exist. But I'm not certain that even I have proven it."

"But you admit there's a chance ghosts do exist."

Cornelius thought about that. He felt it was important to get his answer right. "Certainly there's a chance."

"If a ghost was nearby but you failed to detect it, would you feel bad about convincing people it wasn't real?"

"Obviously, if I was mistaken I would—"

"Then be careful. Some ghosts can't be detected by your methods."

Cornelius was tempted to run around to the other side of the fountain and confront the stranger. To at least see him face-to-face. But something told him that would be a bad idea. So instead, he started walking back to his equipment. Over his shoulder, he heard the stranger say one last thing.

"By the way, Crystal Lux loves ghosts."

Aspen

Aspen rode the WEB Train to the fourth floor, Jamison at her side, embracing the ride by listening to Soul Asylum's *Runaway Train.* When they reached her father's room, Rufus was standing guard as he often did. It had taken some effort on Aspen's part, but the hospital board of directors had given permission for Rufus to be in the hospital under the classification of a service dog.

"If the love that dog gives my dad isn't doing him a service, I don't know the definition of the word," Aspen had said in her meeting with the board. *Sentry,* she had written that night.

She grabbed Rufus' cheeks and flapped them around, something she remembered doing as a small child. Jamison followed suit, even nuzzling his face against the dog's cheek.

"How old is this dog?" Jamison asked, scratching behind Rufus' ear.

"We got him when I was a kid, so at least twenty I'd guess."

"Twenty years? I've never heard of a dog living that long. Especially not a huge one like this."

"Me either, but here he is."

Aspen located the hand sanitizer on the wall. Finally, Rufus had spent all his energy and curled up in a corner—spinning circles to mat down a bed of imaginary grass. Aspen smirked and turned her attention to her father.

He was a slender form under white sheets, which reached his chest. Tubes breathed for him and pads monitored his heart. There were IVs and whirring machines.

Aspen didn't see any of it.

When she sat next to her father's side, all she saw was the familiar stubble of his chin and the still-strong curve of his jaw, though the pull of skin made it more defined now. He had grooves in his face, shooting out from his eyes, which he had sculpted with smiles. Aspen loved the wrinkles and couldn't remember her father's face before them. She loved how his dimples reached the lines of his eyes when he smiled. So many words in her journal, from every phase of her life—good and bad—were about this man. *Guidance. Smothering. Unconditional.* She took his hand and stroked its rough skin.

"I'd like you to meet Jamison," she said without introduction. She simply continued each conversation, hoping he could hear. Maybe, as far as he could tell, she never even left. "He's a television reporter covering everything that's happening." She motioned for Jamison to come over. When he got there, Jamison put his hand atop her father's. The sight of it made Aspen's voice crack.

"Maybe it's just wishful thinking," she said. "But he seems like a genuinely nice guy. I think you'd like him." She looked at Jamison and smiled. "I think I might like him. I'm still not sure how I'm going to admit that to Claire."

Aspen turned her gaze to her father and yearned to hear the gentle rumble of his voice. *Please, wake up.* She sat in silence and watched Rufus' enormous body rise and fall with each breath. Then she stared at Jamison's hand covering her father's. She didn't like to speak if her voice might be choked with tears. She didn't want her father to hear the fear and sadness.

But she felt it. When you love someone so dearly, and you know you might never hear him say "I love you" again, it hurts. She imagined how he must have longed to hear her say the words back, only to be disappointed over and over again. *Can't* appeared far too many times.

So for the thousandth time, she recommitted herself to what had become her life's goal since her father lost consciousness. She would be there when he awoke. She would tell him she loved him. She would make things right, no matter what sacrifice of her time that required.

Aspen put her head on her father's chest. She felt the soothing thump of his heart against her cheek. She tried to synchronize the rhythm of her heart with his. Maybe then, their hearts would beat as one. Maybe then, she could give him some strength. Maybe then, she could bring him back and keep him in her life just a little bit longer. Just long enough for *Can't* to become *Redemption*.

Jamison

Without a family, figuring out how to act was something a man had to learn on his own. Jamison had never had a sick relative in the hospital. Actually, he was pretty sure visiting Aspen's father was his first time in a hospital since he was born. But when he had seen Pike there, so helpless he couldn't even breathe for himself, Jamison hadn't even thought. He'd just gone over and held his hand.

No one had taught Jamison to do that, and for all he knew he'd messed it up, but trying to comfort someone who needed it just felt like the right thing to do.

He felt similar as he took Aspen's hand in the hospital hallway. Of course, he wanted to hold her hand. But mostly, he just wanted her to be okay. He knew she loved being there for her father, but he could tell it was emotionally draining too. He was about to suggest that she go home for a while, but as they exited the hospital an explosion of shouts and shrieks erupted.

At first, Jamison thought they were cheering for them—the timing of their exit was so perfect. But apparently it was just coincidental, because the real commotion was at the town square. When Aspen realized the source, she hesitated. Jamison knew her last experience there was engrained in her mind.

"What if it *is* your father this time?" Jamison said. "Let's just check it out." Aspen still hesitated, so Jamison squeezed her hand. "I'll be right there with you."

She nodded and they jogged there, still holding hands, as if now that they had started, they couldn't stop. When they got there, the crowd parted for them.

"Oh, great," Aspen said. "Just perfect."

Two Greek Gods with short, spiky hair and form-fitting tee-shirts strutted forward, scowling. Jamison wasn't sure what he'd done to make them mad, but one look at their chiseled physiques and he was willing to apologize for anything. Well, almost anything. When their eyes went to his hand, interlocked with Aspen's, Jamison suddenly felt a lot tougher than he was.

"What's this, Aspen?" one of the behemoths said. "Are you two together?"

"We'll put that one in the 'None of your business' column, Blaise," Aspen said.

"Sure looks like it," Blaise said, nodding toward their hands.

"You and Ryder can go ahead and think whatever you want to think," Aspen said, nodding to the man standing next to Blaise. The two could have been identical twins. At least their muscles were identical in their enormous size. "Why's everyone cheering?"

Blaise and Ryder continued to glare at Jamison, but through gritted teeth, Blaise decided to answer. "That guy said he might have found a ghost."

He pointed to Cornelius, who stepped forward, and all eyes turned to the ghost hunter. He cleared his throat and Jamison noticed a sideways glance toward Crystal, as if she was the only reason he was putting himself through the agony of speaking in front of everyone.

"There was a large and sudden decrease in levels of a recent helium blast," Cornelius said. "Now, that's not irrefutable proof. But very often a disturbance like that is caused by supernatural phenomena. Namely, ghosts."

The cheering erupted again and for a moment, everyone's attention was diverted. It was at that moment that a reflection from the teeter-totter caught Jamison's eye and he noticed something out of place, or maybe forgotten. "Why are those there?" he asked. "Do they belong to someone?" He pointed to a pair of running shoes, wedged beneath the handle of one side of the teeter-totter.

Everyone's attention shifted to the edge of the playground and Aspen rushed to the teeter-totter. She yanked the shoes from beneath the handle and sighed, as if relieved. "These are mine. Or at least, they were. Years ago." She looked straight at Jamison and said, "These are from my father." Then she looked inside one of the shoes and pulled out an envelope.

And that's when Crystal Lux fainted on the spot.

Cornelius

What happened next changed the life of Cornelius Brown, PhD. forever.

The fame he had expected after the Discovery Channel documentary appeared in an instant. Elderly men, middle-aged women, children of all shapes and sizes—everyone jockeyed for position to shake his hand. To pat him on the back. To look into his eyes as if they were friends with the great ghost hunter. The man who had proven the existence of ghosts by predicting an appearance down to the second.

Cornelius knew he hadn't done that—he had only suggested it could be likely at what turned out to be a very fortunate time. But no one needed reminding of that just now. This was the biggest moment of his life—except for maybe being named Lego Robotics Captain in third grade. Then Crystal Lux regained consciousness, and the biggest moment of his life was quickly redefined.

Crystal's eyes were still bug-like, as if losing consciousness couldn't dampen her excitement. Cornelius bent over her to help her up, but she immediately wrapped her arms around his neck, pulled him down on top of her, and kissed him with more passion than the scientist thought was biologically possible.

Aspen

With half the crowd cheering for Crystal and Cornelius and the other half fixated on Aspen, she opened the envelope and saw her father's skinny-looped writing.

"Read it out loud!" a man shouted. He wore a Team God tee-shirt and everyone around him looked equally excited. Apparently, Cornelius' feat had convinced some of them God could work through ghosts after all.

Jamison squeezed her hand. "The letter was written to you. It's your choice, not theirs."

Aspen considered her options. Say no and feel the wrath of the entire crowd—although she didn't even know most of them, who had come for the spectacle more than to witness the strength of a father's love. Or she could read it, letting everyone hear her father's words, which were meant for her.

She was about to fold the note and hide it safely away in her journal when an old man caught her eye. The man was stooped and bushy-haired. His eyes were pleading, as if he had witnessed too much tragedy in his life and was searching desperately for hope. For a sign that love still mattered in this world.

So she decided the word for the day would be *brave,* then turned her gaze back to the letter her father had written her and read in the strongest voice she could muster.

Dear Aspen,

The things that give us pleasure change, as we change. When we're young, it's a favorite toy. Then maybe successful competition or getting the prom date you wanted. By the time you're a parent, the greatest pleasure is seeing true happiness on your child's face.

There is a phase many kids go through, typically around middle school, when that happiness is hard to find. You went without it for what felt like eternity. But one day, when you were thirteen years-old, I saw it return. And my life felt full once more.

Since that day, you have been the picture of health and vitality. Maybe I take too much credit, but I like to think I had a hand in it.

So thank you. Thank you for being who you were and for becoming who you are. Thank you for following my advice by taking care of yourself.

And remember, it's important to take care of yourself no matter what—even when your father is lying on his deathbed.
I'll love you forever.
Daddy.

When Aspen read her father's final words, she closed her eyes and pictured him. Not in the hospital bed, but as he had been. When she had been young and he had been strong. She focused on the mental picture until she heard clapping. It started as a few scattered claps, then more people joined in. It steadily grew until a wave of applause covered the town square.

When Aspen opened her eyes, she found the elderly man whose expression had impacted her before. The man was weeping, smiling, and slapping his hands together for all he was worth. His voice was drowned out by the noise, but he seemed to be mouthing the word "Bravo."

Aspen grabbed Jamison's hand. "I want people to know about this. It's such a hopeful story. I want to spread it."

She followed Jamison's gaze to the hill outside town, where a KTRP live-truck would soon be speeding over the precipice. Jamison put his arm around her shoulder and said, "I think I can help you with that."

Jamison

Jamison didn't know how the shoes got there. And he didn't know how Aspen's father kept writing letters that referred to things happening now, as well as his own condition. He wanted to believe it was a miracle. That her father was an invisible ghost sneaking around putting things on various playground toys and writing notes to go with them. But he couldn't.

He'd simply never witnessed magic before. Except the disappearing father trick. Granted, that one was pretty convincing. But as far as mostly-dead-guys tip-toeing through town, unseen by hundreds, maybe even thousands of people, while his hospital gown flapped open-backed in the breeze? Jamison just didn't buy it.

Still, he had seen the same thing Aspen saw after she read that note.

They had witnessed pure joy. A belief that Aspen's father was speaking to her, guiding her. And if Pike Collins could do it, maybe their loved ones were still among them too. Maybe there was reason to hope after all.

So when John Hammerstein said, "We're joined live by Jamison Hightower," Jamison had no hesitation. No regret.

"That's right John, I'm back in Sparkling Pond, where lightning has struck again. For a second time, Aspen Collins has received something from her father, Pike, also known as The Ghost. And Aspen, you're convinced it was your father who left these shoes for you. Why is that?"

Jamison tried to give a gentle look to calm her nerves, but she didn't need it. Aspen was all grace and confidence. "When I was about thirteen, I went through a couch-potato phase. All I wanted to do was watch TV. My dad took me to a 5k race where we jumped through rivers, climbed hay-bales and slid down mud-slicked hills. We had a blast together and ever since that day, I've been very active. Until my father was put in a coma. Since then, I haven't been exercising much. So my father sent me these shoes to remind me to take care of myself."

"And how can you be sure that's the message he's trying to send?"

Aspen held up the note. "He told me."

Jamison turned sideways and gestured to the town square behind him. Cornelius Brown, PhD. was shuffling his gadgets, checking levels, reading data results. "One of the country's preeminent ghost hunters is right here in Sparkling Pond, searching for proof that Ms. Collins' father is, in fact, the one leaving the objects and the messages. For now, all we can say is, if there is another explanation, no one here has been able to find it.

"Reporting live from Sparkling Pond, I'm Jamison Hightower."

He bounce-and-winked, J.D. gave the all-clear, and then Aspen tapped him on the shoulder.

"You did great," Jamison said to her. But she just smiled and flipped the note over to the back side. She pointed to small, barely legible scribbles in the bottom right-hand corner.

Ride a galloping horse.

Jamison

Horses, to Jamison, were like gladiators. Strong, mythical, and something he would never come in contact with. But with one swipe of his pen, Pike Collins, or whoever had written those notes, was about to introduce Jamison to the equine world.

Aspen mentioned a widow who lived in a nearby farmhouse and had always had horses. So they headed straight there, not wasting any time since again, Aspen was paranoid about missing the daily meeting. This time, Jamison was too. He'd been given permission to attend and was looking forward to seeing what was so important.

They entered through a gate and saw a teenage boy shoveling hay into a cow trough. They passed by several barns of various sizes and Aspen knocked on the door.

"Aspen Collins! What a pleasant surprise," a woman said through the screen.

"Hi Erma. I'm sorry to bother you."

The woman dried her hands on a small towel. She looked over Aspen's shoulder, at the crowded town square, and her eyebrows crinkled slightly. "Not at all. Come in, come in."

Aspen and Jamison followed her into the entry way, with boots lined up along the wall and a rust-stained sink near the door.

"I know it's a strange request," Aspen said. "But we were hoping to ride one of your horses."

"My horses?" She seemed to consider it for a moment. "The key is not to spook them. Hold out your hand and let them sniff it, like a dog."

Jamison was a bit confused. Was this woman saying yes? Shouldn't there be liability waivers to sign and intensive lessons first?

"Stalliony is probably the fastest out there," Erma continued. "She's the one that's all black."

"Stalliony?" Jamison said.

Erma looked to the sky, as if needing divine support. "My daughter was six when we bought her. We'd just finished reading *The Black*

Stallion. What can you do?" Her eyes bounced from Jamison to Aspen. "You two don't have kids do you?"

The butterflies swarmed in Jamison's stomach again. "No, ma'am," he said. His cheeks were suddenly feeling hot and he was grateful when the boy who had been feeding the cows creaked open the screen door and said, "Done with my chores, mom. Can I go over to Connor's now?"

"Sure, honey," Erma said. She blew her son a kiss and he ran back into the yard.

"Thanks mom," he yelled over his shoulder. "I love you."

Jamison was about to ask more about the horses when he noticed all the color drain from Aspen's cheeks. She looked sick, or maybe considering the situation, like she'd seen a ghost. She swallowed hard and looked to the floor. Jamison had seen that move on people he was interviewing when they needed a minute to compose themselves before they could continue. He'd once interviewed a Tibetan monk who stayed in that pose for a full minute on live-air while Jamison and the viewing public waited for him to rejoin them.

Erma stepped into the dining room and pointed out the window toward a pasture. She continued the conversation as if she hadn't noticed her son's interruption.

"And the white one with brown spots is a bit slower, but also feistier. Her name is Mr. Ed." Erma's eyes went to the floor this time and she shook her head. "There's no excuse for that name. Ride at your own risk, of course," she said, in place of a waiver.

"Of course," Jamison said. "Stalliony and Mr. Ed. Thank you, Erma."

Jamison turned to leave and bumped straight into Aspen. She looked around him like she didn't even realize he was there. "Can I ask you something, Erma?" she said. "It's a little personal."

"Of course. No secrets here."

There was a long pause in which Jamison thought Aspen must have changed her mind about her question. "Your son, just now, he said that he loves you."

After a moment of silence, Erma tilted her head. "Yes?"

"Well, I was just wondering. Do you think you'd still know that he loves you, even if he didn't say it? I mean, if he never said it?"

"Why on earth wouldn't he say it?" Erma asked. "I'm his mother." She chuckled as if it were a trick question, but when her eyes met Aspen's, her face turned curious and then a bit sad. She seemed to consider the question with difficulty, as if it were something she had never thought about before. "The correct answer, of course, is that love is about actions, not words. That saying he loves me isn't necessary at all."

Erma pursed her lips, as if trying to keep her next words in. But in the end, her honesty seemed to win the battle. "But if that were the whole truth, how could you explain the thrill I get deep down in my chest every single time he says it?"

Aspen looked to the floor again, as if she was too ashamed to show her face. "I couldn't," she said.

Aspen

Why on earth wouldn't he say it? I'm his mother.

Why, indeed. It was rhetorical. A question so ludicrous it shouldn't even have to be asked. As if the thought of a child not saying "I love you" to a parent was such an absurdity no one in their right mind would consider it possible. *Shame* seemed the only possible word for the day.

Aspen went to the pasture. She rode the horse. She made it gallop, like her father had instructed. It should have been amazing. It should have been an experience like nothing she had done before.

But it wasn't. She couldn't focus on the moment. On the beauty and the adrenaline. She was distracted by a pervasive, overpowering thought.

That she was the worst daughter in the world. And she didn't deserve the miracle that was happening to her.

Jamison

Jamison couldn't account for Aspen's lack of enthusiasm while she had ridden Mr. Ed. Or for her general change in mood that seemed to come out of nowhere. Or her question about Erma's son. None of it made sense, but he couldn't dwell on it. Unfortunately, he had a phone call to make.

"Can I speak to Mr. Harris, please," he said when someone in the newsroom answered. When Harris picked up the phone, Jamison tried to make his voice upbeat. "What'd you think?"

There was a grumble on the other end of the line and Jamison was pretty sure Harris was cursing out whoever summoned him to take the call. But his hand must have been over the phone because all Jamison could hear was a kazoo. At least he wasn't swearing at him, Jamison thought. And then Harris started doing exactly that. Jamison held the phone away from his ear, wondering where the kazoo effect was when he needed it. Finally, Harris got to his point.

"I'm not sure we understand each other, Hightower. I said I want hard news. Not some woman talking about her relationship to her daddy. I don't care if you have to burn the town to the ground. If you want to keep your job, give me NEWS!"

The dial tone was like therapy for Jamison's eardrums.

The Ghost

My strength is weakening. I've been able to do it alone this long, but I can't anymore. I need help. There are too many moving parts. Too many things I hadn't anticipated. I have to figure out something that will take some of the load off my back.

The back of a ghost isn't as strong as I had hoped.

Cornelius

Being a celebrity agreed with Cornelius Brown, PhD. Since the moment he had predicted the miracle of the running shoes, his life had changed. *Cuddley Cal's* had presented him with a giant teddy bear, which was too big for Cornelius to lift, but he hadn't planned on keeping it anyway. He gave it to Crystal, who shrieked, cried, and ever since had been dragging the teddy bear by its head—the only way someone her size could maneuver it—everywhere she went.

Having spent most of his life in academia, Cornelius surprised himself at his ability to play to a crowd. If things were beginning to feel too calm, too settled, Cornelius would prepare the Helium Blaster and yell, "Everyone please hold still for a moment. If you all do exactly as I say, we'll stay below the acceptable risk threshold."

He would send a blast of helium toward the middle of the playground, scurry over to his Atmospheric Density Tester, and yell something like, "Levels are increasing. This is definitely a hot spot." Or whatever felt right at the time. As it turned out, he had a talent for saying exciting things.

The crowd would become restless once again, questions would be cast toward him from all corners, and most importantly, Crystal Lux would swoon and blink rapidly at him. With every hour that passed, he became more and more convinced that The Ghost was real.

Cornelius saw Crystal crossing the playground, returning with a Styrofoam cup of apple cider from the stand near the spring rider. She would take a step, then heave the head of the teddy bear even with her. Step, heave. Step, heave. Cornelius rushed to help.

He knew what would happen next. They would sit side by side and share the cider. They would talk about the excitement around them and Crystal would compliment Cornelius on his intellect and daring.

Then he would return to the Helium Blaster to twist levers and push buttons, proving that everything she said about him was exactly correct.

Jamison

It was the second time Jamison had ridden the hospital train and both times he half-expected to be dropped off in Wonderland or Oz. Maybe Narnia. The place just had that feel.

He had never had a family gathering for Thanksgiving, but what he saw as he stepped out of the train reminded him of all the "Home for the Holidays" commercials. A long table, covered with plates and glasses, and lined with chairs occupied by smiling, laughing, chatting people. An enormous bear-dog scurrying around everyone's chairs, snatching scraps dropped accidentally or snuck under the table secretively.

As they took their seats, several clinks of a spoon against glass silenced the conversation and the attention of everyone around the table focused on the gray-haired doctor at the head. The man's badge read "Dr. Morrison" and Jamison immediately pegged him as the attending physician.

"Thanks, as always, to the Sparkling Pond Rotary Club for the delicious food," Dr. Morrison said. "It's nice to know our residents will be sufficiently well nourished for another twenty-four hours of thankless work."

A smattering of polite laughter suggested the joke had been overused, but the attending physician commanded enough respect that everyone still responded. "Now, down to business. Dr. Limon will update us on Mr. Collins' status."

A pimply man with bags dragging his eyes down grunted as he stood, as if it took all his effort. His scrubs hung loosely, rolled up several times at the arms and legs. But when he spoke, it was clear, confident, and professional.

"Pike Collins' vitals remain strong. Heart rate, blood pressure, body temperature and respiratory rate are all within normal ranges. The current level of Isoflurane appears sufficient to sustain his current comatose status. However, the latest CT and EEGs suggest a new development of—"

"Since we have a guest with us today," Dr. Morrison interrupted. He nodded in Jamison's direction. "How about we take it down a level? What say you give a short, succinct summary of the situation?" He nodded to Jamison again. "This man has no idea what's going on with his friend's father. Enlighten him for us. In English."

"Of course," Dr. Limon said. He faced Jamison, and the rest of the eyes in the room followed.

"Three years ago, Mr. Collins was diagnosed with brain cancer. At the time, we considered surgery, but decided there were too many risk factors. However, an acute event a few months ago forced us into it. The surgery itself went well, but his brain began to swell dangerously post-op." He looked to Jamison, as if unsure how much lay people understood. "That means after the operation. The medical team decided an induced coma was the best option to treat the brain swelling."

Aspen sat next to Jamison, focusing on every word as if she had never heard them before. She was leaning forward, and Jamison realized she was trying to glean something new from what Dr. Limon was saying.

"Over the past three months, a major complication has arisen. The brain cancer has spread to other organs, specifically the pancreas, and is growing unabated while he is in a comatose state. Now we're unable to bring him out of the coma because the brain swelling is so severe he likely wouldn't be able to function, and unable to leave him in a coma because the pancreatic cancer is quickly killing him.

"With deepest sympathy to our friend Aspen, her father is in the final stages of terminal cancer. These meetings are less an attempt to save his life and more of an attempt to figure out the best time to bring him out of the coma, such that his brain is functioning well enough to communicate and the cancer has not yet resulted in death. That time appears to be fairly close at hand."

Dr. Limon turned back to the attending physician. "Sir?"

"Good," Dr. Morrison said. "Although it would have been better to say something along the lines of, 'I'm sorry that Aspen's father is going to die of cancer very soon. We're hoping to facilitate a final meeting for the two of them before he passes away.' Nothing else is needed."

"Thank you, sir," the resident said. He sat down and immediately resumed eating.

A couple things clicked into place in Jamison's mind. Aspen's insistence that she not miss a meeting. Her reluctance to canoe the Mississippi. If they decided to bring her father out of his coma and she wasn't there, she could miss her opportunity to speak to him one last time.

And yet, she had put her life completely on hold—she couldn't go anywhere for more than a couple of hours. To Jamison, it seemed out of balance.

The meeting ended abruptly after the doctors decided they could wait at least another day before attempting to bring Aspen's father out of the coma. The medical staff hurried to their next destination while Rufus sniffed the floor for snacks.

Jamison was lost in his thoughts about Aspen and her father when she nudged his elbow with hers. "What's wrong?"

Jamison had seen Aspen's temper and had no interest in witnessing it again. So he tried to tread carefully. He started with a shrug, as if it wasn't important. "I get why you would want to talk to your father again. I mean, who wouldn't? But you had all those years with him, and you've known for a long time that he's sick. Is it really worth all you're sacrificing for one last conversation that might not even happen?"

"Yes," she said immediately. Her cheeks dipped in like she was chewing them, trying to decide how much to say. "I have to tell him that I love him."

Jamison touched her hands and immediately felt short of breath, a shot of adrenaline speeding his heart rate. "He's the perfect father, right? I'm sure he knows you love him."

Aspen's eyes flashed, as if he had just slapped her. Tears sprang down her cheeks, as if she had been on the verge of crying all along. She shoved Jamison's hands away and ran into her father's hospital room, leaving Jamison alone, his hands empty.

Jamison stood perfectly still, afraid that any movement might cause an earthquake. He was staring at Rufus, but his gaze was inward. He searched his words and actions, trying in vain to figure out what in the world had just happened.

Aspen

There are four kinds of secrets, Aspen knew. Two good, two bad.

The first kind is meant to deceive. The lying teenager. The unfaithful spouse. It results in betrayal and pain.

The second is meant to exclude. The topic of the secret doesn't even matter. The fact of it is enough to accomplish its task.

The third is meant to surprise. A fiftieth birthday party. An unexpected visit. It's a necessary evil to enhance a gift.

And the last is the kind of secret Aspen kept—a secret meant to protect. It's easily rationalized because of the possible consequences if it didn't exist. The truth is so scary it needs to be shrouded in secrecy, kept inside and guarded. But the motivation behind it, the reason to keep it, is benevolent. Even noble.

So why, Aspen wondered, did she feel so terrible about it?

Cornelius

If ever there was a night for a ghost sighting, it was this night. Cornelius shuffled with his equipment as Crystal watched nearby, sitting in the lap of the giant teddy bear from *Cuddly Cal's* and sipping her Honeycrisp apple cider. A full moon shone so brightly upon the scene that the stadium lights were barely needed. The tornado slide sparkled in pale moonlight.

But a wave of voices disturbed the peace. It started by the monkey bars, and by the time it reached Cornelius, it was loud enough to distort the readings on his Atmospheric Density Tester. A large group of people arrived shortly after and stood next to Cornelius, close enough to him and his equipment for it to feel threatening. A man with a thick black beard stuck his chin in the air and everyone in the square fell silent.

"My name is Tom and I represent the Free Thinkers." The crowd exchanged confused looks. Team God and Team Ghost were well known, but a third group? "We, as Free Thinkers, take on as our mission, the proliferation of common sense amidst stupidity."

"What are you talking about?" someone yelled.

Cornelius shuffled his feet to put some distance between himself and Tom. He wasn't sure why the man had decided to make his announcement so close to his equipment, but something about it made him uncomfortable.

"We believe all of you have forgotten, or conveniently overlooked, the one indisputable fact in all of this. There is no such thing as ghosts."

Now the crowd began grumbling and Cornelius heard a few curses cast at the leader of the Free Thinkers. He pretended to look the other way and took another step away from Tom.

"Furthermore," Tom continued. "We think it's obvious what is happening here."

When Tom turned and stared at him, Cornelius finally understood. Crystal's voice screeched above all others. "Oh no you don't!"

But Tom was undeterred. "Only one man here has the experience and the knowledge to pull off a giant hoax like this. Only one man could be behind it."

Crystal Lux bared her fangs like an attack dog. "You don't know my Cornelius! He would never do something like that. He's a professional."

"He's a fraud," yelled one of the Free Thinkers near Tom.

Cornelius started toward Crystal—he had to stop her before this got ugly. But she was too fast, and stuck her pointer finger right into Tom's face. "Shut your mouth, sir! You don't know my Cornelius."

Cornelius finally reached Crystal, put his arm around her, and retreated to the shelter of the equipment. The Free Thinkers, apparently deciding they weren't looking for a physical fight, shifted closer to the teeter-totter where they staked out their territory and began setting up camp.

Looking around the moon-lit playground, Cornelius didn't' like what he saw. Whereas the Team God and Team Ghost people had always created a sense of tension, the introduction of a new group— especially one that accused him of a hoax—made the tension feel as if it could snap without a moment's notice.

The Ghost

I'm concerned that this could get out of hand. It was never intended to become a circus. It was never supposed to cause fights. Something tells me I should pull the plug right now. I've shown Aspen that she's loved. I've accomplished at least part of my task. I should call it good enough and stop. Be done with it.

But I know I can't. Because one thing is beyond any doubt—I'll never have another opportunity like the one I have now. And I find that I just can't let that go.

Day Four

Jamison

Jamison had been able to go to college on a scholarship for underprivileged kids. Back in J-school, his favorite professor had asked him why he wanted to go into journalism. After all, for most people it was low on pay, high on demands, and comes with no job security. Why would Jamison want to put himself through that?

"I just want to tell people's stories," Jamison had told him.

The professor had liked that answer, and Jamison had received an "A" in the class. But he wasn't sure how the professor would have reacted if he had been a better journalist himself and asked just one follow-up. "Why do you want to tell people's stories?"

The answer—so Jamison wouldn't have to remember his own—may have given the professor pause. Jamison's story, to that point, had not been a happy one. Most of the time, he wished more than anything to go back and rewrite it from the beginning.

That thought—of having a fresh attempt at life—reminded Jamison of his newest friend. He poked into the kitchen, where Claire was up early fixing another breakfast for an army, and said, "Claire, what does Holly Torrey do all day?"

Claire's eyes widened in surprise. "Holly Torrey?"

"Yeah. Her parents died, right? And since I've been here, I haven't seen her around town playing with other kids. I just wonder what she does."

"What did you do all day when you were young?"

"That's what has me worried. She's a sweet kid."

"She's certainly that. But to answer your question, I don't know what a normal day is like for her."

Jamison scratched the line between his lower lip and chin. "Do you know where she lives?"

Claire's gaze wasn't accusatory, but it was frank. "It's a wonderful thought. But you should take care. Holly doesn't need a father-figure for a week. She needs one forever. And I don't think that's in your plans."

She was right, Jamison realized. As usual, she had seen right to the heart of him. What was he hoping to accomplish? To ease his conscience? To live vicariously through an eight year-old girl? It wasn't something he'd really thought about. He was just feeling his way through, like walking through a dark room with his hands outstretched, guided by nothing but a sixth sense that may or may not exist.

As he considered it, Jamison realized it was probably about him as much as Holly. The way he saw it, children that grew up in a house without love, grew up not knowing how to love. Maybe he just wanted to prove that his own loveless childhood didn't define him. That he wouldn't perpetuate that cycle. That he was capable of kindness to a child, despite never receiving any when he was young.

Claire was still looking at Jamison, but her look had softened. It was as if she had read the thoughts as they had entered his mind, a talent Jamison was pretty convinced she had. She beckoned him with two bony fingers. "She gets up bright and early, far as I know," she said. "Maybe I should go with you."

And so she did, and their pace couldn't have been slower if they'd been like the boy from Altura he'd done a story on, whose mother gave in when he begged for a baby elephant and ended up carrying it to school on his back. Jamison was called in to cover the story when it grew too big, the novelty wore off, and the principal refused to allow it on school grounds anymore. It had proven to be one of his more controversial stories.

They ended up in a quiet neighborhood. One with no tricycles or plastic baseball bats strewn across the yards. Jamison knocked on the door and it was Holly's footsteps that pattered to it and answered.

"Jamison!" she screamed. Just the sound of that voice reminded Jamison why he loved her so much. She lunged at him, wrapped her arms around him, and pressed her face into his stomach.

"Hey there," Jamison said. "I'm happy to see you, too."

"What are you doing here? Want to join us for breakfast?"

"Claire's got something cooking back at her place," Jamison said. "I just thought it might be fun to hang out with my friend for a bit."

Holly turned to the interior and yelled, "DeDe, Papa, I'm going out to play."

"With who?" an old voice said from inside.

"Don't worry, Claire Lyons is here." Holly bolted from the house, leaving the door wide open. "So what do you want to play?"

"Just a second," Jamison said. He nodded to Claire and she walked into the house with him. Jamison leaned into a linoleum-floored kitchen where an elderly couple was frying bacon and brewing coffee. "Sir, ma'am," he said. "My name is Jamison Hightower. I met your granddaughter the other day and we seem to enjoy each other's company. With your permission, I'd like to spend some time with her this morning. I promise to bring her home soon."

The man and woman both turned immediately to Claire—the epitome of trustworthiness and wisdom in town. Claire's nod was as good as gospel.

Holly was waiting just outside the door. "What do you want to play?" she asked again.

"Whatever you want," Jamison said.

"Anything?"

"Sure. What's your favorite game?"

"You can't tell anyone, because it's, like, so first grade."

"You have my word."

Holly checked over her shoulder, then whispered, "Lions."

Even though Jamison hadn't played hide-and-seek, he had been theoretically familiar with it. But Lions? "I don't think I know that one. Is it hard?"

Holly giggled and rolled her eyes. "It's easy. We just pretend to be lions. We chase prey and play around. It's literally the funnest game ever."

"Okay," Jamison said. "Does Claire get to play?"

"Of course," Holly said. "All friends are welcome, remember?" A warmth Jamison couldn't quite describe filled his chest when she said, "I learned that from you, Jamison."

He was in serious risk of shedding a tear when Holly dropped to the ground and changed her voice to a high-pitched squeak that was still supposed to be a lion's roar. "Watch out for the hyenas. They're our enemy." Her voice sounded like Chewbacca in falsetto and Jamison did his best to imitate it.

"Don't worry. I'll fight them off."

Ouch, he thought. Apparently Chewbacca-ing was a talent that developed over time.

Holly knelt up and put her hands on her hips. "No Jamison, you gotta be on your hands and knees. Like real lions." She used her real voice—her scolding voice. Apparently, she'd forgotten her concern that others might find out what game she liked.

Jamison was tempted to point out that they weren't real lions. And even if they were, real lions didn't walk on hands and knees. But he was learning how to avoid her eye-roll so instead, he crawled through the grass and gave a growl that made Holly giggle. God, he loved that sound.

Jamison supposed Claire should be forgiven for her lack of *Lions* skills. Even he felt a bit awkward on his hands and knees and he accidentally stepped on Holly's hand with his knee.

"Oops, sorry," he Chewbaccad to her.

Holly pretended to lick her paw. She looked at Jamison with her best sad expression. "I want to forgive you. But I can't. I just don't know how."

Holly dropped her character for a moment and looked to Claire. In her normal voice, she said, "Just like Ms. Aspen with her daddy, right?"

At first, Jamison assumed he hadn't understood her correctly. But when he played it back in his mind, he heard the same confusing words again. A glance at Claire confirmed it. Her gaze was thoughtful, penetrating, and a bit sad.

Holly had moved on as if nothing had happened. She was busy trying to convince Jamison that zebras were the tastiest prey. But he couldn't focus. His thoughts were consumed by Aspen.

After such a short time, Jamison felt so much for her. And yet, he seemed to know the least about her.

Cornelius

Everything would have been just fine if not for the Free Thinkers. Tom, their apparent leader, wouldn't stop scowling at Cornelius from beside the Tornado Slide. And Crystal, who turned out to be feistier than a miniature Doberman, snarled right back. It was time to bring this entire thing back to the whole reason he'd come here—to impress Crystal Lux. No, that wasn't right. To prove the existence of a ghost. Cornelius needed something big, something dramatic, to undermine Tom and the Free Thinkers, and prove to Crystal that he could handle himself competently in times of adversity.

Several police officers patrolled the town square now, so Cornelius didn't feel too bad about leaving Crystal with his equipment for a while. He paced through the grassy open space of Sparkling Pond until he found the best possible option—Lenny's Electronics and Repair.

A man with a name tag that read *Lenny* was sorting boxes of DVD players behind his check-out counter. Cornelius stopped in his tracks and stared. The man could have been his identical twin. Lenny even absentmindedly touched his pocket-protector when he was thinking. Eerie. Best to keep Crystal away from this shop in the future.

Cornelius perused the shelves, picking up a charging adaptor of some sort, then putting it back down. It's not like he was here to browse. He kept up his charade for a few more minutes, until his nerves were as steeled as possible. Then he approached the counter and waited for Lenny to notice him. When Lenny looked up from his DVD players, Cornelius stared at his Doppelganger. They studied each other in silence for a long moment, eyes moving over spectacled faces, collared button-down short-sleeved shirts, and stiffly parted hair. Then Cornelius leaned in conspiratorially.

"There's something I need help with." He licked his lips and shot a glance to his right, then his left. "But here's the thing—no one can ever know I was here."

Jamison

Jamison had grown up eating the cheapest things he could get his hands on—not exactly a training ground for a food critic. But when Claire Lyons cooked, it didn't take a genius to realize she was born to be a chef. When Jamison and Claire got around to eating the breakfast she had made earlier, it was *blanquette de veau* with black truffles and fresh blueberries. Jamison knew he could sit there all day and do nothing but stuff his face.

And that's just what he did, much to the delight of his hostess. Then he leaned back in his chair, sipped his coffee, and marveled at how lucky he was to have met her. Claire eased into the chair on Jamison's left and said, "How are you enjoying your stay, Jamison Hightower?"

"Very much, thank you. Largely because of you. You've been too kind."

"Too kind?" Claire tilted her head. "Personally, I've never liked the saying. The way I see it, it's just not possible."

"I suppose you're right." For a moment, Jamison couldn't help but wonder what it would have been like to have Claire as a grandmother, but the thought was too painful and he pushed it from his mind. "So you learned to cook authentic French food by taking one class in 1980-something?"

Claire's eyes sparkled. "Well, not just that. George and I went to Paris once. Long ago. Everything was so perfect and romantic. We walked under the Eiffel Tower and strolled by the Seine. We gazed at the beauty of Notre Dame and spent hours poring over the art in the Louvre—not that we understood any of it. The only thing that really takes me back there is the food.

"So I started messing around a bit, tinkering here and there until it tasted right. Somewhere along the line, I got it pretty close."

"Well I think you're amazing," Jamison said. "I really do think you should start that restaurant."

Claire's expression turned wistful. "I have just the place picked out, actually. Right next to The Bent Spoon, on the north side of Paula's

Prairie Cookies. A nice little café with outdoor seating where people can sip a cappuccino or an espresso and talk with a friend over a crepe, just like in Paris. A little slice of heaven."

The thought seemed energizing. Her posture straightened and her eyes brightened. She even rubbed her hands together, as if plotting a diabolical plan.

"You should do it," Jamison said. "Really."

Claire's papery shoulders crinkled a bit. "Oh, it's just a dream. I could never."

"What's stopping you? Not the quality of your cooking, obviously. And it wouldn't be that hard to find someone to take care of the business aspects."

Claire studied her fingers. "I guess I'm just afraid of what would happen if it didn't work out."

"You're afraid of failure?"

"Having the namesake of the entire town attached to me is a lot of pressure. If the restaurant of Hank Lyons' granddaughter went broke? Well, I don't know if I could handle the looks I'd get walking through town."

"I'm not really smart enough to give much advice," Jamison said. *Because no one in my life has had any worthwhile advice for me*, he didn't say. "But I do know this. A year from now, you could be in the same situation, or you could own a cute little French restaurant. But either way, that year will go by."

Claire's eyes misted over a bit, as if his little attempt at philosophy had hit home with her. She was looking at Jamison like he had never been looked at before. As if she was proud. Claire nodded hard. "You're right. In fact, I'll make you a promise right now. In one year from now, I will have my restaurant."

Just claiming it—making that statement—seemed to lift her up. And it was contagious. Jamison felt uplifted just being near her. He wasn't sure how he could play a part, but he resolved—if only for his brief time in town—to do whatever he could to help make Claire's energizing dream come true.

Aspen

Aspen had wanted to avoid the town square, and especially the playground, ever since Holly Torrey had made the first discovery there. A crowd had shown up immediately and Aspen didn't want to be part of the spectacle. The false alarm had reiterated the point. *Viral* came to mind for word of the day.

But her father was speaking to her. And for whatever reason, he had chosen to continue to speak to her from the playground at the square, despite the crowds. Since Aspen felt the need to be close to him—not just his comatose body—she braced herself and headed for the playground.

She was still a hundred yards away when someone at a picnic table saw her and pointed. A dozen people rushed toward her and she wondered whether she should turn and run. But when they arrived, all wearing Team God tee-shirts, they smiled and all seemed to want to touch her arms, her hands, and even her cheeks. Some of them were mumbling under their breath and when Aspen realized they were praying, she sped her pace and hurried to the park.

When the Team Ghost people realized who it was, they came over as well. Although they didn't seem to worship her, they did offer her lemonade and brownies and asked if she would like to sit with them for a while.

The attention could have made her feel wanted, and maybe she should have even tried to enjoy it. But she couldn't help but feel sorry for them. The people seemed desperate, as if they were empty and searching for some sort of meaning to fill the void.

Aspen accepted some lemonade from the Team Ghost people—she was too skeptical of the brownies to accept one—then touched a Team God member on the sleeve in apology, since she could sense the rivalry between them. She had to admit, there was a certain magical feel to the place, with stadium lights surrounding them, hundreds of people excitedly waiting for another miracle, and the knowledge that her father was speaking to her here. They had even brought in a giant, 200-inch, Ultra-HD TV, which was perched on a stand where everyone in a two hundred yard radius could watch Jamison's daily live-shots. But just as Aspen was starting to wonder if she should enjoy the spectacle, a harsh voice broke her from her reverie.

"You're not special," it said. "You know that, don't you?"

Tom, the leader of the Free Thinkers, was yelling from a group of picnic tables near the tornado slide, where his group was camped out. His eyes flicked to the God and Ghost groups next to Aspen, as if trying to decide if it was safe to approach her.

"You are nothing special because there is nothing special going on here. In fact, you're probably in on it."

Several other people near Tom joined in yelling at her. One man mockingly claimed the tornado slide was actually a magical gift from his dead grandmother. Another started digging a hole and shouting that he was looking for buried treasure. Someone threw an egg toward Aspen and it smacked against the picnic table she was sitting at, splattering yoke onto her shirt.

The people around her yelled back and a few even walked over to confront the egg-thrower. Aspen wanted no part of it and snuck away amid the growing chaos. When several people started yelling she looked over her shoulder and saw two people wrestling on the ground, throwing haymakers and trying to pull each other's hair.

Aspen sped her pace, putting as much distance as possible between her and the town square. For the first time in her life, she felt unsafe in her hometown. She was angry at the Free Thinkers, but not just for their cruelty. She was mad that they didn't believe what was happening. At first it was the Team God people, and now the Free Thinkers. So many people thought she was a liar.

She needed to prove them wrong. And if she didn't have the credibility to make the Free Thinkers believe, she would have to find another way. Cornelius Brown was too infatuated with Crystal Lux to even see straight—he wouldn't be able to help. What Aspen needed was an independent, objective person. Not a ghost hunter, but someone qualified.

She opened her journal and flipped to the last page. She pulled a pen out of the binding, licked the tip, and wrote *Proof.*

Jamison

Jamison tried to exude confidence as he guided Claire by her elbow and walked along the main path in town, past shops and eateries. It wasn't so much about being able to catch her if she fell, which was what made him worry he might hurt her with a grip that was too firm. He realized it was more about the presence. About simply being there. To let her know, psychologically as much as physically, that he was there to care for her. That she could count on him.

Claire pointed to an empty space next to The Bent Spoon. "Right there," she said. "The kitchen will be right in the middle of the tables. I hope people will like to watch me prepare their food, but really I want it like that so I can watch them. People are so interesting, don't you think?"

As a guy who loved to tell people's stories, Jamison could wholeheartedly agree with her. "And some outdoor seating, too?" he asked.

Just then his phone rang in his pocket, which was about as welcome as the six-foot prairie rattlesnake an old couple from Wabasha found in their bathtub, without a clue how it got there. They'd called the station and asked for Jamison by name to tell their amazing story.

"Hightower," a voice stabbed at him before he could even say hello. Jamison's heart rate skyrocketed and he pulled the phone away from his ear to look at the time. Somehow, he'd let the morning get away from him.

"Mr. Harris," he said, turning his back to Claire in embarrassment. "I'm on my way to the live-shot now. Is J.D. there already?"

"You're not on your way. You forgot all about it. I can tell by the cracking in your pitiful voice."

"No, really. I—"

"I don't want to hear it, Hightower. Luckily for you, there's been a change of plans."

The next few moments of silence were torture for Jamison. On one hand, he wouldn't be punished for being late for his live-shot. But what if the change of plans involved being called back to Rock Prairie?

"...top of the six," Harris' voice said.

"What?" Jamison asked. His mind exploded in so many different directions whenever he talked to Harris, he always ended up coming off as a bumbling idiot. It was no wonder Harris hated him, really.

"Top of the six?" Jamison repeated. "My live-shot?"

"You do realize this comes with more pressure to perform, don't you?"

"I'll be ready," Jamison said instinctively.

"You'd better be," Harris said, and hung up.

Jamison stared at his phone, trying to wrap his mind around the fact that he'd be doing the live-shot at the beginning of the six o'clock news. This story must be getting a lot of positive feedback from the public. A terrifying thought.

"Sorry about that," he said to Claire. "So, outdoor seating?"

Claire had bent over to pick wildflowers to give Jamison privacy on the phone. She stood now with a bright bouquet of purple, blue, and yellow blossoms. Thankfully, she ignored the phone call and was describing how the tables would wrap around the building, providing options for shade or sun at all times of the day, when Aspen tapped his shoulder, looking as if she had been running.

"We need a private investigator," she said.

Jamison thought about apologizing for whatever he had said after the meeting that had made her so upset, but he figured if she had forgotten about it, he would too. Then he tried to figure out how a private investigator would help what Claire's menu should look like when he realized she was talking about the miracles. "Okay," he said. "I'm sure we could find a good one in Minneapolis. I'll help you look this afternoon."

"Oh, you don't need to go through all that," Claire said. "I know of a wonderful private eye right here in Sparkling Pond."

"Really?" Aspen said. "Who?"

"Rad Collie."

Aspen laughed out loud and waited for the rest of the joke. After a moment of awkward silence she said, "You can't be serious. Rad Collie? From Dangling Cliff Adventures? The old man's high more often than not."

"Well, he has a medical condition," Claire said. "And watch who you're calling old. Rad's younger than me, you know. Besides, people used to call from all around for his expertise."

Aspen shook her head, like something was stuck in it. "Rad Collie, Private Eye. I know you can't judge a book by its cover, but you can usually figure out if it's fact or fiction."

"Just give him a chance," Claire said. "I promise, you won't be disappointed."

Rad

Rad Collie was in the middle of an epic story when his phone rang. If there was one drag about having your own business, it was having to answer the stupid phone. How many times had he been building up to the part where he had furnished a tourniquet for his own broken humerus, or treated his climbing buddy's High Altitude Pharyngitis with a Jolly Rancher, only to have the phone interrupt the climax of the story?

"Just a second, dude," he said to whoever was enthralled with his story. He picked up the stupid phone. "Rad Collie's Dangling Cliff Adventures. Dude, it's Rad."

The voice on the other end was one he hadn't heard in a long time, but hearing it didn't shock him nearly as much as what it said. "Huh? And you're calling me?"

After several minutes of listening, Rad hung up the phone and returned to the showroom to find his customer gone. Still, there was no reason to waste a good story, so Rad picked up where he had left off. If hiking boots and carabineers could hear—and Rad wasn't at all sure they couldn't—they were in for an epic climax.

Aspen

Aspen couldn't believe she was doing this. Although she admittedly didn't know much about Rad Collie, she knew enough. He owned Dangling Cliff Adventures, but as far as anyone could tell, he never sold anything. Anyone brave enough to walk into his store would have to sit through hours of stories while trying to ignore the stench of incense. No one had much doubt what the curling smoke was masking.

Rad had found his place in Sparkling Pond lore as a serious mountaineer, although it was long ago. He had even made an attempt at Mt. Everest in his youth, but had turned around after reaching the Hillary Step. Not because of bad weather or exhaustion, he had told anyone who would listen. But because he really wanted a beer.

The only mention of Rad in Aspen's diary had been December 22nd, age nine, when Arlen McHenry caught a stomach bug and Rad somehow ended up filling in as Santa Clause at Santa's Workshop in the town square. *Creepy.* It was the year she had learned the truth about Santa Clause.

And now, despite all common sense, she was about to step into his shop and ask him to be a private investigator for a personal matter. Jamison strode next to her with his video camera perched on his shoulder, in search of footage that might enhance his live-shot that evening.

Aspen felt calmer just looking at the crooked smile on Jamison's face—as if this were all a little joke. She was almost able to convince herself it would be okay—Claire had recommended Rad, after all. But then she and Jamison neared the entrance to Rad's shop and heard his voice. It was confident and resounding—a voice to make sure everyone in the cheap seats could hear.

"So I kicked off my skis, tossed my poles, and swam along the top of the avalanche. My buddy saw two of my fingers sticking up through the snow, and dug me out. Two fingers!"

Aspen watched Rad face the wall, apparently talking to a pair of hiking boots. And that was enough. She strode toward the exit but bumped into Jamison, his eye pressed to the filming camera. It gave Rad enough time to notice her attempt to flee.

"Aspen Collins," he said. He grabbed her shoulder and steered her inside. "Great to see you out and about. How's your old man holding up?"

"Um, well, they didn't wake him last night," Aspen said. She shot Jamison a desperate look, but he was hidden behind the camera. Some help he was.

"Great, great," Rad said. He flipped his long, gray hair out of his eyes, pulled a brown bandana out of his back pocket and tied his hair back. "Didn't know you had a camera crew these days. Just let me tidy up a bit. I need to look good for my fans, right?"

Rad grinned into the camera and checked himself out in the reflection of the lens. He licked his thumbs, wiped down his eyebrows, and stuck out his lower lip in satisfaction. *Inexplicably Vain.* "So are you going on an adventure somewhere?" he said. "I can outfit any kind of excursion. Half price for mid-week trips." His eyes did a double-take of Jamison's camera and his body tensed. "Some restrictions apply, of course."

"Actually, no," Aspen said. "We're here for something else." She racked her brain for an excuse to leave. Finally, she sighed and dropped her hands to her side. "The thing is, Claire Lyons said you used to be a private investigator."

"That's right, dude. Best in the business. I was a certified researchist manager."

Rad's eyes flashed to the camera again and he squirmed in his chair. "I mean, assistant manager."

"Well, I guess I was looking for someone like that. But I know you have your store to run, so I can find someone else." Aspen grabbed Jamison's arm and pulled him toward the door, but Rad scrambled in front of them and blocked the way.

"No, no. The store pretty much runs itself, you know. I can figure out your dilemma stuff. No charge."

"Oh," Aspen said. It was like dealing with a toddler dressed up as

Batman. Sometimes they just need to feel important. It's up to the adults in the room to prevent a tantrum. "Okay, I guess."

"Just follow me to the back here. Oh, wait here just a second. I got a few, ah…" His eyes darted to the camera. "Just wait a second, dudes."

Rad ran through a doorway behind the cash register. He moved some things around, humming the whole time, with some words Aspen had never heard mixed in. "Okay. You can come on back now."

Rad sat in a rusted folding chair pulled up to an old wooden school desk. He could have been a second grader, Aspen thought, and then realized that was true on several levels. He would be the kid responsible for the folders standing on desks, foiling any attempts to cheat. Aspen pulled up another folding chair while Jamison filmed from the corner. Rad's calloused hands and dirty fingernails rested on the desk.

"So what's going on?" Rad asked. His face was screwed into an uncomfortable-looking serious expression.

Aspen turned to Jamison for help. His eyebrows shrugged behind the viewfinder. "Well," Aspen said. "As you probably know, things have been appearing in the town square. Things for me."

"Uh huh," Rad said. "I've seen it all on the news. You looked hot on TV yesterday."

Aspen cocked her head to the side. He's a second grader, she reminded herself. Probably best to treat him like one, with all the leniencies that involved. "So anyway, we're trying to find proof that my dad is actually sending these things."

"Oh, it's him alright," Rad said.

The feet of the chair screeched on the linoleum as Aspen scooted forward. "How do you know?"

Rad's head snapped up. He swallowed, glanced at the camera again, and screwed on his serious face. "Simply the ratio of event, to, probabilication…mostly it's trade secrets you pick up on the job. So let's move on. You seem doubtful."

Aspen sighed and rubbed her eyes. Simply being here was ridiculous. But she was here, so she might as well be honest about it.

"I'm sure it's him. I don't know how, but I know he's behind it.

But…"

Rad leaned back and slapped his cheeks gently, moving his lips in and out to make varying tones, almost like music. "Lightning can be six times hotter than the surface of the sun," he said. "Fifty-thousand-degrees."

Aspen stared at him, trying to decide if he was completely insane or just weird.

"Dude, I was in the Rockies once with a climbing buddy? We got caught in an electrical storm up there and my buddy got fried. Lightning hit the ground thirty feet away and flowed like a wave on a pond until it lit him up. When I got to him, he was toast. But a little CPR action brought him right back."

"That doesn't sound possible," Jamison said from behind his lens.

"Actually," Aspen said. "Everything he said is possible. But I don't understand its relevance."

"Like your dude said, it sounds impossible. Kind of like you getting old junk from your dad when he's about dead. Amazing things happen."

"I know," Aspen said. "But I'm trying to find out how. How is it possible for him to write these things in the notes? He's writing about things that are happening today."

"It isn't possible," Rad said. "But why would that mean it's not happening?"

Aspen chewed the inside of her cheek for a moment. "I guess because, no matter how much it seems like there's no other explanation, it's still hard to believe. I mean, I studied medicine. In medicine, it's all about science and math. Real, provable answers to every question."

"Every question?" Rad asked. "Never heard of a cancer patient given six months to live, but ten years later, still living cancer-free, and you docs can't explain it? Or a dude who has no heartbeat, but after they call him dead his heart starts beating and he runs the Boston Marathon or some moronic thing like that?"

"Everyone's heard stories like that. But that's all they are to me—stories. I mean, I've never actually seen anything like that happen, so it's hard to believe."

Rad raked his fingers down his face, like he was the philosophy teacher and she was now the second grader. "Dude, you just have to open your eyes. You're seeing it right now."

Aspen

Aspen dug an old pair of shoes from her closet and jogged through the flora of the Sparkling Pond Cemetery. Her father called her "the slow-dance runner" because of the way she eased left and right while she jogged, in time to the music in her head. She'd even been known to spring an occasional pirouette if the tune needed to escape the confines of her soul. *Marathon,* June 6th, age 21.

But now, Aspen couldn't escape the turmoil she felt. She thought of her father, lying in his coma. She thought of Rad's words—*You're seeing it right now.* And she thought of Jamison. More than anything, she thought of Jamison.

Then her thoughts were distracted by a maple deep within the cemetery, its leaves the color of fire. The red was so dense it made the early autumn sky around it glow. She wondered who was responsible for planting it, and decided it was likely Crystal Lux. When the breeze picked up, she could imagine hearing Arlo Guthrie singing through the rustle of leaves, as Crystal likely would.

The music of the Sparkling Pond Cemetery was only legend to most citizens, but Aspen wondered now if it could be real. At dusk, just as the top of the sun dips below the horizon, could the wind rustling through leaves actually create music?

Several Sparkling Pond residents had made that claim, and not just Rad Collie and his friends. Mrs. Littleberry insisted she heard Perry Como—her husband's favorite when he was alive—singing through the branches of his tree one night. A group of teenagers sprinted out of the cemetery last spring, insisting they had heard Lady Gaga through a flowering Lavender Azalea. And William had sworn under oath he had merely been singing along with Bing Crosby—sober as a Walleye on the line—when he had been arrested for disturbing the peace late one night.

Aspen had never heard real music from the flora here, and she spent more time amid the trees and flowers than anyone. Then again, maybe she was experiencing a different kind of magic.

She climbed the hill until she felt the shade of her mother's cherry tree. She leaned against the trunk and tried to organize her thoughts. Thoughts about the messages from her father. About what was happening to her town. And about her feelings for Jamison—and the secret she held from him.

She looked down on Sparkling Pond through the blanket of cherry blossoms and shook her head. "What should I do, mom?" she said. "What should I do?"

Jamison

Jamison had learned to follow the straight and narrow. When you're qualified to do only one job and your boss for that job makes a weekly habit out of threatening to fire you, you better learn to be a rule-follower. Your survival depends on it. Literally, he realized, as he thought about the offer from RISK-TV.

But every once in a while—not often, but occasionally—even he could recognize that rules were made to be broken. And this was one of those times.

He walked next to Holly, who was hobbling on crutches because her leg was in a cast to just above her knee. She seemed a bit embarrassed when Jamison had asked about it—something about falling while playing—so he hadn't pushed it.

Despite the cast, Holly turned the walk into some sort of spy game. She ducked and dodged in place, as if she was hiding behind trees and jumping over logs. Her fingers were shaped like a pistol, causing her to continually drop her crutches and have to pick them up again. Of course, there was no secret mission. She and Jamison were just walking up a hill in the Sparkling Pond Cemetery. But they did have the ashes of her puppy, Baxter, in a sealed Tupperware container, safely secured in the backpack Jamison wore.

It was a great day for a planting.

They were on the opposite side of the cemetery from the cherry tree Aspen sat beneath, but Jamison saw her in the distance. He and Holly crouched a little lower, hoping she wouldn't see them. Jamison had every intention of telling Aspen after they were done. In fact, he had wanted to invite her along. But Holly had been adamant. This was something she wanted to do with Jamison, just two best friends.

"Here's the spot," Holly said. She pointed to the crest of the hill. "They're right there."

Jamison rested his hand on her shoulder and gave a little squeeze. There was nothing he wouldn't give to pour all the strength he had into her. Not only did she need it more, she also deserved it more. "Go ahead," he said. "Baxter and I will wait here."

Holly's shoulders slouched and she limped toward a pair of small bushes atop the hill. Jamison looked to the ground to give her privacy. A few minutes later, she came back and said, "They're doing okay. They say they're happy Baxter will be with them. It'll feel more like a home." But her eyes were full, nearly brimming over with sadness.

"Then let's send him home," Jamison said.

This time he joined her and they walked to the top of the hill. He pulled a handheld shovel from the backpack, set the Tupperware on the grass near the bushes of Holly's parents, and dug a small hole, six inches deep and six inches wide. Perfect for a dogwood tree.

When the hole was finished, Jamison stood and watched while Holly dumped the ashes of her beloved puppy into the ground. Then together, they removed a bag of topsoil from the backpack and filled the rest of the space with several handfuls. Finally, Holley dropped two seeds on top. Then she stood next to Jamison and said, "Will you say a prayer for him?"

A prayer? Jamison was pretty sure he hadn't even heard the word until he was twenty. If he even made an attempt, it was sure to come out as the most sacrilegious thing Holly had ever heard. Unintentionally, certainly, but would that really matter?

"It's okay, Jamison," Holly said, again surprising him with her perception. "Prayers don't have to be memorized. Pastor Adams says the best prayers are when you just talk to God. Just say what's in your heart. Please?"

With that face, she could have asked him to take her to China and he would have started digging a hole. "Okay. Well, what was Baxter like?" Jamison asked. He was stalling as much as he was trying to get information for his prayer.

"He was really smart. He'll probably be a teacher for other dogs in heaven. And he peed on lots of stuff. He really liked doing that."

Fair enough. Jamison cleared his throat and said the first prayer of his entire life. "Baxter, we will miss you. May your heavenly students refer to you as Professor Pees-on-Trees. May your bladder always be full. And may the trees of heaven be fertilized with the sweetness of your urine for all time. Amen."

Holly giggled hard, spilling tears from her eyes. "Yeah. He'll like that."

She stared at the hole filled with Baxter's ashes and the smile slowly dropped from her face. She cocked her head to the side—the weight again, pressing down on her. "I'm sorry I couldn't help you feel better," she said. Her voice cracked and Jamison could barely hear what she said next. "I'll miss you Baxter. Thanks for being my friend, even when no one else would. I'll never forget you."

She and Jamison stared at the dirt for several moments, holding hands. Then Holly launched herself against him, wrapped her arms tightly around him, and together they cried for the soul of a little girl's lost companion.

Aspen

The late morning sun warmed Aspen's shoulders and she realized she should have applied sunscreen. Jamison's hand in hers warmed her heart, and she was starting to realize there was no protection for that. *Infatuation*, November 17th, age 17, she thought, then pushed it from her mind.

Claire had told her about *Lions*. To hear her tell it, Jamison was the best thing to happen to Sparkling Pond since a traveling circus hiked into town the year before Aspen was born. Of course, Aspen got the sense that Claire had an ulterior motive.

Limping next to Aspen and Jamison, Holly kept her casted foot elevated and hobbled on her pink crutches. Aspen noticed that the cast had only two signatures—Jamison's and Holly's own.

Holly told the story of how she hurt herself with animated swinging of her arms. So far, there had been a dramatic fall, fear that she would die, and pain that was literally anguish. But the details were still a bit fuzzy.

"So you just fell while playing?" Aspen asked.

"Yeah. I mean, I guess I was trying to do a cartwheel."

Aspen still couldn't picture how attempting a cartwheel could result in a broken ankle. "And you just landed wrong or something?"

"Exactly," Holly said. After a few more paces, she added, "Well, I mean, I was on top of the Hank Lyons fountain at the time, so I guess it was probably the fall off that did it."

Jamison burst into laughter next to Aspen, and she tried to bottle the sound for safekeeping. "That might have had something to do with it," Jamison said.

Holly beamed at Jamison like she might melt on the spot. "Last year, in third grade, Lizzy Hampton's dad talked to our class about his job as an accountant. But I already know what I want to be when I grow up."

"What's that?" Aspen asked. Who could follow the path of a child's mind?

Holly grinned up at Jamison. "I'm going to be a TV reporter so I can be just like Jamison."

Aspen noticed the absence of Jamison's laugh this time. "Oh, I don't think you want to be like me," he said.

"Why not?" Holly said. "You're old, you can do whatever you want, and you even have a couple wrinkles."

"Oh?" Jamison said. "You wish you had wrinkles?"

"Of course. They're dignified."

Aspen enjoyed the fact that with Holly around, giggles seemed to be part of the air. And she enjoyed the feel of Jamison's hand wrapped around hers as they eased through town. Holly couldn't move very fast on her crutches, but Aspen didn't mind. The slow pace made it feel like a stroll in the park. After Aspen's last experience in the town square, they left a wide berth around the edge and headed toward the lake. Suddenly Holly bounced ahead quickly and called over her shoulder.

"Beat you there!"

Aspen and Jamison kept the same slow pace. She breathed in the humidity, thought about the man at her side, and how his way with Little Holly Torrey had changed her mind about him completely. He seemed determined to take Holly under his wing, but where did that compassion come from? He hadn't learned it as a child because he never had the example. She decided it was something innate within him. As if all he had to do was unlearn what he had been taught about love being nothing more than the ability to make women swoon with a bounce-and-wink. If he could do that, the gentle kindness of the real man would shine through.

The thoughts intrigued her and she stared into his eyes as they walked. Jamison noticed her look and stopped to face her. *First Kiss, September 5th, age 15.* Sometimes she wished she could just turn her mind off.

They stood just inches apart and Aspen moved even closer, so she could feel the warmth of his breath on her cheeks. The feel of Jamison's chest pressing against hers. She ignored the pounding of her heart, closed her eyes, and lifted her lips toward his.

And then he was gone.

Sprinting through the grass faster than Aspen had seen anyone run. He splashed through the river, ignoring the flat crossing-rock in the middle. And then Aspen saw why. At the edge of the lake, two pink crutches were half-submerged. Several feet from the shore, Holly splashed and flailed in a failed attempt to swim while the cast restricted her movement and pulled her under.

Her head bobbed a few times and her arms swung wildly. But in seconds, Jamison had reached her. He lifted her as if she were weightless and carried her to shore. He set her down and sat her up gently.

"Are you okay?" he asked. As Aspen neared, she saw fear in his eyes. Even the smell of the lake seemed tainted with his panic.

"Fine," Holly said. She coughed once and her clothes were soaked through, but she was obviously unharmed.

Jamison waved Aspen over but she couldn't move. She stared from Holly to Jamison and tried to control her emotions, tried to contain her tears. *Disillusioned*, August 1st, age six. A big word for a small girl. Then again, it had been a big event.

When Aspen stumbled, she realized she'd been walking backwards, putting distance between herself and what she had seen. When Jamison cocked his head in silent question, she turned away and sprinted as fast as her legs would take her.

Jamison

For the life of him, Jamison couldn't figure out why Aspen had run away. He desperately wanted to chase after her, but Holly was drenched, embarrassed, and on the verge of tears.

"Let's get you home," Jamison said. "Get you some dry clothes."

He handed Holly her crutches and lifted her off the ground. He carried her to her grandparents' doorstep and nudged the door open. "Hello?" he said.

Her grandparents were in the TV room and stood quickly when they saw Jamison and Holly. "She fell in the lake," Jamison said. "I'm sorry."

"I'm fine," Holly said. "It was my fault, but Jamison saved me."

Jamison set her down and she hobbled toward her grandma. "I have to go," Jamison said. "Again, I'm very sorry."

He dashed out the front door and ran around the town square again. There was no doubt in his mind where he would find Aspen.

Aspen

A riot was underway in Aspen's mind. Thoughts she didn't want to have—knew she shouldn't have—pounded her psyche unrelentingly.

She tried to remember what had happened—Jamison had noticed Holly struggling in the lake and saved her. But her mind's eye cast her back further. To the secret she held so tightly. Her father. Aspen as a young girl. The power of moving water. And that poor little boy who should still be alive.

She ran toward home. Toward safety, privacy, and seclusion. But to get there, she would have to go near the town square, where people were always on the lookout for her. So she veered west until she passed through the cemetery gates and up the hill to her mother's cherry tree.

There, she cried until no tears remained. She leaned her head against the trunk of the tree and closed her eyes, fighting to keep her mind empty. Several minutes later, she felt someone sit next to her and knew it was Jamison. She felt his hand on her knee and the squeeze that replaced words.

They sat like that for five minutes, maybe ten. Aspen wasn't sure. She was steeling herself for the explanation she knew Jamison deserved. When her heartbeat returned to normal and her mind had slowed, she finally spoke through choppy breaths.

"I have a secret," she said. "My father isn't perfect. Not even close."

Jamison remained quiet, allowing her to continue at her own pace. "Don't get me wrong," she said. "He's the best dad I could have possibly asked for. He really has been the perfect father. Except for one day. One moment, actually, that changed the way I've seen him ever since."

It was the best day of her life.

Their new puppy, Rufus, pranced into the water, chasing the white tops of waves, only to tuck his tail between his legs and run when they crested and crashed in front of him. Aspen saw her mommy with a hand covering her giggles, so Aspen laughed too.

"What a weirdo, right mommy?" Aspen said. What a great puppy.

What a great everything. The sun was warm, the lake was cool, and it stretched all the way to the other side of the world. A few other families walked the shore and Aspen smiled at a boy around her age as he splashed in the water.

She grabbed her mommy's hand and then her daddy's and squeezed as hard as she could. "I love you, mommy and daddy." She felt squeezes back as her mommy said, "I love you too." Her daddy squatted down to her level and looked right into her eyes. "I love you too, kiddo." He kissed her forehead and ran off after Rufus, as if something had just given him lots of energy.

Her mommy smiled at him, then her mouth turned into an "O" and she covered her lips with her fingers. "Look, Aspen." She rushed forward and picked up a shiny rock, then sat cross-legged on the beach. Aspen joined her, sure to take the same position and look as much like her mommy as possible.

"What is it?" Aspen asked. "Can I see?"

"Of course, sweetie. Look, it's a Lake Superior Agate."

Aspen crinkled her nose. "That's a funny name. But it's really pretty."

She ran her finger across the smooth surface, dazzled by the waves of purple and red.

"It's the Minnesota state gem," her mommy said. "It was formed by volcanic eruptions from a billion years ago. The red comes from all the iron around this part of the state."

"Yeah, it's pretty," Aspen said. "Can I keep it?"

"Sure," her mommy said, and Aspen squeezed her in the biggest hug she could. Only one thing could make this day any better.

"Can we make a sand castle?" Aspen asked.

Her mommy looked at the shore and said, "I don't think this type of sand will work, sweetie. It's too rocky here. But I bet daddy would show you how to skip a rock on the water."

Aspen looked knowingly at her mom. "Rocks can't skip, mommy. They're too heavy. They sink."

Her mommy laughed and although Aspen didn't know what was funny, she always loved it when her mommy laughed. "That's true, rocks do sink. But if you put a little special magic on them, they can skip right off the top of the water like they have wings."

Aspen tried to envision it. Giant boulders hitting the surface of the water and bouncing high into the puffy clouds, feathered wings flapping. Amazing. "Can I learn?"

Her mommy laughed again and when Aspen followed her eyes, she saw her daddy, wrestling in the water with Rufus. Daddy always won those wrestling matches. He was the strongest daddy in the world.

"Looks like I get to teach you," her mommy said. "First, look for a flat rock. Small enough that you can throw it easily, but with enough weight that the breeze won't blow it off course."

Aspen began her search, trying to replace the image of a boulder with a smaller rock bouncing over the water in the same way she might skip to school. She found a handful that seemed smooth and small, but not too small. She brought them to her mommy and opened her hands to show her.

"That's perfect," her mommy said. "Now turn sideways to the lake, bring your arm back, and flick it side-armed. Like this."

Her mommy took a funny looking step, like she was about to fall over, but then her arm whipped around and a rock shot out of her hand. Aspen watched it rotate as it hovered over the water. When it bounced off the surface and sailed into the air, Aspen shrieked. Three more times it bounced before skidding across the water and finally disappearing into the invisible below.

Her mommy's laugh was pure joy. "Oh, that was fun. You try now."

Aspen faced sideways and brought her arm back, but it felt weird. She tried to throw the way her mommy did, but the rock hit the water with a "plunk" noise and sank out of sight.

"That was great," her mommy said.

Maybe it was. She should try again.

So she threw another rock and, even though the same thing happened, she could tell it was better than the first one. She tried four more times—until she ran out of rocks. On the last try, it might have skipped a little bit, once. But probably not.

"Can I go swim with daddy and Rufus," Aspen asked.

"Of course. But stay close to daddy, okay?"

Aspen was already sprinting into the water, toward where her daddy was throwing rocks to Rufus, who chased them, dunked his head under the water, then looked back for another thrown rock. Aspen pulled her legs out of the water with each step as she ran toward her daddy, then jumped on his back and pulled him over. They both splashed into the water and had to beat away Rufus' slobbery licks as he seized the opportunity to pounce.

After they wrestled with Rufus for a few more minutes, Aspen lay against the rocky bottom so only her head was above water. She crawled around, swam *a few strokes when it was deep enough, then crawled again when her feet touched rock, bouncing with the waves.*

"Aspen, stay close," her daddy said.

She saw the boy she had smiled at earlier. He was swimming too. He was out a bit further and seemed to be having fun. It must be even more fun out there. So Aspen swam out toward him.

"Aspen, stop!"

She heard her daddy's voice and didn't know why he sounded mad. He never got mad. So she turned around to swim back right away. She reached forward, pulled her arm through the water and kicked like they had taught her in swim lessons. But she didn't go anywhere. In fact, she could have sworn she went backwards.

She reached again and pulled, and this time she was sure she was going the wrong way. It didn't make any sense. The waves were going toward the shore, she was swimming toward the shore, how could she be getting farther away from it?

She looked behind her and the enormous sea of blue caused all her muscles to tighten. She saw the boy struggling to swim back too, but it was like an invisible wind was pushing him away.

Aspen's mind shut down, her muscles froze, and her vision went blurry. She realized her vision was warped because she was under water. A fresh wave of panic pushed her arms and legs back into action and she struggled to the surface. Her father was swimming toward her fast, and yelling. Something about "sideways" and "along the shoreline" but it didn't mean anything to Aspen.

Seeing her daddy had calmed her some. So she turned back toward the boy, so close to her now, but still unable to make any progress toward the shore. He seemed to be tiring and his eyes were circles. The noises he made scared Aspen. She had never heard grunts like that—like he was gurgling mouthwash.

Aspen was kicking and pulling as hard as she could now, just to stay afloat. She was being pulled toward the boy. Soon, they would crash into each other. But just before they did, she felt her father's strong grasp wrap around her waist. She buried her face in his shoulder and knew she was safe. She felt the presence of the boy very near. Her daddy would save him too. He was the strongest daddy in the world.

Her daddy seemed to drop into the water farther and Aspen went under. She swallowed a mouthful of water and when she felt her face break the surface she coughed and gulped for air. What was her daddy doing? She swung her head around and saw the boy reaching toward her daddy, his eyes as round as ever.

Her daddy reached to the boy and Aspen was sure he would save him too. But what happened next made Aspen scream and slam her eyes shut. Instead of pulling the boy into his safe grasp, her daddy put his hand on the only part of the boy still above water—his face—and pushed him away with such force that blood spilled into the lake water around them. Her daddy yelled but she couldn't tell what he said. Then he began to carry her away, but the boy wasn't with them.

Her daddy swam sideways for a while. He breathed hard and his pulls and kicks were jarring. After a minute, he switched directions and he carried her to shore easily. When they reached the spot where Aspen had skipped rocks, her mommy ran to her and wrapped her in a towel.

No one said anything, instead they turned to the lake and saw the boy's parents sprinting into the water and swimming hard toward where he was. But Aspen searched the water and couldn't see him. She knew it was too late. The boy's only chance to be saved had reached out and pushed him away.

Her daddy ran back into the water and joined the other parents, searching for the boy who was gone. He stayed out there forever, looking for what wasn't there anymore. Finally, the three adults came back to shore and Aspen saw her daddy talking excitedly, but his shoulders were hunched over like he was carrying a sand bag. She was sure the other man would push her daddy the same way her daddy had pushed the boy. Instead, the woman ran away, in the direction of the parking lot. The man walked in circles.

Aspen's daddy jogged back to her. He squatted next to her and Aspen could see that he was afraid. Weird that she could recognize the look even though she'd never seen it on him before.

"Are you okay?" he asked.

Aspen didn't respond. Was she okay? She was alive, she was breathing, she was scared, she was confused. But mostly, she was furious. "You should have saved him, too," she said.

Her father started crying. Another thing she'd never seen. Blood dripped from his hand. "I'm sorry, Aspen." He looked like he was going to say more, but stopped. He probably couldn't say anything more, he was crying so hard. It made Aspen even madder. Finally, her father managed to say something. "I love you so much."

Aspen tried to look at her daddy but all she could see was the boy as he drifted away. She could imagine him sinking under the water, but she could never imagine telling her daddy she loved him ever again. She knew perfectly well—his love for her had killed that boy.

She had learned something. Love isn't beautiful and pure, like her parents had told her. It's dangerous and people get hurt. Love comes at a price—a price an innocent boy paid with his life. And Aspen knew she wanted nothing to do with that kind of love.

So she decided right then and there—she would never say those words to her father, ever, ever again.

Aspen

At 730-feet, the S.S. Edmund Fitzgerald was the largest ship on the Great Lakes. With a deadweight capacity of 26,000 long tons, it was strong. Reliable. It was dubbed "Queen of the Lakes" and "The Mighty Fitz."

But on November 10, 1975, on a journey across Lake Superior, the Fitzgerald ran into a winter storm with 70-knot winds and waves topping 35 feet. Without so much as a distress signal, she sank 530 feet, to the bottom of the largest freshwater lake in the world, taking 29 souls with her.

The strength of the Mighty Fitz had proven little more than an illusion.

Aspen's father had once been a mighty ship, capable of loading his back with the weight of the world and the adoration of his daughter. Every daughter's father is the strongest, their mothers the prettiest. For a while. At some point, the illusion is exposed.

Now, Aspen's illusions lay at the rocky bottom of Lake Superior, next to the bones of a once-seven-year-old-boy. Cursed to spend eternity in a cold, dark, watery grave. Right alongside the mighty S.S. Edmond Fitzgerald.

But there was one big difference between the fate of the Fitzgerald and what Aspen had witnessed in the waters of Lake Superior.

The tragedy of The Fitz and her crew had been the result of an accident.

Jamison

Shards of bark dug into Jamison's spine. His hand still rested on Aspen's knee and he was moving his thumb back and forth, hoping to give her some comfort. What a terrible, terrible thing for someone to have to witness.

"For years, he tried to explain," Aspen said. "But explain what? Why he chose me? I didn't want to hear that, to have to face the guilt that comes with that. So I never let him speak about it. Any time he started to, I would just start screaming until he stopped.

"Seeing you dive in after Holly like that? It made me think, what if my father had acted like you? What if he had gone to the extent you did to save someone you barely know?"

Jamison sat up straight and faced Aspen. "This was different in so many ways, Aspen. I didn't risk my life like he did. I only had one person to save. I didn't have to worry about my own child dying if I made the wrong choice." And I don't have to live with the guilt that torments her now, Jamison thought.

"I know. I know all that is true. But still, he let that boy die. And I'm not afraid to say it—I haven't forgiven him for that. I don't understand how someone can choose to let someone die like that."

"But if he hadn't, you all would have died."

"Then we all would have died! But you can't just choose like that.

You can't play God. To sacrifice a human life? You can't do that!"

It was becoming clear to Jamison that Aspen was more complicated that he had realized. And that her relationship with her father was more than what everyone in the town square saw. A loving father guides his daughter with notes and objects from her past—that he could comprehend. But then he found out it had been years since she had told him she loved him, and that she had never forgiven him for what had happened years ago on Lake Superior.

"Then why do you even bother going to the meetings every night?" Jamison asked. "If you haven't forgiven him, and that's why you couldn't tell him you love him before, why does it matter if you're there when he wakes up now? Why not just let him die in peace?"

"You don't understand."

"Then explain it to me," he said. "Please."

Aspen wrung her hands together and chewed her cheeks. "With the exception of that one moment, my dad really was the perfect father. It was a mistake not to tell him I love him. The biggest mistake of my life. What happened at Lake Superior that day doesn't change that. Even if I haven't forgiven him, he deserves that much."

"He deserves more than that. He deserves your forgiveness."

"No he doesn't! That boy looked to my father for help, and he killed him. Don't you understand that? He killed him."

Jamison breathed out for a long time, wishing he could blow her words away with the breeze. "You seem pretty sure about what's right and wrong."

"That's because I am."

"And what about all those things that aren't black and white? That are morally ambiguous? What about those situations when no matter what you do, it can't be perfectly right?"

"I don't believe they exist."

"What?"

"Some things are right, some things are wrong. End of story. That doesn't mean there won't be sacrifices involved with doing what's right. But it doesn't change the fact that it's right."

"You're hiding, Aspen. You hide behind things."

"What are you talking about?"

"Claire told me why you didn't like me at first. About how you were mad that I didn't believe you, but you wouldn't just come out and say it. Why don't you just come out and say it this time? And don't give me that holier-than-thou stuff. What is it you really can't forgive him for?"

Aspen closed her eyes for a long time and Jamison wondered if he had pushed too hard. But then Aspen answered him in little more than a whisper.

"He was my daddy. He should have saved us both."

"But how could he have—"

Aspen stopped him with an outstretched open palm. She stared at him with tears in her eyes.

"He didn't even try," she said. "He should have at least tried."

Aspen

Aspen was lost.

She had wanted to forgive her father, but hadn't been able to. She wanted to let go of the grudge she held, but couldn't. She wanted to free herself of the anger and bitterness she felt when she thought about that day, but she didn't have the power.

If she wasn't in control of her own thoughts, her own actions, or her own emotions, who was she? Nothing more than a pawn to some greater power, whose will she must bend to? Was she even her own person?

She felt deep in her bones that she was. That the real Aspen was within her, struggling to show herself.

Every life charts its own course, she knew. Sometimes, we all fall of track. To find the way back, we must first find ourselves. But when Aspen looked at the course of her own life, she saw an unwillingness to forgive, a grudge held, and resentment toward the one who loved her the most.

And no matter how hard she looked, she couldn't find herself there.

Jamison

A few minutes before 6pm, as Jamison was about to start his live-shot, a Team God member pushed a Team Ghost member, who smacked into J.D., who bumped into the camera and knocked it off the tripod. Jamison heard the anchors back at the station throwing it to him as J.D. scrambled to replace the camera in time.

Two police officers immediately grabbed the men and put them in handcuffs. Others, who were rushing to join the fight, retreated back to their own camps and peace was restored for the moment.

Jamison pictured Aspen at the Physicians Team Meeting and wondered how it had gone, or if it was still going on. Protected from the chaos outside.

"Sparkling Pond is now home to three separate groups," Jamison said into the camera. "Each group thinks a different entity is responsible for the messages from Pike Collins to his daughter, Aspen. One group thinks it's a heavenly miracle from God. Another believes it's the work of a ghost. And recently, a third group arrived, claiming the entire thing is a hoax."

Jamison turned his body and motioned behind him. "As you can see, the groups have each claimed territory for themselves, spread around the playground at the town square where the objects have been appearing. Fights between the tribes are becoming more and more common, and just a few hours ago, the Sparkling Pond Police Department called the sheriff's office for back-up. Now, there are twenty officers in town, trying to keep the peace. But if things continue on their current path, even that number might not be sufficient.

"For now, relative peace is holding. It seems no one wants to go to jail before Cornelius Brown, PhD., the famed ghost hunter, gives what he is promoting as an academic lecture on the situation, tonight in the Sparkling Pond town square. Several rows of seating are being set up and tickets are being sold for a hundred dollars each for the lecture, which begins at nine o'clock sharp this evening.

"Reporting live from Sparkling Pond, I'm Jamison Hightower, KTRP news."

Jamison

Jamison was no private investigator. He would leave that to Rad Collie, unsettling as that thought was. And he was no ghost hunter. He would leave that to Cornelius Brown, PhD., at least when he wasn't gawking at Crystal Lux. But as a reporter, he had learned how to roll over a stone or two, and in this case, he'd found someone right there in Sparkling Pond that he and Aspen should see.

He knocked on the door of Aspen's house and heard her call, "Come in." She was at her dining room table, apparently going through her mail. But the way she was looking at the letter in her hands...well, if someone could look longingly at a piece of mail, she was doing it.

"What do you have there?" Jamison asked.

"Oh, it's nothing," Aspen said, and she folded it twice, then slipped it back in the envelope.

Now Jamison's curiosity was really piqued. What could it be, other than another note from her father? But if those were starting to come by post, that would mark a pretty startling change in Pike's methods.

"It's just a letter from my old school," Aspen said.

"Can I see it?" Jamison wasn't sure why he was prying so much, other than because he felt like he could tell when she was hiding something. Aspen hesitated, then tossed it onto the table. Silent permission. Jamison removed the letter, unfold it, and read.

Dear Aspen,

I'm sorry to bother you with another letter from one of us at Mayo Medical School. I know others have contacted you as well. We don't mean to pester you. But please understand how rare it is to have someone with a perfect MCAT score, an IQ of 150, and someone with your social graces, all wrapped up in one. Forgive us our attempts to woo you back, but it's rare to find such genius, and we would love to see you return, whenever the matters in your personal life make that possible.

Please accept my apology for our persistence that borders on obsession.

And please don't hesitate to contact us if you decide you'd like to return.
Yours in medicine,
Dr. Kenneth Keystone

Over the past few days, Jamison had read some of the most intriguing, most unexpected letters he could imagine. But this one was right up there. "A perfect MCAT?" he said. "An IQ of 150? He's talking about you?" That explained how a single word could conjure memories of every day of her life since childhood.

Aspen shrugged like she seriously didn't think anything of it. "I told you I went to medical school. I just didn't finish because I came home when my mom had her accident."

It seemed every time Jamison thought he had a grasp on who Aspen Collins was, she would blow it right out of the water. "Who's this Dr. Keystone? One of your old teachers?"

"You haven't heard of him?" Aspen said. "He's probably the most famous brain surgeon in the world today."

Of course he is, Jamison thought. "And you're telling me this guy is begging you to come back?"

"Looks that way, huh? It's really not that big of a deal. They make me sound better than I am."

"Oh, you mean you're not Hippocrates reincarnated? Could have fooled me."

Jamison couldn't figure out if he was in awe or intimidated. Either way, it was a novel feeling—normally the whole TV thing meant he had those effects on others. But actually, he liked this. It took some pressure off.

Just then his cell phone rang. He looked at the display and his arms tensed. He'd been expecting another call from RISK-TV, which would have been bad enough. He quickly silenced the ringer and shoved it back into his pocket.

"Not someone you want to talk?" Aspen asked.

"Nope." He tried to shake it off, but every time this happened, it would get to him.

"Want to talk about it?"

"There's nothing to talk about," he said. But as soon as the words left his mouth, he heard how hollow they sounded. Aspen deserved more than that. "It was my mom," he said. "She has a hard time taking a hint."

"Wait," Aspen said. "Your mom just called and you ignored it?"

Jamison didn't want to get into it, but he didn't see an easy way out. "She wasn't exactly the perfect mother," he said. "She was in and out of rehab for most of my childhood, so that made it hard to be there for her son. But who cares, right? Everyone sees me on TV and loves me, so what do I need her for?"

"You need her because she's your mother."

"Trust me, she doesn't even know what the word 'mother' means."

Jamison wished she'd drop it, but he could tell she wasn't done. "But she called you now. That couldn't have been easy for her."

"I don't care. Look, you don't know what it was like for me growing up. If you did, you'd never talk to her again, either."

"But Jamison, she's your mother. Whatever happened, and whatever attention you get from the people who see you on television…they could never replace your mother. They don't love you like she does."

"This coming from the person who refused to tell her father she loves him."

"Yeah, well at least I'm trying now!" she yelled. Her anger rose quickly and burst from her. "At least I'm doing something about it!" In the long moment that followed, Jamison saw the fury in her eyes calm. "I'm sorry," she said. "I guess you hit a sore spot. But I shouldn't have snapped at you."

Jamison heaved a big sigh, wondering how he hadn't realized how raw their emotions were. But how could they not be? Somehow, he and Aspen had found themselves in extremely personal, extremely sensitive territory. "Me too," he said. "I started it."

Jamison searched for a way to get back on firm ground. To change the subject so things could get back to normal between them. Then he remembered the whole reason he came.

"Do you know Gus Macken?" he asked.

Aspen took a deep breath, as if to put their short disagreement behind her. When she answered, her tone was light again. "I've always been a baseball fan. You can't be a baseball fan in Sparkling Pond and not know Gus Macken."

That didn't fit with the Gus Macken Jamison had found in his research. "Why do you say that?"

"He spends just about every waking hour at the baseball field in town. He's the public address announcer for every team we have, little league through town ball. He's been doing it ever since he retired."

Retired? Jamison had missed that nugget of info in his research, too. "Do you know what he used to do?" he asked.

"For his career?" Aspen said. "I don't think so. He's always been a baseball guy to me."

"He was a federal agent, once up on a time," Jamison said. "For the last fifteen years of his career, he worked from here in town. The government would send him samples, he'd write up a report, and send them back."

"Samples of what? What did he do for them?"

Jamison knew he wasn't Perry Mason, but it was still fun to see Aspen's face when he said, "Among other things, he was an expert in handwriting analysis."

Cornelius

Cornelius had never imagined that this trip to nowhere Minnesota would turn out so perfectly. Yet here he was, with thousands of people clamoring for a look at him, jockeying for position near his equipment so they could see what a true ghost hunter did.

And then there was Crystal. With the beginning of their relationship, his life had taken on new meaning.

He wrapped the tie she had bought him around his neck and began to flip and twist it into a knot. For a long time, he had thought about what his lecture should entail. What should the format be? Should he just give a speech, or prepare a power point presentation? Should he open it up for questions from the audience?

In the end, Crystal had come up with an idea of her own. It took a while to grow on Cornelius—he was a professional, after all. Even if the stranger was right and there was a ghost here that his equipment couldn't detect, her idea seemed a bit too…dramatic. At first.

But all she had to do was ask. Cornelius would do anything for her. Anything at all. And she had, indeed, asked. So Cornelius had gone to Lenny's shop and learned about the finer points of creating a remote control for a device that wasn't initially made to be used remotely. He learned about the modifications that would be necessary, but he did so without raising any red flags. He still had some reservations about the plan, but he knew that in the end, he wasn't about to say no to Crystal.

He cinched his tie tightly, just like Crystal liked, and focused on his lecture. And he thought about the extra drama he had planned. One thing was perfectly clear. It was going to be a night the town of Sparkling Pond would never forget.

Aspen

"The ballpark's just across the river," Aspen said.

She led Jamison, carrying his camera by his side, past Norske's Lefsa Shack and crossed a footbridge spanning the river. On the other side, the crack of a wooden bat echoed in her ears. *Crackerjacks*, July 7th, age 12.

It seemed odd that a game would be going on. That there were people in town not at the playground searching for ghosts and awaiting another miracle. With the sun dropping low on the horizon and the stadium lights starting to glow in the evening dusk, the night almost felt normal.

On the field, a grizzled man in his thirties with a bushy black beard slammed a pitch into the right-center field gap. Two men rounded third base, one after the other, and cruised in to touch home plate.

"Let's go up there," Aspen said, pointing to the public address booth.

Jamison heaved his camera onto his shoulder and followed her. As they climbed the steps to the booth, an elderly man leaned into a crackly microphone. "Now batting, first baseman Kyle Kelley."

Aspen tapped lightly on the door and opened it a crack. "Can we come in?" she asked.

Gus Macken waved them in, then leaned into his microphone.

"Summary for the inning; 2 runs, 2 hits, no errors. After six complete, it's Rochester 7, Sparkling Pond 4."

Gus leaned back and swiveled in his chair. "Well hello there, Aspen. Can't say I'm surprised to see you. Kind of figured you'd come by sooner or later."

"Hey Gus," Aspen said. "This is my friend Jamison. He tells me you used to do some handwriting analysis."

"Right as rain." Gus swished his lips back and forth, crunched, then spit a sunflower seed shell into a Pixie cup. "Just one minute," he said. He flicked the microphone on. "It's time for the seventh inning stretch. A-one. A-two. A-three. *Take me out to the ballgame…*"

Gus sung the entire song in a horrendous a cappella. Then he turned off the microphone and swiveled back to them. "Sorry. Got two minutes. Do you have the documents with you?"

"They're right here," Aspen said. As she fished them out of her pocket, Gus stared at Jamison.

"Jamison, she says? Jamison Hightower, right?"

"That's right."

"Hey, can I have a quick autograph. My granddaughter loves you." Jamison scribbled his name on the game-day program Gus held out, and Aspen realized she didn't mind quite as much. It wasn't his fault Gus requested an autograph, and it would have been rude to refuse. When Jamison had finished, Aspen set two sheets of paper next to the microphone.

"This is a note from my father." She set out the note that had come with the shoes. "And here's something of his I found in a drawer. An old shopping list, it looks like. I'm trying to figure out if they're both written by him or if someone else could have written the note."

Gus slid some oversized reading glasses onto his face and transformed from a baseball public address announcer to a professional handwriting analyzer. "This will suffice as an exemplar."

He hunched over the documents and talked to himself while Jamison filmed and Aspen reminded herself to breathe.

"Could you talk us through it?" Jamison asked.

"Sure as sunshine. The slants, curves, size of the letters—it all seems to match up."

"Does that mean they're from the same person?" Aspen asked.

"Not necessarily," Gus said. "The real secret is in the lines that connect the letters and the angle of the writing. And, of course, the biggie—letters that are formed differently depending on where they occur in a word." He peeked over his glasses for a moment, then bounced between the two documents, studying with the lenses, then without them. Finally, he set the papers down on the desk.

"These documents were indeed written by the same hand."

Aspen squeezed the journal in her hand. *Confirmation.* After a pause, she asked, "How sure can you be?"

"Handwriting analysis can only be as accurate as the analyzer," Gus said. "But I feel confident that there's a greater than ninety-five-percent chance that I'm correct. That's the best I can do."

A ninety-five percent chance her father had written her the letters. It was what she had expected, but still. To hear it spoken aloud took her breath away.

"Can you tell when each was written?" she asked.

Gus spit another sunflower seed into the cup, then grabbed another handful and shoved them into his mouth. "That's a much less exact science," he said through the seeds. "All I can tell you is that the note appears to have been written much more recently than the list. But you probably already knew that. I'm sorry I can't be more specific."

Aspen nodded. "Thank you, Gus. How much do we owe you?"

Gus smiled at Jamison and held up the game day program. "The autograph will be plenty."

The Ghost

The notes to Aspen are real, and all of Sparkling Pond knows it now, after their trip to see good old Gus Macken. Of course, it's old news to me, having watched the words pouring from pen to paper. And yet, I can't help but feel a huge sense of relief.

I knew the letters were authentic, but Gus didn't. He wasn't there when

they were written—trust me, I know. What would have happened if he had
made a mistake? If he had said they weren't authentic, or even that he couldn't
be sure? I'll tell you what would have happened. Doubt.

People would have begun to wonder if maybe the notes were just a decent
forgery. If maybe what was happening wasn't miraculous.

And after all, what good is a miracle if no one believes it?

Aspen

As Aspen walked back across the river, the authenticated note that
proved the miracle was real rested in her pocket. As long as she kept
her distance from the craziness at the square, the entire situation
somehow made her feel invincible. So she took Jamison's hand, and did
something she never thought she would do.

"So Jamie," she said.

"Jamie? I haven't been called that since…well, never actually."

"Huh. I kind of like it. Besides, no one else calls you by your real
name, so why should I?"

"Fair enough. But are you really going to call me Jamie?" Jamison
closed his eyes and whispered so Aspen could barely hear him. "Please
say no, please say no, please say no."

"Okay, I get it. No Jamie. So then, Jamison," Aspen said. "I was
wondering if you would be interested in joining me for dinner this
evening, after I go to the meeting. Assuming, of course, they don't wake
my father."

When Jamison didn't answer, Aspen's mind started to spin.
Miscalculate, February 18, age 22.

"Of course," Jamison finally said, as if it were difficult for him to
spit it out, and Aspen breathed a sigh of relief.

"Great. Be at my house at seven." She walked away so she wouldn't
have to figure out if she should give him a hug, kiss his cheek, or
something else. Asking him to come over already said everything she
wanted to say.

Behind her, Jamison's voice sounded awed. "I'll be there."

Jamison

The most beautiful woman Jamison had ever seen had asked him out.

He analyzed her tone, her posture, her exact words—maybe she meant it as friends, or maybe it was a business meeting to talk more about the things that were appearing. But in the end, it seemed about as clear as could be—Aspen had asked him on a date. He felt like he had just won the lottery.

But first, he had another very important commitment. Specifically, a grudge match. A best-of-seven tournament against Holly in the old board game, SORRY. It didn't take long for them to learn something about each other—neither of them liked to lose.

Claire was rocking in a swinging bench that hung from the porch, her eyes closed and the sunlight on her face. And across from Jamison, Holly rubbed her eyes like a business man after a fifteen-hour day.

"Why can't I just pick a 1 or a 2?" she said. "I swear this game is rigged."

They'd been playing for an hour, had finished three games, and she had destroyed Jamison in all three. So he was pretty sure her suspicions were unfounded. Apparently winning wasn't enough—she wanted to beat him into the ground.

"Just don't give up," Jamison said. "Persistence pays off."

Jamison internally cursed at himself, but he couldn't help it. He knew Holly was short on role models and he just wanted to fill the roll while he was there. True, it would be nice if he could come up with something memorable that would really stick with her and make a difference in her life. But he just kept spewing clichéd phrases at every opportunity. *If at first you don't succeed, try, try again. If you can't say something nice, don't say anything at all.* They sounded as ridiculous to Jamison as they surely did to Holly, but he never knew he was going to say them until after it was too late.

"Hey Jamison," Holly said. "Get this. A man wakes up in the hospital after a serious accident. He yells, 'Doctor, Doctor, I can't feel my legs!' So the doctor says, 'I know. I amputated your arms.'"

Holly slapped her leg, her rolling giggles so pure they sounded fake. Jamison gave her his game face and tried not to laugh, but when he looked at Claire, they both began to roar.

"Finally," Holly said, back to the game. She moved one of her pieces out of the starting circle. "How long until you go to Aspen's house?"

"About an hour." Jamison pulled a card and moved eleven spaces.

"You going to try to get to second base?"

There was no way he heard that correctly. "What do you mean?"

"Jamison, I'm eight years-old. I'm not a little kid anymore."

Jamison's mind was suddenly like an erased chalkboard. He couldn't have spelled CAT if he had tried. The combination of confusion and shock had shut his brain down completely.

"I do read books, you know." Holly said. She rolled her eyes, as if Jamison's reaction was just what she had expected from a clueless adult. "For the record, I don't think you should. Second base can lead to home runs and only married people should hit home runs. At least that's what the older kids say. I don't really get it though. I see kids playing baseball in the sandlot by the town square all the time and I'm sure I've seen lots of home runs. No one gets in trouble for it, they just have to chase the ball."

Jamison had absolutely no idea how much Holly understood or didn't understand about anything. And he certainly wasn't going to ask. If ever there was a time to focus on SORRY, this was it.

"Are you going to marry Aspen?" Holly said.

Jamison bounced to his feet and almost tripped over the bench of the picnic table. "I need some lemonade. Don't you want lemonade? Claire, do you have any lemonade?"

Claire's eyes were still closed and her face pointed toward the sun, but she bounced with suppressed laughter. At least someone was getting a kick out of this. "In the refrigerator. There's iced tea too, if you'd rather."

Jamison escaped as fast as he could and poured himself some lemonade in the kitchen. If he had thought he was prepared for kids, he was kidding himself. How was a person supposed to answer a question like that?

But now that he was by himself, he couldn't stop wondering. What would happen with Aspen during their date? How should he act? Normally, he'd be the charming Jamison Hightower and everything would be great. But with Aspen, things were different. More complicated. He didn't know who to be. And he couldn't remember the last time he was so nervous for a date.

Jamison finished his lemonade, braced himself, and headed back out to the deck. He made sure to ask a question about the position of one of Holly's game pieces as he walked outside, before she got an idea to ask anything else. They finished the game—a fourth straight loss—and Jamison tried to remember she was just a kid. He shouldn't get too worked up about getting swept.

"I want a rematch," he said. "Tomorrow. Same time. Same place. Be here."

"You're on," Holly said in her high-pitched, little-kid voice. She shuffled through the playing cards like they were a gangster-roll of cash. "Anytime you're man enough," she said. "Your money's always good here."

Aspen

It was official. Aspen Collins was infatuated with James Smith. She knew better than to think of him as Jamison Hightower. And her father had taught her better than to think she was in love with him. *Imparted Wisdom,* May 30, age 24. Love was like a building constructed by two people. Hard work was the foundation. Respect was the frame. Time provided the walls and roof for protection.

But she willingly admitted she was infatuated.

Of course, there was the issue of his relationship to his mother. Aspen could never be with a man who couldn't show respect to his mother. Because someday, he would end up treating his wife the same way. *Inevitable.* But she held to the hope that Jamison would change his ways. And she was learning not to underestimate him.

After the five o'clock meeting, she put on an outfit she rarely wore. In fact, she couldn't remember the last time she had. The skirt was a bit shorter than what she normally wore when she dressed up, with a slit reaching well above her knees. The blouse plunged in front to reveal more cleavage than anything else she owned. Watching Jamison's reaction to this outfit would be better than a good book and a hot bath. She smiled, put it on, then bounced downstairs and started on dinner.

She was building a fire in the hearth when a knock came at exactly 7 o'clock. She grabbed her wine glass and went to the door. When she opened it, a chill in the air told of colder days to come.

Jamison smiled when he saw her—a wide grin that brightened his expression. She was happy to see he hadn't brought his camera.

"Good evening," he said, and brought a bouquet of flowers from behind his back. "I found these on the way over. You don't even need a florist around here."

Aspen put her nose to a blooming purple flower and closed her eyes. You couldn't beat the scent of wildflowers in early fall. It reminded her of the Sparkling Pond Cemetery. *Butterscotch,* March 10, age 25. "They're perfect," she said. "Thank you."

A breeze blew through Aspen's hair and she breathed it in. Outside, the sun had set and stars were gleaming on a moonless night.

"Dinner won't be ready for a while," she said. "Would you like to go for a walk?"

They strolled into the grassy streets. As if pulled on a true north setting, they started toward the lake hand in hand. She looked to the town square in the distance, where even more people had gathered for Cornelius' lecture, which would be starting before too long. Each stadium light was pointed to a different playground toy, with a large group of people staring at it, waiting for another miracle. The chatter that reached Aspen was anxious and muted. Moths flew themselves into the lights, bounced off, and took another spin. *Mob mentality.*

Aspen and Jamison turned away and minutes later, they arrived at the waterfall that plunged in a musical tumble. With the cooling of the air, steam rose from the water, fogging the starlight. It was one of the few times of the year the lake could provide a perfect cover. Aspen looked to the glow from the town square and decided they were far enough away.

"Are you a trustworthy man, James Smith?"

Jamison stared at her like he was trying to figure out where she was going with that question. "Definitely."

"Then turn away, and don't peek. You promise?"

Jamison nodded, then turned from the lake. His head started to move toward her, but flicked back. Aspen watched him for a few moments, then lifted her blouse above her head. She peeled off all her clothing and folded each article into a neat pile. She set the pile next to a big tree where she wouldn't lose it in the darkness. She took a deep breath and considered *impulsive,* or maybe *regret.* But she took two nimble steps toward the water—keeping a safe distance from the waterfall—and leapt as far as her legs would propel her.

The water was warmer than the air, but when it enveloped her entire body, it gave an invigorating chill. Her breath caught as she plunged under water, then kicked slowly until she reached the surface. She began to breaststroke in a circle, forcing her blood to flow and warm her body. "You can open your eyes," she yelled over the splash of the waterfall.

With no moon, Jamison was a faint silhouette on the shore. She heard him rustling around, and then a splash twenty feet away threw droplets onto her face. When he reached the surface, he swam near her, careful not to cross an invisible barrier.

"So beautiful," he said. They tread water, staring at the other's silhouette in the dim light of the stars. Jamison's wet hair covered his eyes and he flicked his head to toss it away. *DiCaprio.* He bobbed slightly, then dipped, revealing the outline of smooth muscles above his shoulders, then sinking to his chin.

Aspen arched her head and drifted onto her back. With darkness as her cloak, she floated away from Jamison, staring at Orion, Cassiopeia, and the Big Dipper. She followed the line at the bottom of the Dipper until she found her favorite star. Polaris. The North Star. Constant and bright and unmoving amid chaos. Watching it flicker gave her a sense of peace she could find in very few places.

Aspen and Jamison swam under the blanket of stars for an hour. Joking, diving deep, laughing, but never touching. Jamison seemed to understand her intent. Despite being so close and so completely naked, this experience was about sharing something she held dear with a person she wanted to know better, and someone she hoped would know her better.

When they finally tired, Aspen nodded to the shore. "I trusted you not to peek last time. Your turn now."

Jamison flashed a crooked grin—even more intriguing with drops of water running the grooves of his dimples. He took a few strokes toward the shore, then Aspen forced herself into a back float, true to her word.

She gave him a full minute, counting the seconds one by one, resisting the temptation to quicken the pace. Then she swam until she felt the sandy bottom between her toes. She climbed up some rocks and found the tree that hid her clothes. She gazed up through the branches at slivers of twinkling sky and focused on the chill of the air against her body, a drop sliding down her thigh.

After another minute of air-drying, she put her clothes on. She searched the darkness and found Jamison sitting next to a tree, staring at the lake. His tie was loose and his top button undone. When he heard her approach, he stood.

"That was amazing, Aspen. Thank you."

When he leaned toward her, Aspen felt her stomach tingle like she was sixteen. His lips brushed against hers, then pressed more firmly. His hand grazed her cheek, then pulled her closer.

When the too-short kiss was over, Aspen didn't try to hide her smile. Instead, she kissed him again, holding onto the feeling as long as she could.

Jamison

It was the best night of Jamison's life.

It wasn't like he'd never kissed a girl. He'd just never kissed a girl like that. With a feeling of respect, admiration, and what he could only describe as the beginning of love. As he and Aspen strolled, hand in hand, ignoring the chaos of the town square, Jamison felt unsteady on his feet. Like his inner ear hadn't quite adapted to his new state of euphoria.

"Why do you go by your TV name?" Aspen asked.

Their fingers were entwined, their pace so slow they might not ever reach a destination. The long pause before Jamison's answer was perfectly natural, perfectly timed to their steps.

"People love Jamison Hightower."

"But it's not who you really are."

Jamison knew he probably wouldn't say so much if they hadn't just kissed, but Aspen had a way of drawing him out. He was speaking before he even realized it. "I guess I'd rather be the guy people adore than the one they think is a loser."

"How do you know they wouldn't love you? The real you?"

Jamison thought back on his childhood. Going from the kid with no dad, to the kid with the druggie mom, to the kid who stayed in the shadows and spent every minute studying and working toward a job he was unlikely ever to get. "If I've ever been loved, I've never seen it."

"Well I'm sure you've been loved."

Jamison's short laugh betrayed more pain than he had intended. Aspen stopped him and looked deeply into him. She brought their chests close together and extended her arm toward the sky, pulling Jamison's arm with it. She pointed toward the stars.

"Have you ever seen the Seven Sisters constellation? Just there?"

"Sure," Jamison said, squinting. "That little cluster, right?"

"Count them."

"What, the stars? I imagine there are seven, considering the name is Seven…well, I just see six right now."

"That's all you can ever see. At once anyway. But move your eyes a little to the side and you'll see another star. But a different one disappears." Her hair brushed against him as she turned to look at him. "Just because you can't see something doesn't mean it's not there."

Jamison looked closely at the stars and realized she was right. No matter where he looked, he could only count six. Sometimes one group of six, sometimes another. He resisted the urge to kiss her and smirked. "If I only see six, I don't believe there are seven. I'd have to see the seventh star."

"You can't just take it on faith, huh?"

Something about the question brought a weight to Jamison's chest. He looked to the dew-covered ground, unable to meet her eyes. "When so much is wrong with the world, it can be hard to have faith in anything."

Jamison got the sense she was unimpressed with his answer, but she said nothing more and resumed walking. They strolled for several moments in silence and had nearly arrived at Aspen's house when a chorus of shouts erupted from the town square. Over the past few days, Jamison had become very familiar with that sound. It was distinct, leaving no doubt as to its meaning.

He and Aspen forgot about the stars and sprinted toward the spotlights.

Aspen

Aspen darted through the mass of people blocking her way—no one bothered to move for her anymore. She struggled past a small scuffle on the outskirts, tiptoed past a group of a hundred kneeling in prayer, and finally reached the clearing where Cornelius' equipment was set up. Crystal Lux was dancing in circles, her hair flying wildly, and a pair of jeans clutched in both her hands.

"I knew it would come again," Crystal said. "The ghost is trying to communicate."

"What happened?" Aspen asked.

Crystal seemed flustered by the interruption. "The jeans," she said. "They appeared out of nowhere. Under the jungle gym. There was nothing there, and then these were there."

"You saw it happen?" Aspen said. She took the jeans from Crystal and felt the blood drain from her face. Jamison placed his hand on the small of her back for support.

"No. But Crazy Willie was on guard."

Aspen stared at the jeans. *Sexuality*, February 14, age 17. "William?"

"Right here, Aspen," William said. He poked the rim of his hat out of his eyes. "It's just like Crystal said it, far as I can tell. It wasn't there, then it was."

Aspen stared at William, as if trying to decide whether to believe him. "Who found the last one?" she asked.

"It was me, remember?" Jamison said.

"And Holly found the first one while she was playing," Crystal Lux said. "The ghost doesn't care who sees him." Then she screamed and pointed at the jeans Aspen held.

Aspen saw the corner of an envelope sticking out of one of the pockets. She ripped it out, removed the letter, and started to read.

"Read it out loud!" someone shouted. But this time Aspen ignored them. Something told her this one might be a bit too personal. Besides, after all that had happened here, she didn't think she owed them anything. So she leaned into Jamison for protection, and the two of them read.

Dear Aspen,

Relationships are the most complicated thing humans deal with. When two people come together with different pasts, different personalities, and different expectations, it's a wonder anyone can find love. Add in the complications of sex, and the result can be explosive in many different ways.

Our society has a strange view of sex. We group it with violence as things that our children shouldn't be exposed to, despite the fact that the two couldn't be more opposite in substance—one born of hate, the other of love; or results—one resulting in death, the other with life. That coupling of sex and violence has created an unnatural fear of a beautiful thing.

Don't take sex too seriously.

On the other hand, we minimize it. Our society glorifies the one-night stand and casual sex. Married couples go through the motions, forgetting the strength and beauty of what bound them together. They don't remember the power of sex until one partner strays.

Don't take sex too lightly.

When Aspen reached the next line, every muscle in her body froze.

Like she had explained to Rad, even though she claimed to know the notes were written by her comatose father, the impossibility of it always left a lingering uncertainty. But what she read next destroyed every speck of remaining doubt.

Jamison seems like a good man. I'm happy you've found him. Just make sure you use both your head and your heart to guide you forward.
I'll love you forever.
Daddy.

Cornelius

The stars were aligning for Cornelius like he had never thought possible. Just when he had started to doubt himself and his theory about detection through helium, the ghost went and solved his problems for him. It had proven, beyond any reasonable doubt, the existence of ghosts. All that remained now was for someone to take credit for the discovery.

Cornelius was up to the challenge. But he needed to do it right. After all, once he proved the existence of the ghost, what more would there be to do? His job would be done, and then what? He needed to figure out a way to be needed. Fortunately, he had come up with the perfect plan for that as well.

The crowd was still electric from the discovery of the jeans, and especially the latest letter—a rumor was spreading that it had named Jamison Hightower by name! A celebration had continued for twenty minutes. But when nine o'clock arrived, Cornelius had no intention of missing out on his opportunity just because the ghost had decided to act. He nodded to Mayor Ohlson, who stepped to the podium which had been set up a safe distance from Cornelius' equipment. Cornelius checked all around his equipment to make sure no one was too close to it, felt the remote control in his pocket, and tried to contain his excitement for what was to come.

"Good evening," the mayor said. The microphone screeched and the mayor tapped on it. "Must be a ghost in the wires," he said. When no one laughed, he cleared his throat and continued. "I know you're all here to listen to our ghost hunter friend, Cornelius Brown, PhD. But before he takes the stage, I have an announcement to make. More of a demand, actually.

"Despite the late start, this crowd is larger than anything Sparkling Pond has ever seen. Now the numbers I don't mind, just make sure to continue to visit our local shops. But the fights that have broken out repeatedly are unacceptable. Our little jail cell is overflowing, our police force, even with help, is overwhelmed. So I have decided to act."

The crowd rumbled with speculation and confusion. "I have requested and been granted access to the National Guard," the mayor said. He lifted a phone from his side. "I have been in constant contact with them, and they tell me they are only minutes away from arriving in Sparkling Pond. So remember, if you cause any trouble, you will have the United States National Guard to deal with. Understand?"

The crickets in the field were amplified by the silence. "Okay then," the mayor said. "Without further ado, Cornelius Brown, ghost hunter."

The crowd erupted in applause and Cornelius waved. He kissed Crystal on the cheek and made his way to the podium, blushing like never before.

The Ghost

When people seek attention, they tend to put their ambitions in front of their concern for others. When they think they're in love the way Cornelius does, they become nothing short of crazy.

Cornelius arrived uninvited. I've never known what to expect from him. And I don't know what to expect now. But I do know one thing—I don't like the looks of what's happening here.

Cornelius

"Thank you," Cornelius said, waving to the crowd as they continued to stand and cheer. "Thank you. Thank you so much. It's an honor to be here."

"We love you, Dr. Brown!"

A wave of cheers rose from the crowd and Cornelius basked in it. He could have stood there all night. Instead, he patted the loose strands of his comb-over and leaned toward the microphone.

"At this very moment that I'm speaking to you, large amounts of helium have been injected into the very air we are breathing. But don't worry, you won't be squeaking like you just inhaled from a balloon." For him, the laughter was immediate.

Cornelius gestured to his Atmospheric Density Tester, and Crystal standing next to it. He secretly reached into his pocket and pressed a button on the remote control.

"Over here is my lovely assistant, Crystal Lux. Ten percent off mochas at the Squinting Café all week, by the way." Crystal beamed at him and touched the ADT seductively. "She's keeping an eye on levels for us. If she—"

"Cornelius!" Crystal shouted, nailing the timing perfectly. She fiddled with some nobs and switches, and an alarm on the ADT blared through the square. "These readings are off the charts," Crystal said. "I'm not sure the machine can take this kind of feedback!"

Cornelius tried to cover his pride with a look of concern. Crystal ran to him and jumped into his arms. "It's going to overload!" she said.

Right on cue, a deafening explosion rocked the square. The Atmospheric Density Tester blasted apart into a thousand pieces, surprising even Cornelius with its violence. Shards of metal flew from the machine—but it looked like it all blew out in the intended direction. He would have to compliment Lenny from the electronics store on the accuracy of his information.

Then, to his right, Cornelius saw a woman clutch her arm and fall to the ground. She cried out in pain and Cornelius knew right away that a stray part had found its way out of the intended blast zone. People went to her immediately, looked at her arm, and helped her to her feet. The woman looked okay. She seemed to have only been scratched. She and the people next to her looked back to Cornelius expectantly.

"I guess that answers our question," he said. "There can be no doubt that we have a ghost here." Singing and dancing broke out all around the square. Cornelius noticed a group of Free Thinkers scowling at him, but apparently the mayor's warning was enough to hold them back. He leaned into the microphone and tried to regain everyone's attention. Except for the Free Thinkers, they all believed he had proven the presence of a ghost. Now, to make sure he continued to be relevant.

"My friends, it's time to move to the next step. More effective communication. What we have experienced so far—one way communication with no visual contact—is extremely twentieth century. It's time to move into the modern age. I have been working on a new, experimental method that could make it possible to actually see this ghost."

For some reason, people weren't listening as intently as Cornelius had expected. People were talking among themselves, and a few were yelling questions at him. Cornelius tried to continue his speech, but a burly young man near the front of the crowd shouted so loudly everyone stopped and listened. "How do we get rid of the ghost? When will it leave?"

Cornelius didn't have a clue. But he wasn't about to admit it. So he cleared his throat and made it up as he went along. "Ghosts of this nature live in the in-between. They cannot survive if the host is fully alive, and they cannot survive if the host is fully dead. In this case, I would say the ghost will leave us when Pike Collins recovers, or dies."

There. He had addressed their concern. Now back to his point on his new, experimental method. But before he could regain his train of thought, a large group started marching out of the town square.

"Where are you going?" Cornelius said.

"This ghost has been haunting this town long enough," said the muscular man who had asked the question. "We're going to get rid of it. Right now."

"No!" Cornelius said. "No, stop. You can't do that. You don't understand."

In complete panic, Cornelius looked to Mayor Ohlson, who was punching numbers into his phone. "Are you here yet?" Cornelius heard him ask. "Good. Go straight to the Sparkling Pond hospital. Don't let anyone in."

Cornelius looked at the mob as it simmered, threatening to boil. "Who are these people?" he said. "The world's gone crazy."

Day Five

Aspen

Aspen awoke to a town in near lockdown mode. Her father was safe, the National Guard having arrived just in time to turn back the angry mob before they could do God-knows-what. Most of the people had been from out of town, but Aspen had noticed a few familiar faces mixed in, taking advantage of the anonymity. The burly Gunnison twins stuck out in a crowd.

The presence of soldiers in her hometown had been a blessing last night, but in the light of the morning, she could see how unnatural it was. Her father was contacting her from a comatose state. She hadn't felt this close to him in years. And yet, the cost of that miracle seemed to be growing every day.

After careful reflection, Aspen decided the risk wasn't worth it. She would put an end to this craziness. She would see to it that today was the day it would end. But first, there was something she had to do.

Sitting outside her house, waiting for Jamison to arrive, she flipped over the note that had come in the pocket of the jeans. *Climb a bluff,* it said. So before the day started and she stopped the growing insanity, she was planning to do just that.

"Good morning," Jamison said as he strode up to her, his camera at his side. He kissed her lips lightly, sending concentric waves through her entire body. "What's on the docket today?"

"Follow me," she said. She took his hand and led him through town, past closed up shops guarded by uniformed soldiers who wouldn't make eye contact. *Unnatural.* When they arrived at Dangling Cliff Adventures, Rad Collie was sitting in an Adirondack chair outside the shop, sorting through a pile of gear and smoking a pipe.

"Morning, dudes," he said out of the side of his mouth. "How's it hanging?"

Aspen nodded and smiled, without a clue how to answer. "We were hoping you might climb one of the bluffs with us," she said. "Something fun, but not too crazy."

"That's music to my ears, dude. I can't stand being all cooped up like a hibernating bear. All these cops around. This peacock has to stretch his wild feathers."

Jamison heaved the camera onto his shoulder and whispered. "I need to be on this guy all the time. Talk about made for TV."

"What's that?" Rad asked.

"Do you have any ideas off hand?" Aspen said. "For, ah, stretching your wild feathers?"

"Follow the leader, baby girl. Just follow old Rad."

Rad gathered a bag of climbing gear and ten minutes later, they were crossing the border of Sparkling Pond, toward the nearby bluffs. Rad carried the backpack full of gear, Jamison filmed occasional bits of video, and Aspen embraced the excitement of the upcoming climb.

"Where are you taking us, Rad?" Aspen asked. "Lookout Mountain?"

"Never heard of it," Rad said.

It wasn't possible to live in Sparkling Pond without knowing about Lookout Mountain, much less to own an outdoor adventure shop. Aspen motioned in front of them to the wave of bluffs dipping and peaking at the edge of town. "It's the biggest one, right there in front of us."

"Oh, you mean Epic Rib Cracker," Rad said.

"I don't think I know that one."

"Same thing, better name. Who wants to climb Lookout Mountain or Pleasant Peak? Lame!" Rad's crooked finger pointed to the peaks. It bounced from one to the next. "That's Epic Rib Cracker. And Blind Man's Suicide. There's Hypothermic Meltdown. Oh, and there's my favorite," he said. "EMT on Speed Dial."

"Okay," Aspen said. "Then we're climbing Epic...Cracked Rib?"

"Epic Rib Cracker!"

Aspen had hiked to the top of Lookout Mountain, aka Epic Rib Cracker, several times. It was a nice hike with a bit of safe scrambling at the top—Class 3 maximum. But after an hour of following the trail, Rad led them to the bottom of a sheer cliff in a place she had never seen. The smooth rock climbed thirty feet before jutting out in a roof of rock that blocked their view of the peak. Next to Aspen, Jamison brought his camera to his shoulder and filmed as Rad pulled three climbing harnesses from his bag.

"Throw these on, dudes."

"I'd love to," Jamison said. "But I have to film."

Aspen held hers in front of her and tried to figure out where her legs were supposed to go. But her mind kept returning to the question of whether climbing with Rad Collie was really safe. And how she somehow ended up alone in this.

"Chicken," she said to Jamison, although remembering his excitement in the canoe, she had a feeling he would love to switch places. She stuck her foot through a hole in the harness and tried to be annoyed at Jamison's smile. Instead, she found herself wanting to kiss him again.

When she had double-backed the waist strap on her harness, Rad sauntered over. He jingled as he walked. Carabiners and belay devices clinked against each other like janitor's keys. He threaded a rope through her harness and said, "Up you go, princess."

Aspen eyed the sheer cliff in front of her without a clue how to proceed. But as she studied the rock closer, she was able to make out tiny groves and juts in the surface, just big enough to stick her climbing shoes into. She took a deep breath and started up the rock wall.

"Your dad left you some jeans, huh?" Rad said. "Know why?"

Climbing was one thing, but climbing and talking? Then again, it was better than being back in town, feeling watched every second of the day. *Refuge.* "Yeah. It means he didn't approve of the outfit I wore on my date with Jamison last night."

Aspen's eyes darted to the camera, but Jamison was safely hidden behind the lens. She wished he would just shut the stupid thing off.

"Showing your stuff, huh?" Rad said. "Wish I'd seen."

Aspen forgot about climbing for a moment. "What did you say?"

"Ah, I hear your old man left you sexy jeans?"

Aspen smothered a grin. Second grade, she thought. Second grade. "They're very conservative, actually. But they're just like the pair of jeans we bought together the day after he talked to me about sex."

"Oh? When was that?"

"I was seventeen. We were at the Daddy's Little Girl Dance and I wore a dress that was way too revealing because I was planning on going out with my boyfriend afterwards."

Rad craned his head so his ear was facing her. His eyes bulged a bit too much. "Go on," he said.

"He told me to think about why I wore the things I did, what message I was trying to send, and to who."

"Crazy coot," Rad said.

Aspen paused on the rock wall. "My father?"

"Of course your father." Rad shook his head hard and changed his tone. "But I'm not here to commentarize on his philosophizing. I'm here to help figure out how junk's showing up at the playground. But I do have to say, I don't get why that dude was so obsessed with how you looked."

Aspen reached for a handhold above her and lifted herself higher. "He wasn't," she said through a grunt. "He was obsessed with preventing society from turning me into someone with no self-esteem and an eating disorder. It was about wanting me to think things through before I acted. To think about consequences. He didn't want to stop me from living, just to live intentionally. It's why he sent the jeans—to make me think more intently about the clothes I wore last night instead of reprimanding me somehow for skinny dipping with Jamison."

Rad coughed, long and wheezing like he was choking on smoke.

"Sorry Rad," Aspen said. "Should have warned you that was coming."

When Rad had recovered, he said, "Your old man would rather you swim naked with a dude than wear a skimpy dress?"

Aspen considered how to explain in a way that would make sense. "Skinny dipping was about fully immersing myself into a beautiful experience. The water, the fog, the thick air and shimmering skies. It was freeing and emotional. The skimpy dress? It was just a skimpy dress, sending a message I probably wasn't ready to send yet."

Rad mumbled something that sounded unconvinced, but Aspen refocused her attention on the climb. The rocky overhang was directly above her now. She clung to the rock and arched her head. She studied the nobs and grooves and searched for a plan, but came up empty. "You might have to help me down, Rad," Aspen said. "I don't think this is beginner-level stuff."

"When are you going to learn?"

"Learn what, Rad? I've never done anything like this before."

"When are you going to learn that nothing's impossible? Things can happen that you might not expect."

Aspen closed her eyes and focused on calming her nerves. When her heart rate had slowed, she tilted her head up and again studied the rocky roof above her. There was a notch in the rock, almost like a hole from below. If she could reach it, maybe she could grab onto it.

"And again, I'm waiting," Rad said.

"This is not the time for your impatience," Aspen said.

Being pressed against the rock thirty feet above the ground made Aspen feel helpless and reliant—and she didn't like it. *Anger* and *Frustration* seemed like pretty appropriates candidates for the day.

Her father was sending her things and she couldn't figure out how. She had never said I love you, and now, his gesture of love had turned the town so crazy the National Guard had been required. She glared at the notch above her and channeled all her emotion into her legs.

She jumped from the rock, as high as she could, and stretched for the groove. The fingers of her right hand slipped inside it and she squeezed the rock as hard as she could. She was hanging from the ledge with four fingers, her feet kicking the air below.

Rad roared in laughter. "Ha! Dangling Cliff Adventures! Dude, who has a camera? Oh," he said when he glanced at Jamison with his high-definition, professional grade video camera.

Aspen relied on instinct and swung her legs a few times to gain momentum, then flipped them over the flat, rocky top of the roof. Before gravity could do its work, she shoved off the ledge, scrambled to get her feet underneath her, and stood atop the peak. She put her hands on her hips and scanned the area below.

It was beautiful, of course, but Aspen was surprised by an overwhelming feeling of happiness. As if, for this moment, all was right in the world. She was reminded of something her father once told her about what makes people truly happy.

It's not watching our favorite TV show or posting a clever Tweet. It's not even sitting at the Bent Spoon as the sun goes down, frozen margarita in hand. People are happiest when they strive, struggle, and then succeed. When we exceed our own expectations.

It's why we go to the moon, and then turn our sites on Mars. It's why we write literature and play music. It's the challenge that makes the success so sweet.

Aspen hadn't felt that glow in a long time. Shuttling between the hospital and the cemetery had become a duty—and not exactly a mentally stimulating one. But in guiding her here, her father had allowed her to live again.

Aspen gazed at the rolling hills and bluffs surrounding her. She felt Rad's approval and Jamison's respect. A wave of pride bubbled up and boiled over and she began laughing.

She whispered, wanting to keep the moment private. "Thank you, daddy."

Cornelius

If Cornelius had been made a superstar by predicting the appearance of the running shoes, he had been made a legend by the explosion of his Atmospheric Density Tester. The woman who had been injured in the explosion hadn't threatened to sue him, she had begged for the chance to sit next to him during his next public event. The people he talked to hadn't been devastated by what had happened, they had been inspired. And the National Guard had prevented anything bad from happening at the hospital. Everything was under control.

That's why Cornelius sat as part of a giant circle, with Crystal sitting to one side and the woman with a bandaged arm on the other. Many Team God and Team Ghost members were in the circle, but the Free Thinkers prowled the perimeter like jackals waiting for the opportunity to pounce.

Cornelius had thought the Free Thinkers would be in jail after threatening Pike Collins like they had. But in the end, the presence of the National Guard had prevented them from attempting anything. And since they hadn't actually done anything illegal, there were no grounds to detain them. So they stalked and they crouched and they glared from outside the circle, one eye always on the nearby soldiers.

"I'd like to share my newest theory," Cornelius said, trying to ignore the Free Thinkers' stares. "As humans, we have a tendency to believe only what we can see with our own eyes. We lack faith when it comes to the unseen. So our next step must be to make the impossible possible.

"What if we could see ghosts with our own, naked eye? We would make believers out of the most skeptical of doubters. We could go beyond proving that ghosts exist and make it possible to interact with them. In short, we could destroy the barriers between our worlds forever."

Cornelius felt a twinge of guilt somewhere in his consciousness, but he quickly submerged it. Sometimes, he knew, you have to show people something that is *not* real, in the name of convincing them of what *is* real.

Crystal had her eyes closed and was swaying like she was in a trance. But the Free Thinkers appeared to be considering attacking him and taking their chances with the National Guard. Cornelius decided to reign it in a bit, for now. There would be a better opportunity to make headlines later today. When Jamison Hightower did the day's live-shot—that would be the time.

The time to take his message from the confines of Sparkling Pond to the very corners of the entire world.

Jamison

"This has to stop."

Jamison and Aspen were picking zucchini and squash from Aspen's backyard garden—food she would sell at the farmers' market only minutes later. They had been working quietly, both deep within their own thoughts. Jamison's had been about Aspen. Aspen swimming in the lake. Aspen standing atop the rocky summit. Aspen leading his hand and pointing toward constellations. As far as what was on her mind—judging by the seriousness of her tone, Jamison figured he was about to find out.

"What has to stop?" he asked.

"All of it. The insanity going on right now. Foot soldiers are all over our town, for Christ sake. How did this happen?"

Jamison didn't have an answer, so he didn't say anything. She came over and took his hands. Her tone was so gentle he could barely hear her.

"You did this, Jamison."

He flinched—that wasn't at all what he'd been expecting. Aspen continued just as softly. "I'm not mad and I don't blame you. I know you didn't intend for all this to happen any more than my father did. But it happened. You told the world about it, and the world invaded our town."

Jamison was so tongue-tied, he probably looked like he was choking. He had never looked at it that way. Like he was the one responsible for turning a beautiful miracle into a national spectacle. He'd only tried to tell the story.

"Only you can put a stop to it," Aspen continued. "I need you to do something for me. Go on television today, for your live shot. Tell them it's over. Tell them it was all a hoax, a fraud, that we were all wrong. Tell them there is no ghost. There's no magic. Make them leave, Jamison. Give us our town back. Please."

The very last thing Jamison wanted was to hurt Aspen. Or this fairy tale town she lived in. In a heartbeat, he was nodding—he would do whatever she needed him to do.

"Of course," he said. "I'm sorry I didn't recognize it sooner."

Jamison hugged her then, and thought about how truly lucky he was to have been sent to Sparkling Pond for a little piece of fluff.

Aspen

Aspen squeezed, smelling the musk of Jamison's neck and feeling the tickle of his whiskers on her forehead. This man was here with her, now, and she felt more alive with him than she had felt in months. At this moment, she didn't want to sit by a hospital bed anymore. She didn't want to give up her own life for something that might never happen. She knew it was selfish, but she couldn't help it. She wanted this man, this embrace, this life. She no longer needed to keep him at a distance. She wanted this closeness, this intimacy.

Aspen knew her father was right about the difficulty and complexity of relationships. But she also knew what her heart was telling her—that standing here in Jamison's arms was exactly where she was supposed to be.

Jamison

Aspen headed to the famers' market to sell the vegetables they had picked. She would be there for the noon rush, while Jamison was doing his live-shot, and they would meet up afterwards at the Squinting Café, where they would take refuge from the crowds and hopefully watch a mass exodus from town—the result of the live-shot Jamison was about to do. He went back to his room at Claire's house and was about to start shaving when his cell phone rang.

"You're off it," Harris said. There was satisfaction in his voice. As if he'd been looking forward to this moment for a very long time.

"I don't understand," Jamison said, even though he did understand. He understood perfectly.

"Then let me spell it out for you. I told you I wanted hard news, but you continued to put sing-songy storybook crap on my air. So I'm firing you. Paul is packing up his gear right now. He'll be coming to take your place for this live-shot, and you can come back here and clean out your desk."

Sometimes our own feelings are hidden from us, Jamison knew. As if they're buried under the ground. It's not until a meteor crashes down and displaces tons of earth that we are able to see those feelings uncovered. What Jamison saw was sheer terror.

What would he be without his job? He was employed, but would become unemployed. Or employed by RISK-TV, which might be worse. He was known, but would become unknown. Mostly, he was loved by those who watched him, and he would become unloved. He would become nobody, with nothing, and no one who cared for him. Just like when he was a kid.

"Sir," Jamison said, as calmly as possible. "I beg of you to give me one more chance. I promise you, I'll come through for you. I give you my word that you'll be happy with my performance." Harris didn't answer, so Jamison kept groveling. "I'll give you hard news. I'll catapult us into second place. I'll do it. Just give me one last chance."

The line went dead without another word from Harris, and Jamison was left to wonder whether another reporter was on the way to town, ready to take his place.

Claire

Claire Lyons sat at the same circular dining table that Hank Lyons himself had. Each chip in the wood and scratch in the varnish represented a memory—most of which Claire couldn't remember. But their existence still gave her a sense of place. They grounded her and made it a home. Life had been lived at this table. Her life, and the life of her families before her.

So many conversations had taken place around it. Serious conversations and light-hearted evenings. Jokes and confessions. Laughter and tears. Everything humans experience—everything that makes us unique—had occurred right around this beautiful piece of scarred mahogany.

Claire had been around for a countless number of those experiences. Over the course of her substantial years, she had become an expert at reading people. She could sense happiness or sorrow, truth or lies—sometimes even better than the people from whom they originated.

So when Jamison said nothing was bothering him, she knew it wasn't true.

Some people were more difficult to read than others. Jamison was like a children's coloring book. He scribbled on his notepad, sighed, then crossed out what he had written and scribbled some more. Most telling of all, a perfectly prepared *chocolate ganache* crepe and a spinach and Swiss *cocotte brioche* sat untouched in front of him.

"Can I help with anything?" Claire asked.

Jamison had to set his pen down. Claire recognized it as a conscious shift, an effort to set aside his frustrations and put on a mask of contentment. Who did he think he was talking to?

"No, thank you," he said. "Just a bit of writer's block. I can't quite figure out how to go about telling this story."

Claire pursed her lips. Lies were easy to detect. She didn't need to analyze a person's voice or hook them up to a polygraph. She could see everything in their irises. And if they wouldn't even let you see their eyes, well, there you go.

"You've done so many stories," Claire said. "Why is this one so different? What makes it so difficult for you to write it?"

Jamison's blank stare pointed out the window. Then he looked directly at Claire for the first time all day. "Competing motivations," he said.

Claire studied his irises. This time, there was no deceit hidden there.

She wondered what his competing motivations could be and how they would manifest themselves. She had a feeling she didn't want to find out, and knew just as surely that she soon would anyway.

Aspen

It was later than normal when Aspen pushed her wheelbarrow into the clearing to set up for the noon rush at the market. She couldn't wait to get through the next couple hours and meet back up with Jamison. The thought of thousands of people walking through the field of clover to their cars in the parking lot brought a smile to Aspen's face. *Homecoming.*

Her excitement cooled when she saw William in the neighboring stand, sitting on an overturned bucket. In front of him stood an easel covered in stretched canvas. He held a pallet of acrylic paints in one hand and expertly maneuvered a brush with the other. He spun mixtures of color, constantly lightening or darkening, thickening or thinning.

While he dabbed at the canvas, his eyes flicked to a painting hanging on display nearby. In it, a cowboy rode a bull and whipped his hat above his head. William's stare darted to it often, but it was as if he wasn't seeing the painting at all, but something inside his mind instead.

He flinched when he heard Aspen's footsteps. She smiled a "good morning" to him, but his eyes stayed low, drooped. He wasn't "Crazy Willie" today. No practical jokes. Nothing that would make the townspeople shake their heads and wonder. Just a deep sadness etched into the lines of his face beneath his flimsy cowboy hat.

"You okay, William?" Aspen asked. She set the wheelbarrow down and flipped another bucket for herself. "You look a little out of sorts. Anything I can do to help?"

Aspen studied his face. Bags sagged beneath his eyes and his mouth frowned like it had no strength left. When he spoke, even his voice lacked the half-crazed sound it usually had. Aspen wondered how much of his usual persona was a mask.

"I'm going to miss him," he said in a low, raspy voice.

Aspen knew who he was talking about. She followed William's eyes to the painting he had been starting at.

"The knight in shining armor," he said. "The man who saved my life."

"That painting is of my father?" Aspen asked. She studied it more closely. The depth and texture he had created using a brush, paint, and canvas created more than a picture or a portrait. It elicited a feeling. Something about the purple and orange in the background sunset, mixed with the determination and confidence in the young cowboy's features. Aspen couldn't look at the painting without feeling strength and hope.

But when she looked at the painting he was creating now, the feeling faded. On this canvas, no forms existed. With wisps of color and shape, hints at depth and movement, William had created sadness.

"He's going to die soon, isn't he?" Aspen said.

She couldn't explain why she asked him. Someone with nearly four years of medical training asking someone called "Crazy Willie" a health-related question? Still, Aspen had a feeling William knew, or could sense, more than she was able to discern from the nightly five o'clock meetings.

William nodded slowly and stared at his painting. "Ever since that day, people treated me different. I know I'm different. But your daddy, he told me all the time I was his best friend, just like always. 'Course, your mom was his very best friend, I always knew that. But he was the one man who always treated me good." William's eyes began pouring tears. He put his face in his hands. Aspen fought back her own tears and rubbed his back. "What am I going to do when he's gone?" William asked. "Who will I be if I ain't Pike's best friend? Nothing but 'Crazy Willie' that's what. I don't want to be nothing but Crazy Willie."

Aspen squeezed his shoulder, with no idea how to answer. *Identity.* Who would she be if not her father's daughter?

Something about the look on William's face—the drooping eyelids and liquid eyes—made Aspen certain she would never speak to her father again. A wave of regret washed over her and she wished more than anything that they had never taken that trip to Lake Superior. Then she never would have seen the lengths to which her father would go to save her life. She could have lived her life unaware of the bad things good people sometimes do.

"If only I could go back in time," she said aloud. "Stop that trip from ever happening."

William nodded and Aspen realized he had been around for so much of her life that talking with him was almost like talking to her father. "Pike wished for that too," he said. "Every day."

Aspen stared at William's knee since she couldn't meet his eyes. "Do you think it's a terrible thing to kill one person so you can save another? In my whole life, I haven't been able to forgive him for it."

William was unexpectedly quiet. *Blissfully Ignorant.* "My father," she explained, then hesitated and swallowed the cry in her throat. "That day he saved me from drowning in Lake Superior, there was another boy. My father tried to save him too, but when he realized he couldn't save us both, he pushed the little boy, right in the face. He saved me, and the little boy drowned. He chose me, and that boy's parents have had to live with that ever since. I've tried not to hold it against him, not to judge him, but…well, he killed that boy. I know he did it for me—to save me. But he still did it."

William's eyes flashed at her, as wide and aware as if he were young again. "Aspen," he said. Then he stared at a spot on the ground like his eyes no longer worked and he was overwhelmed by an internal vision. "No, no," he said in a moan. "Oh no, no, no."

"William, are you okay?" Aspen wondered if he needed medical attention. His face had turned a sickly white, almost green.

William took her hand as if to keep her where she was, to prevent her escape. "In his whole entire life, Pike Collins ain't never done anything like that."

Aspen's shoulders drooped and she hung her head. Of course, William wanted to believe the best about his friend. And she knew she should let him. He was old and frail himself and the last thing he needed was to have his perfect vision of her father shattered. And yet, she couldn't stop herself from saying what she knew to be true. "He did that day."

William flicked his head back and forth, his resolve strong. "Aspen, you need to listen to me, girly. If you think your daddy pushed that boy he tried to save, then you're wrong. You don't know what happened."

"William, I was there. I saw it."

"What did you see?"

Aspen flinched, not wanting to remember. But as soon as her eyes closed, the vision came back to her. "We dropped below the surface and I knew he was struggling with the weight of two of us. So he pushed the boy away and swam off. Pushed him really hard, right in the face. The boy's mouth was bleeding from it. I can still see the blood in the water, William."

"Not the boy's blood."

William's words made no sense. Of course it was the boy's blood. She had seen what her father had done. Who else's blood could it be?

"Your daddy's blood," William said.

Aspen's throat tightened and flashes of white appeared in her vision. What he was saying couldn't be true. And yet, a sliver of self-doubt began slicing its way into her mind. She had never heard her father's side of it. She had never allowed it, screaming in a tantrum every time he had tried. She hadn't needed to hear it, she had seen for herself. But now the exact moment when he had pushed the boy became fuzzy. Was it still a real memory? Or had her mind filled in the gaps left by the real experience?

"Pike reached out to the boy, that's true enough," William said. "But not to push him, to grab him." William's eyes were clear, focused. "The boy was panicked. Scared out of his wits. Didn't know what he was doing. He bit your daddy's hand. Hard. That's where the blood came from."

The water pulling her in the wrong direction. She and the boy nearly colliding. Her father's strong grasp around her waist. All of it was so clear. And then he reached for the boy to save him, but pushed him away instead. It's what her mind always saw. In the adrenaline of the moment, could she have been wrong?

"No," she said. She couldn't believe it. Not only because she had seen what had happened, but because if William was right, she had been holding a grudge for her entire adult life for something that had never even happened. That thought was too terrifying to contemplate. "I saw him, William. I saw what he did."

William shook his head slowly. A serene gesture that was certain and unmovable. "You think you saw. But I was the one that saw. I took your daddy to the hospital when you all got back while your mother stayed with you at the house. I saw them stitch up the wound. I saw with my own two eyes. Bites, punctured all the way down to the bone. Bled like a river."

Aspen felt her mind collapsing in on itself. She couldn't fathom the consequences of what William was saying. Her father had done exactly what she had accused him of being too afraid, too weak, to do. He had tried everything he could to save the boy. None of it had been his fault. There had never been anything to forgive.

"Why didn't he tell me?" Aspen was sobbing now, but she didn't care. She was with William, which was as close as she could get to being with her father.

"He tried," William said. "You never let him. He surely would've forced you to listen if he knew what you thought he did, but you had just witnessed something terrible. You saw a boy drown. You were scared and Pike didn't want to make you relive that. But he never could have guessed that you thought he pushed that boy. None of us could."

Aspen buried her face in her hands. She felt William's tentative touch patting her shoulder and thought about how her father must have felt every time she refused to say "I love you."

She would go to his side and never leave it again. Not until she spoke with him. Not until she explained. Not until she told him that she had been the cause of their only rift, not him. Because she had believed a lie. Because she had fought with all her might, rather than let him teach her how to forgive.

Tammy Wellington

Across the field, sunlight filtered through a fourth floor room at Sparkling Pond Hospital. A team of doctors and nurses responded to alarms originating from machines attached to Pike Collins. The physicians huddled together and spoke quietly but urgently to each other. It was obvious a decision would have to be made. Nurse Tammy Wellington watched from nearby, listening closely.

"We induced this coma as a last resort," one of them said. "We never expected it to lead to recovery."

"We had hoped," Dr. Morrison whispered. "Even if we wouldn't say it out load. We always hoped."

The conversation continued. Calm, controlled, but tense. Several ideas were floated. Each was rejected as little more than a prayer. In the end, there was only one option available.

"What happened?" Dr. Morrison said under his breath. He glanced at a clock ticking seconds away on the wall. "And why did it have to happen now?"

"Will he make it until five o'clock?" a doctor asked.

Dr. Morrison shook his head. "I don't know." He glanced at the team of doctors around him. "We'd better start. Immediately."

He strode to the door and stuck his head out.

"Is anyone out here free right now?" he asked.

Tammy tapped him on the shoulder. She should be the one to do this. "I can be," she said.

"Call Aspen Collins," Dr. Morrison told her. "Tell her to get here as quickly as she can."

Tammy removed her phone from her pocket, wasting no time. She didn't have Aspen's number in her phone, but she was certain she could contact someone who did.

"Please," Dr. Morrison said, getting her attention again. "Please hurry."

And with that, Tammy began scrolling through her contacts.

Jamison

Nobody's perfect. Jamison knew when he arrived in Sparkling Pond that there was no such thing as The Perfect Father. Pike Collins wasn't perfect. Jamison knew *he* certainly wasn't perfect. And Aspen wasn't perfect either.

Which meant it was possible she'd been mistaken. It wasn't out of the realm of possibility that she was just wrong. Maybe what was happening to her town would go down as the most exciting time in the town's history. Maybe the crowds, the craziness, even the soldiers, were actually a good thing. After all, it wasn't a boring place to be anymore, right?

At least that's what Jamison told himself when the red light started blinking and he went on the air. Him, not some other reporter who had come to take his place. Not yet. He still had one more chance to prove himself. So, with an ache forming in his stomach, he launched into his attempt to prove himself.

"Over the past several days I've told you about the sleepy town of Sparkling Pond and its insistence that one of its own—Pike Collins—is sending messages to his daughter. The Ghost, as they call him, is believed by some and doubted by others, but one thing is for sure— he's about to get more interesting to everyone."

Jamison nodded to Cornelius, who patted his comb-over and walked to Jamison's side. "Today, the nation's leading ghost hunter, Cornelius Brown, PhD., joins us to make an unprecedented announcement. Dr. Brown?"

Cornelius' eyes were wide and glazed, looking almost drugged. He licked his lips and swallowed. "Last night, through helium detection technology, I was able to prove that ghosts truly do exist. But today, I've made an even bigger discovery."

"And what's that, Dr. Brown?"

Cornelius rubbed his hands together and leaned closer to the microphone. "I have invented a concoction, a blend of helium, sulfates, and cooled nitrogen. When this formula comes in contact with a supernatural, post-humanoid being—a ghost, if you will—it makes the being visible to the naked, human eye."

Jamison knew he still had time to stop the madness. All he had to do was call Cornelius a crockpot, look into the camera, and tell the viewers of Minnesota and the millions who were sure to Google the story that the entire thing was a hoax. That they should go back to their own lives and leave Sparkling Pond alone. That was exactly what he told Aspen he would do. It was what she expected him to do.

But it wasn't what he did.

"Is this something you can prove to us, right here, right now?" he said. And with that simple question, Jamison knew his betrayal was complete.

"You'd like to see a ghost?" Cornelius asked. He was practically drooling.

Cornelius bounced his eyebrows and Jamison felt like he had been punched in the gut. Is that what he looked like every time he bounce-and-winked? An attention craving, off-his-rocker idiot? Jamison could no longer summon any excitement, so he just nodded.

But that answer wasn't good enough for Cornelius. Jamison was so confused he barely noticed when Cornelius took the microphone from him and spoke into the camera. Jamison couldn't focus on the words. He saw the thousands of people watching, entranced. He looked at the National Guard troops, standing sentry at each storefront, patrolling the playground, guarding the entrance to the hospital in the distance. He looked toward the cottages in town, where smoke curled from several chimneys—people too scared to come out of their homes because of what was going on. And he saw his own face staring back at him from a giant, high-definition screen, looking to all the world like a villain.

And Jamison realized he had lied to himself. Aspen had been right—this wasn't some moment that would go down in history as an exciting time. Because of what Jamison had brought, it would be a stain on the town forever. And he was the reason why. His complete, conscious, intentional betrayal.

The thought made him sick. It was time to take the microphone back, look into the camera, and say whatever needed to be said to clear this town of his poison. He reached for the microphone, but before he could snatch it from Cornelius' hand, a fist came out of nowhere and blasted Cornelius off his feet. Blaise Gunnison stared down at him with his fists clinched.

And then all hell broke loose in Sparkling Pond.

The mob of Free Thinkers who had threatened Pike the night before now turned their aggression toward the Team Ghost members. Most Team God members turned and ran, but the Team Ghost population dived into the fray against the Free Thinkers. Another sound bellowed through the town as dozens of National Guard troops, in full riot gear, left their stations around town and began marching toward what was turning into an all-out war.

Jamison couldn't even tell who was fighting who, and he tried to find J.D. with the camera to wrap up the live-shot, but J.D. was gone and Jamison didn't know where. He scanned the area, trying to figure out what to do, when a fist connected with the side of his head and he fell to the ground hard.

Jamison tried to stand but was dizzy from the punch. Then someone stepped on his hand—someone else kicked his stomach. In that moment, Jamison was sure he would either be trampled or beaten to death. But the mob seemed to forget him; he became lost in the clutter of people. Everyone was either running wildly or diving into the fray. Through blurry vision, Jamison was able to see through the mob, to a small group of people who had watched the live-shot from a distance. And the hole in his stomach became an immense void.

Aspen stared at the spectacle, wide-eyed, with her hand covering her mouth in shock. Next to her, Claire pulled the arm of his friend, Holly Torrey, trying desperately to get her away from the fighting. And Holly, sobbing and screaming soundlessly, looked right at him. He read her lips perfectly.

Jamison!

Claire managed to get Holly to go with her and thankfully, they were able to leave the area. Jamison stood and shook his head clear as the fighting raged around him. He looked back toward Aspen and met her eyes. She stared at Jamison through a well of tears and shook her head. He could see in her eyes that his betrayal was complete. Then she turned from him and ran away.

Tammy

Nurse Tammy Wellington had always liked Aspen Collins. Well, since sophomore year anyway, when Aspen first spoke to her. Tammy had been sitting in the locker room after the Chiefs girls' basketball team suffered a rare loss. The loss stung Tammy more strongly than any of the players. Ever since second grade, when she had attended her first game, she had been a Lady Chiefs fan. She had always dreamed of one day wearing the Crimson and Gold. She hadn't let her pudgy legs and lack of ability stop her from playing a part.

"Get me some water," Stacey Canterbury said. Tammy knew she didn't mean to be rude. It had been a hard game. A hard loss. She hurried to a water bottle and handed it to Stacey.

"Out of my way, fatty," Lauren Adams said, hip-checking Tammy. Tammy wished she hadn't fallen to the floor. She had learned that calling attention to herself was the worst thing she could do. But Lauren had hit her pretty hard.

Tammy looked around at the girls. Each one looked disgusted. Like Tammy had cost them the game. Her mind flashed back, panicked that she had done something wrong—been slow with a water bottle or a towel. Maybe something else a team manager was supposed to do that she had neglected, causing her team to lose. She couldn't think of anything, but there must have been something. The girls all looked irate. And they were all staring at her.

Except Aspen Collins.

Aspen looked like she might throw up, her disgust was so complete. Tammy knew she was upset about the loss. But instead of vomiting, Aspen began screaming. "What is wrong with you guys? Are you completely callous? Do you really think this is cool?"

Tammy wondered if Aspen needed some water, but didn't want to call attention to herself. But then all the girls started flicking their eyes to Tammy, then darting them away again. Tammy had assumed Aspen was talking to her teammates about the game. But realization came slowly—she was screaming at them about how the girls were treating *her.*

"You think we're all big star athletes and that gives us the right to pick on people we see as inferior?" Aspen continued. "Tammy's done nothing but help us. Selflessly. And you all think you can step on her because it makes you feel better about yourselves after a loss? It's pathetic. She has more heart than any of us and if she were out there playing tonight instead of us, I guarantee we wouldn't have been embarrassed like that. We should all learn from Tammy, not insult her."

Aspen walked directly to Tammy and said, "If I've ever been mean to you, I want you to know I'm sorry." Then she wrapped Tammy in a sweaty hug.

Aspen Collins—All-State forward, Prom Queen, everybody's best friend Aspen Collins—had just turned Tammy's world around. She tried not to let her tears drip onto her shirt and mix with Aspen's sweat. She vowed never to wash the shirt again.

In the next twelve years, Tammy had grown a lot. She had matured. But she had never forgotten. And now, she finally had a small way to show Aspen the gratitude she had always felt. She would break the news that they were waking her father. She would be a small participant—a team manager—in this drama they had worked so hard at for so long.

To let Aspen speak to her father one last time.

The Ghost

There's one thing I need to make clear—I didn't actually believe Jamison Hightower would betray us like that. Not in that way.

When I saw Aspen's eyes, I could tell that she hadn't either. And certainly it's true, Jamison deserves some responsibility for what has happened in Sparkling Pond. He did have an opportunity to fix things, and instead made it worse. But it's not Jamison Hightower who deserves the blame.

It's me.

I'm the one who brought him here. I'm the one who set the wheels in motion. I'm the one who has brought this horror upon my beloved hometown.

Aspen

Aspen tore through the grassy streets as fast as her legs would take her. She tried to transfer all her agony and disappointment into movement. First she found out the truth about what had happened in Lake Superior, then Jamison stabbed her in the back. Her entire world was coming apart at the seams. She would run and run and never stop running. But somehow, Jamison caught up with her. His hand grabbed her shoulder and she spun on him.

"Get your hands off me."

Why did he look so sad? He had wronged her, not the other way around. He should be celebrating the promotion that was probably coming his way. But his eyes drooped like she had never seen before.

"Aspen, I'm sorry. You weren't supposed to—"

"I wasn't supposed to what? Witness your total betrayal? I don't know why I trusted you. I don't know why I ever even talked to you. In fact, I never want to speak to you again."

The sound of gunshots echoed through the town. In the middle of the fight, someone had shot into the air. The attempt to calm the crowd only made them more unruly. Aspen glared at Jamison—the cause of all of this. Why did he look so contrite? The softness of his eyes almost made her feel sorry for him. But sorry for what? *Self-inflicted Wound.*

"I understand," Jamison said. A tear gathered in the corner of his eye and Aspen fought the urge to caress his cheek and wipe the tear. "I can do that for you. I can disappear from your life and never return. If that's what you want."

"Good. You do that."

Aspen continued staring at him. She knew about his insecurities and how the people who were supposed to love him had let him down. She knew she had an opportunity to show him a kind of love and devotion he had never experienced.

Then there was a sound the likes of which had never existed in Sparkling Pond. The grinding of gears. The combustion of fuel. The spewing of black exhaust. Aspen pressed her hand to her heart. An army tank was rolling through her town. She turned on the man in front of her, using all her self-control not to slap him.

"Get away from me, Jamison Hightower."

And she turned and ran away.

Tammy

Tammy double-checked the phone number and dialed again. Where was she? Her home phone went unanswered. Her cell went straight to voicemail.

She left an urgent message, but leaving a message and hoping for the best wouldn't cut it. They had already stopped the Isoflurane. There was no telling how much time they still had, but it wasn't much.

Tammy shouted, "I'm going to find her" over her shoulder, and sprinted for the WEB Train.

Jamison

The fight in the town square had turned into a war. From the outskirts of it, Jamison couldn't even tell who was fighting whom. In one moment, it seemed to have morphed into everyone against the National Guard, but then another fight would break out among the Free Thinkers and Team Ghost, and suddenly the soldiers found themselves breaking up a fight between two people who, moments before, had both been attacking them.

The chaos only continued to grow.

Jamison sprinted toward Claire's house, although he wasn't really sure why. Familiarity? Maybe he needed to be near the strength she always emitted. But when he got there, Claire wasn't home. So he ran to the house of Holly's grandparents. He had to be sure she was okay. That Claire had been able to get her to safety. But the door there was locked too.

Jamison slammed his fists against the door. "Is anybody in there? Can you hear me?"

A gunshot blasted near the square and Jamison flinched. He certainly wasn't out of range if the shooters decided to turn their targets onto people. "Please," he yelled to the door. "I have to know you're all okay."

There was movement in the window—a shuffling of curtains. And then the face of Holly's grandfather peeked through. He didn't say anything. Didn't mouth any words. And he didn't have to. His message of rage was written all over his wrinkled face.

Jamison stumbled away from the house and watched the carnage taking place in and around the playground. He knew in that instant the fate he deserved. The least he could do was attempt to tell the story of someone in need on the way out. They called reporting for RISK-TV a suicide mission. If that was true, he was just the man for the job.

He tilted his head to the sky and screamed with every ounce of breath in his lungs. "I'm sorry! Don't you understand? I'm sorry!" But no one was listening. Holly and her grandparents were locked safely in their house. The people in the town square were busy hurling rocks at soldiers and throwing seemingly random punches at each other. No matter. Jamison wasn't speaking to anyone in specific. He was speaking to the entire town.

"I didn't mean for this to happen!" he screamed into the air.

But it was futile. No one heard him. No one cared. He watched the fighting continue, the tanks crushing wildflowers, the yelling and screaming. And he said again, quietly, to himself, "I didn't mean for this to happen."

Tammy

Tammy stepped out of the front doors of Sparkling Pond Hospital and screamed at the sight in front of her. Her town had turned into a battle ground. There were tanks, soldiers, masses of people—and everyone was fighting. What were they all fighting about?

This was supposed to be an easy search through town. There were only a few places Aspen could be. But this changed everything. How was she supposed to find Aspen in the midst of a war? It wasn't safe here.

She went back into the hospital and closed the door behind her. But she couldn't take her hand off the door-knob. She owed Aspen more than that. So she took a deep breath, pushed forward, and stepped back into the chaos.

Tammy knew most people in town, like everyone else did. She knew Crazy Willie lived in a cottage nearby, and that he knew Aspen well. So she ran to his doorstep and knocked hard. After several moments, it creaked open and William pressed the rim of his hat out of his eyes.

"Excuse me, sir," Tammy said. "I'm sorry to bother you, but I'm looking for Aspen Collins. It's urgent. Do you know where I can find her?"

The cowboy's eyes misted over, which was strange. But he gave Tammy directions to Aspen's house and rushed back inside. Tammy jogged in the direction Crazy Willie had told her and pulled out her cell phone. One of her coworkers answered and Tammy heard the tension in her voice. They had started sensory stimulation. It wouldn't be long now. The window was opening, but even if it worked, it wouldn't last long. The cancer was quickly finishing its work.

Tammy hung up and stuffed the phone in her pocket. She sprinted to the house Crazy Willie had described and rapped her knuckles against the door.

Aspen

What does it mean to love another? Aspen wasn't sure she knew. In just a few short days, she had grown to feel strongly for Jamison. She thought she knew him. She thought she could count on him. She had begun to imagine what life would be like with him. If she could somehow keep him in Sparkling Pond. Somehow be with him forever.

But he had betrayed her. He had betrayed the town. He had even betrayed her father.

Thoughts of her father just created more panic in her mind. Would they even have a five o'clock meeting this evening, with everything that was happening in the town square? Would it be safe? What if it was the day they decided to awaken her father from his coma, and she wasn't there?

It was then that she heard the roar.

The sound—so foreign until recently—was like a song she could recognize from the first note. The entire mob in the town square could recognize it as well. For a moment, the fighting stopped. People wrestling on the ground paused to see what the roar was for. Soldiers, unaccustomed to hearing the excitement behind the sound, lowered their riot-gear shields and looked to the playground. And Aspen, who was nearing her house, turned and sprinted back into the mass of people.

The volume grew as she neared the town square. On the side of her consciousness, she realized people were staring at her puffy eyes and wet cheeks, but she didn't care. If something had appeared, nothing else mattered.

When she got to the merry-go-round, Ryder Gunnison was waiting for her, surrounded by countless people. He had a black eye and his lip was cut. But he seemed more upset about what he was holding in his hand than about his injuries. He held out an envelope, which Aspen took, then reached out his hand and dropped something into her palm.

"I don't know how it got here," he said.

Aspen opened her hand and saw a small rock glinting in her palm. It was purple with swooshes of pink and red flowing through it. She recognized it right away. A Lake Superior Agate.

She squeezed the stone in her palm and tore past the gaping crowd, furious that even her father was preventing her from escaping Jamison Hightower.

Tammy

Tammy was beginning to panic. Aspen wasn't at home. Things at the hospital were progressing too quickly. And here she was, sprinting around Sparkling Pond, unable to find the person she so desperately needed to find.

All the people racing around didn't help anything. There was a giant roar minutes ago, as if Bono had just taken the stage, and then everyone within earshot—which was basically the entire town— stopped fighting and sprinted toward the town square, too distracted to answer Tammy's questions.

The only thing she could do was go to the store Crazy Willie had said to try if Aspen wasn't at home. So she turned around and jogged back the other way, hoping she would find Aspen at Rad Collie's Dangling Cliff Adventures.

Rad

The whole town had gone crazy. Everyone was spazzing out over something. The place was like a freakin' Phish concert.

Rad cleaned up the store a bit, mostly in back. Not much made Rad nervous—and a good, old-fashioned riot usually made him feel right at home. But something about this was different, and it made him uneasy.

When he had hidden everything that needed hiding, he thought about grabbing a beer and pulling up a chair at the entrance to Dangling Cliff Adventures. Watching the circus for a while. But then he caught sight of Aspen running through the grass, making a bee-line toward his shop.

After all the distance she had covered to get there, she wasn't even breathing hard. She just ran straight up to him, opened her palm to show him some random rock, and said, "I need to talk to you."

Rad cursed in his brain and put on his professional, thoughtful face. He nodded, like an intellectual, and led her inside.

Cornelius

Cornelius feared for his life. But more than that, he feared for his equipment. Just as it looked like a tank was going to plow over all his possessions, another miracle had happened and calmed things down.

Cornelius was taking advantage of the relative calm to hide what he could under whatever playground equipment might provide shelter. He was shoving a small gamma ray detector under the merry-go-round when Jamison Hightower walked by, looking more beat up than any of the Team God members Cornelius had seen, despite Jamison not having any physical injuries. Cornelius would have thought he was wandering aimlessly if not for the look on Jamison's face.

"Where are you going?" Cornelius asked.

Jamison heaved a sigh, as if stopping to talk was beyond his abilities. Then he looked toward Cornelius, but avoided eye contact. "Away," Jamison said. "For good."

Jamison's face wore a mixture of determination and resignation. Cornelius had seen that look before—on people who were being haunted and couldn't stand it for another minute. He wasn't sure how Jamison was being haunted, but Cornelius knew this much—in any situation, that look was not good.

Okay, so maybe he had taken the ghost sighting scenario a bit too far. He sure couldn't have predicted the craziness that followed. He had a welt the size of an apple on the side of his head from that oaf that clocked him, and it looked like many others were even worse off.

Cornelius knew he couldn't undo what he had done during the live-shot, but maybe he could at least help restore some sort of order. He found a National Guard soldier and pulled him aside. Then he scanned the crowd. "Him, him, and…him," Cornelius said to the soldier as he pointed. "They're the instigators."

The soldier nodded, said he'd keep a close eye on them, and strode away. Maybe Cornelius' tip would help calm things down. He sure hoped so. His equipment wouldn't be replaced easily.

Jamison

The End.

Jamison had always loved the clarity of those two words. At the culmination of a book or movie they would let you know, in no uncertain terms, that you had reached the finish line. That there was nothing more to come.

He didn't bother to straighten his skewed rearview mirror as he gazed at the chaos from Sparkling Pond—that enchanted place without a single road within its borders. And he realized those words—the end—were about him. Like a paperback tossed over the edge of the bed. Lights flicked off. Eyes closed and ready to drift away. His story, too, was coming to an end.

He scrolled through his incoming calls, not worrying too much about how long his eyes were off the road. He found the number for RISK-TV and called it. They answered quickly, as if anticipating his call. As if they knew he was bound to fall, and would inevitably accept the job in the end.

Aleppo, they said. The most dangerous Syrian city at the moment. Making it the most dangerous city on the planet. The only difficulty would be deciding which heartbreaking story to cover. There were so many stories that needed to be told. So many people whose only hope was to have someone like him tell their story, and hope someone watching cared enough to act.

He would have to tell as many stories in the shortest time possible. If the history of RISK-TV reporters in Aleppo was any indication, he wouldn't have long.

The End. To Jamison, those words had never sounded so sweet.

Aspen

The sound of the battle raged into Dangling Cliff Adventures as Aspen slipped through the open front door. She passed by Rad, who craned his neck outside and shook his head. "No wonder we don't see more miracles," he said. "People don't have a clue how to handle it when we get one."

He closed the door and latched a dead-bolt, then Aspen followed as he sauntered to the back room and sat behind the desk. He slouched back and kicked up his feet as if there was nothing wrong in the world.

Aspen slammed the agate onto the scarred surface of the desk. Rad ignored it while he wiggled a bit, arranging himself on the chair. But Aspen couldn't sit. She towered over him, pacing.

"What's got you wound up like a pissed off King Cobra?" Rad said. He shook his head. "Er, I take it there has been a development?"

Aspen had to keep moving. Stillness allowed her mind to wander, and she knew where it would end up. So physically, she paced. Emotionally, she dug. And mentally, she flew.

"My dad left me this," she said.

"And—"

"This time, he doesn't know what he's talking about."

"Easy, sleazy," Rad said. He put his palms out toward her. "You got to learn how to chill. Why don't you rest your weary bones on that chair there and we'll...we'll converse about the developmentations you mentioned."

Aspen's entire being still yearned for action. Or distraction. But Rad had a mellow way about him that was contagious. She risked calming down a bit and was surprised to realize she was able to focus on the stone. She sat, her body completely still except for her bouncing right foot. *Confined.*

"Better, no?" Rad said. He folded his hands together and slouched in the chair. "So why'd he leave you a rock?"

Aspen scoffed. It came out as a mixture of a short laugh and a deep chortle and sounded like a cough or a sneeze. She took a moment to control herself, then said, "Forgiveness." She felt like spitting on the beautiful stone.

Rad sat silently staring at her. She wished he would say some of his weird things so she could stew in her thoughts, but he just waited. Finally, she gave in.

"Something happened when we went to Lake Superior for a camping trip when I was young. My dad did something, and I never forgave him. I never bothered to see it from his perspective. Even now, it took finding out that I was wrong about what truly happened for me to even consider his side. And all along, if I could have had the smallest bit of empathy, I would have seen the terrible situation he'd been in. The awful decision he was forced to make. Without time to think, without time to weigh one option over another. I thought he chose me, and I never forgave him."

She stared at the cuts that ran through the wood desk, unable to force herself to look at the agate. *Remorse.* "I screwed up. Even if there had been something to forgive, I should have forgiven him a long time ago, and I'll have to live with that for the rest of my life. But now, with this rock, he's trying to tell me to forgive Jamison. And I can't."

"Why?"

"Because it's completely different."

"How?" Rad said.

"Didn't you see the news today? Don't you see what's happened to our town? It doesn't fit this time. He doesn't deserve forgiveness. He doesn't deserve a second chance. Even before I knew the truth, I knew that what my father did was for me. But everything Jamison did was intentional and deliberate and cruel."

"Interesting," Rad said.

"Interesting? Really? That's what you've got for me? Interesting?"

"Well, I don't figure you want to hear what I really think."

Aspen had a feeling he was right, but still, she raised her eyebrows and tossed her hands as if to say *Let's hear it.*

"I think you're to blame for all that mess out there as much as Jamison."

"Excuse me?"

"You just said it," Rad said, his hands up in defense. "You should have forgiven your old man. Told him you loved him. But you didn't. And look what it made him do."

Aspen hadn't thought of it that way before. And now that it had been pointed out to her, she wondered why she hadn't.

"It's always easier to blame other people," Rad said, answering the questions in her mind. "But no one's completely innocent."

Rad continued to slouch, but Aspen sat at attention now. She felt that pit in her stomach that was becoming all too familiar.

"You know," Rad said. "The speed of light is a hundred-eighty-six thousand miles per second."

Consumed by confusion and nagging guilt, Aspen wasn't in the mood for one of Rad's weird tangents. "I really don't care about the speed of light, Rad."

"You should. Because even going that fast, it takes the light from the sun 8.3 seconds to reach us. The next nearest star is Proxima Centauri, and it takes light from that star 4.3 years to reach us. For stars in other galaxies, it takes millions of years from the time its light leaves the star until we can see it."

Aspen squeezed the bridge of her nose and rubbed her eyes. If he had a point—and he very well may not—he sure was taking his time getting to it.

"Any of those stars could have already gone supernova," Rad said. "The biggest explosion in the entire universe. But we won't know it for years, because the light has to travel through space. So even if the star has been blasted into smithereens, we see it twinkling calmly in the sky for millions of years."

"So?" Aspen said.

"So, the only thing we see is the face that star is putting on. We can't see what's going on behind the starlight until millions of years later, when the star finally tells us its secret." He leaned forward, his eyes blazing now. "Just something to think about, dude."

The last of Aspen's anger seeped out under Rad's gaze, leaving her exhausted. A small spark of hope flickered through the fatigue when she realized she hadn't read the note. So she slid the stone off the desk, shoved it into her pocket, and started to leave. To read her note in private.

"Thanks, Rad."

As sunlight hit her face—light from 8.3 seconds in the past—Aspen blinked, waiting for her pupils to adjust. The shouts and grunts of fighting in the town square had resumed as soon as she'd left the square, so Aspen slid around to the back of the building. The realization that she was hiding in her own hometown threatened to stoke the fire inside her again, but the allure of the note was more powerful. She unfolded it carefully and read:

Dear Aspen,

I have failed you, and I'm sorry. I tried to be the perfect father, but I wasn't.

Some people say intentions don't matter. That our lives are judged on our actions—what we actually do and say, not what we wish we had done or said.

While I understand that sentiment, I can't wholeheartedly accept it. You see, I didn't want for any of that to happen at Lake Superior. I think that's true of most people who hurt someone they love. But sometimes, we hurt people whether we want to or not.

That day at Lake Superior consisted of my very best moment— when I saved you from being pulled out by the rip-tide. And also my very worst—when I was unable to save the other boy.

But how would you like to be judged by your very worst moment? To have your life forever defined by that single weakness? And if you were given a chance at redemption, can you imagine your motivation to be remembered for something better?

Aspen, my baby girl, I'm going to die soon. Very soon now. But before I go, I'm going to ask for more than I deserve. I wasn't able to save that boy, but you can save me. By forgiving me for my weaknesses, my shortcomings, you would set me free. You would grant me redemption.

We all need forgiveness for something. Me. You. Jamison. Everyone.

Give it. Those who hold a grudge strap a weight upon their own shoulders. Those who forgive are free.

Free yourself. I beg of you. And in the process, you will free me.
Love always,
Daddy.

Aspen flipped the note over and looked to the lower-right corner, where she saw the word "Breathe."

She eased her eyes closed, rested her head against the chipped brick of the building, and forced as much air into her lungs as possible.

An unexpected sense of peace swept over her immediately as she exhaled. She was hit with the realization that she hadn't taken a truly deep breath in a long time. Angry breaths are shallow. Anxious breaths are choppy. The pure, satisfying breath that filled her lungs now rejuvenated her spirit. For a brief moment, her attention was inward, on her breath, her mind, and her soul.

The experience was surprisingly freeing.

She thought of Rad's words and wondered whether she truly understood Jamison as well as she thought she did. And then she remembered her father's words from the note.

We all need forgiveness for something. Me. You. Jamison. Everyone. Give it.

It was her father's dying wish. And Aspen knew she had to grant it. But how? That was the question that stumped her as she crept back to the front of the building, slightly crouched as if expecting an attack. The situation in the town square had escalated and was out of hand. How could she possibly find and forgive Jamison in all this chaos?

When the realization hit her it was so obvious she couldn't believe she hadn't thought of it right away. She could kill two birds with one stone. If she could find Jamison.

Aspen began jogging toward Claire's house, praying she hadn't already missed her chance.

Tammy

Tammy cursed. By the time she had been able to weave through the crowd, the middle-aged hippie said she had missed Aspen by a minute. At least she was on her trail now. She had almost caught up with her. The hippie seemed sure he knew where Aspen would be. Claire Lyons' house—the big old cabin right near the lake.

Tammy's phone buzzed and she answered. It was Dr. Morrison himself this time, which got Tammy's attention real quick. Air was whistling through the phone so she stopped jogging to hear him better. "Can you repeat that?" she said.

When he did, Tammy immediately hung up and tried Aspen's phone again, now even more desperate to get in touch. But the call wouldn't go through. Instead, she heard a recorded message that said all cell towers in the area had been shut down by order of the National Guard until further notice. They were sorry for the inconvenience.

Tammy replayed the doctor's response in her head over and over. The words made her sprint faster than she ever had before.

The Ghost

So much has happened. So much of it unexpected. I'm not sure what I'm doing anymore. We're off script here. And my illusions of control are long gone.

Aspen

Aspen sprinted past Team God and Team Ghost members as they pushed and shoved each other, some swinging their fists wildly while others attempted to break up the brawl. National Guard soldiers looked on, having failed in their attempts to break up the fights without using excessive force. Shooting warning shots into the air didn't seem to have any effect. The soldiers seemed paralyzed by uncertainty, surprised that the presence of armored men with guns wasn't enough to stop the violence. The Free Thinkers only added fuel to the fire.

Aspen finally broke through the crowd and into open grass. She could see Claire's house in the distance. And then something caught her eye. An envelope, lying in the grass. Not accompanied by any object. Not causing a stir in the town square. Aspen picked it up, opened it, and was amazed to see her father's handwriting.

Jamison is in danger. Don't let him go.

She stuffed the note into a pocket and sprinted the rest of the way to Claire's house. When she burst in, Claire was sitting at the dining room table, but she was alone.

"Is he upstairs?" Aspen asked. She started running up the steps until she saw Claire shake her head.

"He's gone," Claire said.

Departed, May 15, age 24. Claire hadn't said that Jamison had "left" or that he had "decided to go." He was gone. And Claire's eyes held more than sadness. There was a focus in them too. Worry, Aspen realized.

"Where?" she asked.

Claire heaved a heavy sigh. "Straight to the airport, with nothing but the clothes on his back. Apparently they'll have a ticket waiting for him. He said something about Syria."

"What!" Aspen exclaimed. "He took the RISK-TV job?"

"I'm afraid so, yes."

"But their journalists die! They send them to places they know they won't come back from, just for the publicity of it!"

"I know," Claire said. "I did all I could to talk him out of it. But when a man in his state of mind makes a decision about something like that…"

Aspen remembered her father's advice and tried to breathe deeply, but her lungs refused to expand.

"I know what he did was wrong," Claire said. "But I've grown to love that boy. And I'm worried about him. I know he wants to tell those people's stories, and I know someone needs to, those poor, poor people. But not for that station. Not Jamison."

As a tear slipped down Claire's cheek, Aspen thought about her father's most recent note—*Jamison is in danger.* And she thought back on their last conversation.

I can disappear from your life and never return.

Good. You do that.

Then, amid the chaos in her mind, she pictured the past few days. A water-drop making its way through the dimples of his cheek while they swam naked in the mist. The warmth of his lips against hers when they were pressed together. And suddenly, the thought of never seeing him again, of never giving him a chance at forgiveness—just like with her father—created a panic that swept through her entire body.

She had to reach him. No longer just for her father. For herself. For her chance at love.

"How long ago did he leave?" she asked.

"Maybe ten minutes? Aspen," Claire said, and she took Aspen's hands with a puff of flour. "Jamison needs you. Find him. Don't let him get to that airport. Only you can save him."

Aspen quickly kissed her cheek and bolted for the door. She flew outside and nearly ran right into the knuckles of someone about to knock on the door. Aspen blinked and realized it was Tammy Wellington, team manager for her high school basketball team and nurse at Sparkling Pond Hospital. Tammy's eyes bulged in recognition and she clutched Aspen's hands.

Aspen knew where she was going. What she had to do. The man she was growing to love needed her, and she would do whatever was necessary, sacrifice whatever it required, to save him. To give him a chance at redemption. It was the right thing to do. Then Tammy squeezed her hand and said, "Your father's awake."

And that changed everything.

Tammy

Tammy saw the pain and confusion in Aspen's eyes, so different from the certainty and determination with which she had defended the 15 year-old Tammy. She had seen, every single day for the past three months, how important this was to her. She knew what it meant.

So she said a silent prayer that Aspen would reach the hospital in time.

Aspen

Aspen tore away from Claire's house, ready to run with every ounce of strength she possessed. But run where? Maybe she could call the hospital. See if there was any way to buy some time. To see if they could keep her father alive a little longer.

She fished her phone out of her pocket and realized it was powered down. Frantically, she turned it on, squeezing it impatiently while it booted up. She scrolled past several messages from Tammy and tried the hospital. But her phone wouldn't work. Something about shut down cell towers.

Aspen put her head in her hands and looked to the left—toward the Sparkling Pond Hospital in the distance, where he father lay awake. Waiting for her. Then she looked right, toward the path that led to the parking lot. The car that could catch up with Jamison, who was driving toward something Aspen couldn't comprehend. Needing her.

How could it possibly have come to this? Going to her father meant she would lose the man she had grown so fond of. Maybe even loved. If he were to die in Syria, she would be responsible. There was no question, no other option. She had to save Jamison.

But going to Jamison meant she could miss her only chance to tell her father how much she loved him before he died. To grant the forgiveness he had begged for. To set him free. There was no question, no other option. She had to save her father.

But she wasn't strong enough to save them both.

Seconds ticked on, refusing to give her time to think. Jamison was speeding away, her father was fading. Aspen sat on the ground and began to cry. She was paralyzed. Neither option was acceptable. She couldn't stand the thought of losing either of them.

But slowly, she realized only one thing would be worse than losing Jamison or her father, and that was sitting on the ground, crying, until they were both gone from her life. She had to act. And she had to act now.

And now she knew the torment her father had known.

She steeled herself. She stood. And she began to sprint with everything she had.

The Ghost

Right and wrong. Black and white. Left or right.

If only life were so simple.

Sometimes there is nuance. Sometimes there is gray area. Sometimes there are complications.

Sometimes no father in the world is strong enough to save two drowning children. Sometimes decisions have to be made, and the consequences accepted.

There is something worse than having to watch someone you love make a decision like that.

It's far more painful when you're the one forced to choose.

Aspen

Aspen's tears blurred her vision. She smeared her right cheek, then left, wiping the drops away. Crying wouldn't help anything. It was too late for that. She had made her choice.

It's like her father used to tell her—you can't change the past.

She tried to rationalize her decision. But no matter how many circles she ran in her mind, she knew she was responsible. If the unthinkable happened, it would be her fault.

If her father died, he would die without knowing of his daughter's forgiveness.

And yet, despite the pain, it felt right. As if she had his blessing somehow. As if, in choosing to find Jamison, she had stumbled upon her father's wishes as well. At least, that's what she tried to tell herself.

She pushed the gas pedal almost to the floor. She had to catch up to him on the road before he got to the airport and through security. The trees blurred past the window, sharpening Aspen's focus. She was so intent on keeping the car on the road and watching for any wildlife that might jump in front of her that she didn't notice the flashing lights until she was nearly upon them. She eased the brake slowly, making sure to keep control of the car. And she fought a knot that had formed directly in the center of her throat.

An image flashed in her mind of Jamison driving off the road, having decided a tree would do better than a bullet in some far off country. She tried to push the image aside, but it persisted. It would make sense, she thought. If he cared about his life so little that he would take the job with RISK-TV, why wouldn't he just put a stop to it now? Why do the song and dance when the answer lay in groves along the side of the road?

Two police cars slanted together in the middle of the road, no more than a hundred yards ahead of Aspen, creating a barricade. She held her breath as she eased her car toward the barricade, terrified of what she might see in the ditch. An officer was out of his car, waving his hands high above his head to make sure Aspen saw him and didn't attempt to pass by. When he jogged up to her window, she slid it down, staring straight ahead.

"Can't go this way, I'm afraid," the officer said. "Probably not for a couple hours, 'till they get the scene all cleaned up."

Panic. April 1, age 11.

Aspen could barely form the word. "Why?"

The officer straightened his hat as he looked at her. "Because there's no room to get by."

"No," Aspen said, steeling herself for the worst. "I mean, what happened? Was there an accident?"

"Are these things really accidents?" the officer said. "Sometimes I wonder. Driving like that, he must have wanted it to happen."

"Jamison?" Aspen said. She didn't expect the officer to know if the man involved in the accident was Jamison or not, but she needed so desperately to know. The uncertainty was more than she could bear.

And then she saw an image of him. Jamison Hightower. James Smith. Like a vision, or an apparition, or another ghost. Walking toward her. A crinkle in his brow.

"The driver?" the police officer said on the periphery of Aspen's consciousness. "I don't know his name, I guess. But every trucker who knows how to drive knows to slow down for that curve. But this guy tipped his load of gasoline onto its side and spilled it all over the place. We're looking at an environmental assessment, Hazmat suits, the whole nine yards. A little common sense would've…"

Aspen didn't hear the rest. She jumped out of the car, nearly knocking the officer over, and ran toward Jamison. His face—not the face of a ghost, but of the actual man she had come to love—still looked at her with confusion in his eyes, until Aspen leaped toward him and hugged him with her entire body.

Jamison

Jamison struggled through the confusion of seeing Aspen. Of holding her in his arms. The last time he'd seen her, the look of betrayal and anger had burned into his consciousness, forever etched in his memory. He couldn't fathom how she'd gone from those feelings to this— clinging to him as if terrified she might lose him. But his confusion was dwarfed by one, overpowering thought—she had come looking for him.

Jamison held her at arm's length, brushed the hair out of her eyes, and tried to sort through everything that swarmed in his head. Regret over his actions, relief that he wouldn't be going to the Middle East— not as long as he was with Aspen—and an unfamiliar feeling he couldn't identify. But he felt it more powerfully than all the others. He focused on it but still couldn't place it. It was new. Foreign. And its strength was uncontrollable.

And then, with the force of a sledgehammer, it hit him. He understood, and he crumpled his face onto Aspen's. It was the feeling of being loved. True love for his true self.

Aspen had seen him at his worst. Using his eyebrow bounce-and-wink to garner attention. Basking in a feeling of superiority because of his fame. Even destroying her hometown for his own gain. And yet she had come for him. She had loved him enough to forgive what he had done.

The cheap adoration of his fans was revealed for what it was—a sham. A fake. A lie. Aspen had shown him a kind of faithfulness Jamison had never even known existed. But he wanted it. And suddenly, he knew exactly what he had to do. Jamison held Aspen with one arm—afraid to let her go—and with his other hand, pulled out his cell phone. He breathed a sigh of relief when he was able to connect to a tower outside Sparkling Pond.

This would be the most important phone call of his life.

Caroline

Was it Sunday? Tuesday? Maybe that was yesterday. It didn't matter. Every day blurred like the day before. Every day burned like the day before. Like the next certainly would as well.

Caroline Smith did the only thing she knew how to do. She cleaned. Even after all these years, even after all she had lost, the drugs still called out to her like a lost friend waiting to be rediscovered.

Her only hope was to wipe it clean. Wipe everything clean.

People must take responsibility for their actions, she knew. But why were others allowed to simply say those words and then move on like nothing had happened, when her entire life had been a lesson in what it actually means?

When Jamison had left all those years ago, she never imagined what was in store. Years of heartache, dozens of phone calls made, hundreds of letters written. All ignored. She had been rejected over and over until the pain of it settled into a constant ache in the back of her head. Well, so be it. She had brought it on herself. There was no one else she could blame.

The phone jarred her out of her heartbreak. The screeching from an old-fashioned wall-hanging phone was the only thing that could accomplish that feat, save for the cleaning obsession. She felt her heart skip a beat, in spite of herself.

Early on, when her hopes had still seemed possible, that sound represented everything she wished for in life. She didn't want money or fame or success. All she wanted was to hear that phone ring, and for her little boy to be on the other end of the line.

As the days turned into weeks, and finally into years, she knew her dream would never come true. Still, for those few wonderful seconds while the phone was ringing, she would set her mind free. Why not? If only one thing gives you hope, if only one event could make your dreams come true, why not allow yourself to live in the fantasy? It's so sweet while it lasts. Years ago, Caroline had stopped answering the phone when it rang. If she didn't cut it short, the ringing would sometimes go on for almost a minute.

Once, three years earlier, it had rung for seven full minutes. Probably a telemarketer giving himself a break from having to make his next call. But for Caroline, it had been bliss. She had leaned against the wall, picturing her son on the other end, imagining their conversation. "You're getting married? I'm invited? I can't wait to meet your kids. When did you say kindergarten graduation is? Of course, I'll be there. I wouldn't miss it."

When the ringing had stopped she had sat for several moments, eyes wide and disbelieving. Then she had cried for three days straight.

It was the sweetest memory of her life.

As the phone rang now, she dropped her dust rag and settled herself for a few moments of ecstasy. But when she tried to imagine how the conversation would go, she couldn't hear his voice. His real voice, not the TV voice. It wasn't there, in her mind. It was gone. The very last remnant of his existence had been pulled from her memory.

Caroline stared at her dust rag. The ringing no longer made her heart jump. Now, it made her sick. But she knew of a cure for this kind of sickness. She had been fighting it for years, and for what? What had she gained? Who would be hurt? Some would call it a relapse, but she thought of it as a reward. She didn't care if she never cleaned another speck of dirt in her life. She would lose herself in the drugs until she was too far gone to realize she was covered in dirt and grime.

Since her hope was gone, nothing mattered anymore. It didn't matter what would happen to her. It didn't matter who would follow the stench and find her body two weeks after she had overdosed. It didn't even matter anymore who was on the other end of the line.

And since it didn't matter, since she didn't care, since there was no way she could feel a single shred of disappointment anymore...she picked up the telephone.

Jamison

On the side of County Road 12, with flashing police lights and the smell of gasoline in the air, Aspen touched Jamison's face.

"Jamison...why?"

Why?

Jamison couldn't count the times he had asked himself that same question in the last hour, but he had yet to come up with a decent answer.

"These past few days have been the most magical of my life. I didn't want that to end."

He took a deep breath, knowing she deserved more. Knowing she deserved the whole truth.

"I did it for myself, Aspen. I did it to save my job. So I could still be the TV guy everyone loves. I did it because I didn't care who I hurt, as long as I didn't get fired. I did it because I was afraid."

Aspen should have been yelling at him now. But her eyes, when Jamison met them, were soft. Was she considering giving him another chance? Was that possible? Or did she just need closure? For a moment, he allowed himself to hope. He took one of her hands, and she didn't pull away.

"But I'm not afraid anymore," he said. "I understand now. I know what you were talking about."

"What do you mean? Understand what?"

"When I look at you, I see it," he said. "The seventh star."

Aspen stared into his eyes and stroked his cheek. "I forgive you," she said. Then she brought her face close and kissed him.

Jamison felt like he had been born again. Like everything was new. It was as if one kiss from Aspen could make all his problems disappear.

If she was willing to be with him, what did it matter if he didn't have a job? He should have seen it before. If he had Aspen, he had everything he needed.

The loud crackle of a police radio startled Jamison out of the kiss. It seemed to surprise Aspen too because she pulled away. Something in her eyes focused, as if coming out of a trance.

"We have to hurry," she said. "He's awake."

Aspen

"He's awake."

Aspen repeated the words, letting them rattle around in her mind. Letting them settle in her soul. She'd longed to say those words. She'd dreamt of it every day. And now, when she was saying them, she was farther away from her father than she'd been since his hospitalization began.

She grabbed Jamison's hand and rushed toward her car, still idling on the side of the road. He seemed stunned, too. As if unexpected events—from her chasing him down to kissing him to telling him about her father—had left him whiplashed and still trying to regain his bearings.

To complicate things further, a loud crackle emanated from the window of a police car, followed by a gravelly, static filled voice.

"All available units to Sparkling Pond. Repeat, all available units please respond to the disturbance in Sparkling Pond."

The young police officer Aspen had spoken to when she'd come upon the scene strode over to the car, reached through the open window, and pressed a button. "Don't you have the National Guard there?"

"Ten-four," the crackly voice responded. "But they've been ordered not to shoot."

"Shoot! You're shooting people down there?"

"Not yet," the crackly voice said. "But it's headed that direction. And if it goes downhill, we're going to need everyone we can find."

The young officer straightened up and looked at the mess all around him. "I've got a gas spill here and—"

"I don't care! We need you here! Now!"

The young officer looked around one last time, then shrugged a little and jumped into his car. "On my way," he said into his walkie-talkie.

Aspen watched the officer adjust the rear view mirror and thought back on her father's note, and on Rad's suggestion that she was partially responsible for the violence in her town. A pit formed in her stomach when she realized the truth of his words. If she hadn't held that grudge for so long, her father would have had no reason to perform the miracle. Without the miracle, there would have been no craziness. Without the craziness, there would have been no violence.

But at the same time guilt tried to weigh her down, another feeling vied for attention. A lighter feeling that saw the entire debacle from a different perspective. Her father's perspective.

Knowing her father as she did, Aspen was certain he'd never want her to sacrifice to be with him. On some level, she had always known that. And when she'd decided to chase down Jamison instead of going to be at her father's side, she hadn't chosen Jamison over her father. She had chosen her future, her life, over her past. Somehow, if only subconsciously, she had known it was what her father would want. That his love wasn't contingent upon her being by his side when he woke up. That he would want her to move on. To live her life.

And now, faced with another opportunity to see her father before he left for good, she knew he would understand that she had to put it off just a little bit longer. She could only hope he had the strength to hold on and wait for her.

"Stop!" she said.

Jamison squeezed her hand more tightly. "What are you doing? Didn't you hear that? He has to get to Sparkling Pond."

Aspen ignored him and ran to the police car. "Stop," she said again. "We need you to let us through first."

The officer didn't even look at her. "Ma'am, there are bigger things going on right now. I'm afraid you can't get past."

Desperately, Aspen put her hand on the windshield, as if she could stop the car with one arm. "You're going back to Sparkling Pond."

"That's right. So step away from the car, please."

"You won't be able to help."

The officer gave her a hard stare and shifted his car into Drive. "Young lady, if you don't want to get arrested — "

"I'm telling you, you can't help. There are too many people who've lost their minds. But we can help. If you'll help us."

"What?" Jamison and the police officer said simultaneously.

Aspen swallowed hard, hoping she knew what she was doing. "I need you to let us through so we can get to Rock Prairie."

The officer's frustration was near a boiling point, but he calmed himself enough to ask, "How is that going to stop the fighting in Sparkling Pond?"

Aspen grabbed the front of Jamison's shirt and pulled his face low to the open window. "This is Jamison Hightower."

The officer's blank stare wasn't encouraging. With embarrassment, Aspen realized she'd just done her equivalent of the eyebrow-bounce-and-wink and had been completely shot down.

"I don't care if he's Kirby Puckett. Now this is your last chance to…" The officer's voice trailed off as he looked at Jamison for the first time. "Hey, are you Jamison Hightower?"

"Yes, sir."

"That's what I just said!"

"From KTRP News, Rock Prairie?"

"That's right, sir."

"This is unbelievable," Aspen said. But she caught herself in time. Ridiculous as the situation was, it looked as if the officer might actually let them pass simply because she had Jamison with her. For his part, Jamison appeared to know his role to a T.

"I don't suppose there's any way you could move that barricade just for a minute so we can sneak by, is there?" Jamison said, all charm.

The automatic locks on the patrol car doors popped up and the officer pulled his seat belt on. "Hop in," the officer said. "I'll give you a police escort."

Baffled and incredulous, Aspen opened the back door and ducked in. Jamison followed behind, looking equally confused.

"Where to?" the officer asked.

"Um, the television station," Aspen said. Then she whispered to Jamison. "Has that actually worked before?"

"Not like that."

The officer flipped on his lights and sirens and swerved into the ditch. He drove around the barricade and the accident, spinning his wheels in the grass until the car jumped back onto the road. As they tore off toward Rock Prairie, the officer looked at them in his rear-view mirror.

"Call me Junior," he said. "And this ride here? It's for Uncle Fred."

Aspen looked at Jamison, who shook his head. "Uncle Fred?" Aspen said.

"Fred Holliday. *Farmer* Holliday, to you. Not one week ago, Jamison Hightower gave my favorite uncle the biggest thrill of his life."

Jamison

The ride back past the cornfields was nothing like the trip Jamison had taken just a few days before. Instead of hydroplaning through puddles with his pants soaked to the knees as his old car struggled to keep its engine running, Junior had the police car shooting over the blacktop and streaking past blurred corn stalks and the occasional car pulled onto the shoulder.

All the while, Junior chewed on the end of a long piece of grass, looking like he'd be more at home in a tractor than a squad car.

"You should've seen Uncle Fred," he said, watching Jamison in the rear-view for longer than could possibly be considered safe. "He called the whole family over to the farmhouse. Everyone within fifty miles. Must have been twenty of us Holliday's piled into his living room— aunts, uncles, cousins. He played and replayed the recording of your interview with him. Over and over and over." After a short silence he said, "Of course, it didn't take long. He only said the one word." He shook his head as if in awe of his uncle. "Never would've guessed Uncle Fred would be a TV star."

Soon, they reached the outskirts of Rock Prairie, with big-box stores and fast food chains dotting the frontage roads. Jamison was about to tell Junior to take the next exit, but the car swerved that way before he could say anything.

"Can you drop us about a block away?" Jamison said. He glanced at Aspen and her nod confirmed that he understood her plan correctly. "We're, ah, hoping to keep a low profile."

Junior laughed like he was in on a big secret. "I don't want to know a single detail, Jamison Hightower. Just promise me you're not going to hurt anyone in there and whatever else happens, my lips are sealed."

"Thank you," Jamison said. And then he was hit with another idea. "I don't suppose you'd be interested in helping us sneak in?"

Next thing Jamison knew, he and Aspen were creeping along the concrete wall of the KTRP News building while a police officer they just met rapped on the front door with his baton. When a scared looking intern Jamison had never spoken to cracked the door open, Junior said, "Son, I'm going to need to speak with your boss."

The intern swallowed hard and opened the door so Junior could step inside. When he then disappeared through an interior door to find his boss, Junior waved Jamison and Aspen over. They crept through the front door, into the foyer, and darted through a door to the opposite side of where the intern had gone. Jamison knew right were they were—the cubicle-filled sales hall. What he didn't know was how they'd get into the studio undetected.

"Just a minute," he said, and cracked open the door they had just snuck through. Junior was bouncing up and down on his toes, excited to be a part of the plan. "Thank you," Jamison whispered. Junior gave him a sly thumbs-up, hidden by his hip. His smile covered his entire face. Jamison wondered if Uncle Fred would believe a word of the incredible story he was sure to hear.

"That was strange," Jamison said when he had closed the door and was back in the hallway with Aspen.

"That was karma." She stretched onto her tiptoes and kissed his cheek.

A loud bang startled Jamison and he ducked, crouching with his back against the wall along with Aspen. Through a thin vertical window in the door at the end of the hallway, John Hammerstein's face glared toward something he must have dropped on the floor. "Owen!" he shouted. "Owen! I need you to clean this up." When he was answered with silence, his face turned purple and Jamison could even see a vein bulging at his temple. "Where's the damn intern? Someone has to clean this up! I've got a newscast to prepare for."

Jamison nudged Aspen with his elbow. "I think I know where the intern is," he whispered. He nodded toward the door through which they had entered. Through an identical vertical window, Owen the Intern's terrified face attempted to explain something to the police officer scowling over him. "Thank God for Junior," Jamison said. He turned his attention back to the other door. "Looks like Hammerstein's out of the way. Let's go."

He led Aspen down the hallway, creeping softly over the threadbare carpet. He peered through the window, scanning left and right, then slowly turned the knob and pushed. Jamison knew the station layout like the back of his hand. To his right was the room where all the portable cameras and tripods were stored. Only one was in there now, which meant at least three reporters and photographers were out on stories. Good news for them, Jamison thought.

And to his left, another hallway, from which they would be exposed to the entire newsroom. But if they could sneak through there without being seen, they'd have access to the only door that led to the studio and master control. Jamison waved Aspen along with him and snuck right to the edge of the wall, barely concealed from the newsroom. He slid his head slowly forward until he had a view. The open floor-plan room was entirely empty except for two people— Owen the intern still looking shaken as he returned to his cubicle, and Harris behind his news director's desk. Jamison felt a chill just looking at him.

Jamison was considering their odds of being able to make sure no one was looking, then darting down the hall and into the studio. But just then, Harris looked up from his desk and his eyes met squarely with Jamison's. He looked momentarily confused, but it didn't take long for the confusion to turn to anger. "Hightower? What the hell are you doing here? I'm calling security."

Jamison didn't waste any time. He grabbed Aspen's hand and tore down the hallway, leaving Harris' increasingly angry voice behind. They sprinted through the door leading to the studio on one side and master control on the other, separated by a wall of soundproof glass.

"In here," Jamison said.

As soon as Aspen was through the threshold, he slammed the door shut behind him. He reached for the lock, but there was none. Just as Harris' irate face appeared in the vertical window of the door, Jamison wedged his foot into the base. Harris slammed his shoulder against the door, but it held. Jamison searched the room.

"Grab that doorstop," he said.

A moment later, Aspen tossed the small piece of plastic to him and he smashed it into the space at the bottom of the door. With his face just inches away, Harris glared at him through the glass. "Hightower, you open this door right now. Do you understand me?"

Jamison resisted the temptation to laugh or stick out his tongue. What he was about to do would be enough. He turned his back on his former boss. "Follow me," he said, and led Aspen to the other side of the glass wall and into master control.

An array of screens and control panels spread out before them and Jamison tried to take it all in. It had been years since he'd been on this side of the camera and technology had changed quite a bit in that time. Fortunately, the important things were labeled.

"I hope you're not expecting me to do anything with all this stuff," Aspen said.

"It's easy. All you have to do is push that button to make my mike live," Jamison said. "And that one to cut into programming and put me on the air."

"And what are you going to do?" Aspen said.

The slamming against the door grew louder, more furious. Rather than giving up, Harris had enlisted help. Jamison could only hope the door would hold out long enough for him to finish.

"I'm going to make things right," he said, and rushed into the studio.

Cornelius

Cornelius Brown couldn't see through the smoke.

The National Guard had tossed smoke bombs into the mob, and one had rolled right up against the Helium Emitter and begun spewing noxious fumes all over his equipment. But at this point, even Cornelius had forgotten about his treasures. Simply staying alive was the immediate goal. Of course, his life was secondary.

Through the thick blanket of smoke, Cornelius spotted Crystal, draping her body over the Atmospheric Density Tester. Cornelius rushed toward her—dodging two large, bearded men as they wrestled each other to the ground—and he grabbed her hand tightly.

"Come with me!" he yelled over the screams of battlers and tank tires. "We have to get out of here!"

"No!" Crystal clutched her arms around the equipment more tightly. Veins stuck out of her neck and biceps. They were the most beautiful veins in the world. "I'm not leaving the ADT. Your work—"

"My work is nothing without you," Cornelius said, shocked by the brazenness of his own words. But if they were going to die here, it wasn't going to happen without one serious profession of love.

His words, or maybe the tone in which he said them, made Crystal relax her grip on the equipment just a little. "Really?" she said. A gunshot rang out somewhere in the distance and both of them flinched.

"Yes!" Cornelius said. He scrunched up his shoulders, as if that could protect him from the chaos around him. "You're the most amazing woman I've ever met and I never want to be without you!"

"You mean it, Corny?"

Cornelius flinched at the nickname, unsure if he would ever get used to it. But if it was what Crystal wanted, he'd try until his dying day.

"I mean it."

She plowed into him then. With his eyes shut, preparing for a kiss, Cornelius first thought she'd been just a bit overzealous. A bit carried away by the passion of the moment. But when he opened his eyes, he realized he wasn't the only one on his back. Crystal lay next to him, having been bowled over by a group of brawling men.

She shook her head clear and met his eyes. And then, as if they were the only two in the world, she crawled over to him, held his face, and kissed him.

It was one of the best moments of Cornelius' life, but it was short lived. A high-pitched, screeching sound overtook all other noise. The entire mob of people clutched their ears at the deafening feedback. Cornelius turned his head toward the sound and saw the 200-inch plasma TV screen laying on its side, in exactly the same knocked-down posture as Cornelius.

Feedback looped again, causing screams of surprise from all around the town square. Then the giant screen flickered and a face appeared, staring at them with a look of urgency.

A small group of people rushed to the giant screen and tipped it back onto its base. Cornelius arrived in time to help tighten a bolt at the bottom, which was bent but still seemed to work. He reviewed his handiwork and nodded his approval. Then he yelled, taking advantage of the brief silence.

"Everyone be quiet," he said. "Jamison Hightower has something to say."

Jamison

In all his years on TV, Jamison had never done anything truly important. Not on a grand scale anyway. Sure, he had given all the Farmer Hollidays out there a place to tell their stories, and their five minutes of fame. But when it came to things that really mattered, he had to admit his contributions had been minimal.

So as he cleared his throat and looked into the camera, he ignored the pounding on the studio door and focused on what he would say.

"This is an urgent, breaking news report, and an exclusive from…" Jamison was so used to saying KTRP that it almost came out instinctively. But as he considered his time at KTRP, the abuse he'd suffered at the hands of Harris, and the ambulance-chasing priorities of the station, he decided to change his words. "And an exclusive story of great public importance."

An especially hard slamming against the door was coupled with a scratching sound, as if the doorjamb was giving way. Harris, and whoever was with him, would surely break in soon. Jamison knew there was only one thing he could control at the moment, so he refocused on his broadcast.

"Last week, I traveled to the town of Sparkling Pond, where a miracle was reportedly taking place. Since then, hundreds of people, maybe even thousands, have traveled to Sparkling Pond to witness the miracle. Recently, things have turned violent in the town. I'm told that as we speak, the National Guard is trying to keep the peace, and local authorities are struggling not to resort to violence as a means of containing violence."

Jamison took a deep breath, steadying his nerves. There was no way to predict how his next words would be received.

"I'm here today, talking to each and every person in the town of Sparkling Pond. And I'm here to say…it was me. There is no miracle."

The gasp Jamison heard came from Master Control, but he imagined it was an echo of the collective gasps coming from Sparkling Pond.

"Some may call it a hoax. Some a publicity stunt. Call it what you want, but know this—it is no miracle. There is no ghost. What's been happening in Sparkling Pond was planned and executed by me, Jamison Hightower, working hand-in-hand with the Sparkling Pond Chamber of Commerce. It was a simple attempt to boost visibility of the town as a means of increasing tourism."

Jamison continued to look directly into the camera, relishing the idea that just came to mind. "Any complaints should be directed to Thomas Harris, News Director at KTRP News. Thank you."

The red light on the camera flicked off and Jamison was left in an eerie silence. Even the banging on the door had stopped, with Harris apparently looking for another way in. Either that, or leaving town before the torrent of complaints could come his way. The creaking of the door to Master Control echoed throughout the studio, and Aspen's footsteps seemed tentative.

Jamison unclipped the microphone from his lapel, pushed his chair back, and walked toward her. She stared at him uncertainly. Jamison grabbed her hands.

"That should do it," he said. "If there's no miracle, people will leave. Hopefully, the fighting is stopping as we speak."

"But the miracle..."

"It wasn't me," Jamison said.

The line between Aspen's eyebrows deepened. "But you just said—
"

"I said what needed to be said to stop the fighting. But whatever's going on in Sparkling Pond, whatever's going on with your dad, I had nothing to do with it."

If Jamison had any doubts about what he'd done, they vanished when he saw the look on Aspen's face. It was a look he could bask in for hours. For a lifetime, given the chance.

It was a look of hope.

Aspen

It wasn't Jamison. It wasn't the Chamber of Commerce. It was her dad. It was a miracle. Just as she had always known.

"Oh, thank God," she said.

Before she could say anything more, the door burst open with a splintering sound, causing Aspen to scream and Jamison to push her behind him. The scowl on Harris' face as he crossed the threshold made Aspen lean in closer to Jamison. Then the scowl, which threatened violence, turned to a sneer, which seemed equally as threatening, if not more.

"I hope you enjoyed that little stunt, Hightower. Because it'll be the last one you ever pull." The sneer smothered his face as he said, "You're going to jail, my friend. Officer!"

Just then, a burly, intimidating police officer in uniform strutted through the door, smacking his baton against his open palm.

When Junior winked at them, Aspen almost collapsed in relief.

"You're coming with me," Junior said to them in a voice so over-the-top Aspen was sure Harris would realize something was wrong.

"You got me," Jamison said, and Aspen elbowed him in the ribs. Why didn't he just tell Harris they were playing him for a fool. But a fool he was, apparently, because Harris' sneer only continued to grow.

Jamison approached Junior with his hands together out in front, as if surrendering himself to handcuffs. Junior, looking as happy as a kid playing cops-and-robbers, willingly obliged. Aspen was sure she heard him giggle as he tightened the cuffs around Jamison's wrists.

"No funny business, you hear me lady?" Junior said to Aspen.

She followed behind as Junior led Jamison out of the studio, down the hallway past the newsroom, and out the front door. They ducked into the back seat and heard Junior's voice say, "Don't worry, sir. They'll be prosecuted to the fullest extent of the law."

It wasn't until they pulled out of the parking lot and Junior tossed the key to the handcuffs over his shoulder that they all burst into laughter.

●   ●   ●   ●   ●

The laughter lasted only a moment. When the excitement and adrenaline wore off, Aspen realized they weren't in the clear. Not by a long shot.

Her father was still waiting for her.

Junior sped back to Sparkling Pond with lights and sirens blaring again, and pulled off the road in view of the Hank Lyons statue.

"I've never met him, of course," he said to Aspen, "but tell your daddy I give him my best."

Aspen put her hand on the burly man's shoulder and squeezed. "Thank you, Junior." She wanted to add more. To say they couldn't have done it without him. That they would never be able to repay the debt they owed him. But the look in his eyes told her that he already knew.

She and Jamison jumped out of the car and ran past the statue. When they reached the town square, hundreds of people still stood around, but no one was fighting. The National Guard was still there — several soldiers were leading a group of handcuffed people away. But there didn't seem to be any threat.

Their plan had worked. With no miracle, there was no conflict.

Aspen and Jamison rushed past the playground and continued as quickly as they could to the hospital. They ran through the front doors and jumped onto the WEB Train. Aspen punched a button and the train sped off.

In moments, they arrived on the 4th floor and hopped off. A rush of nausea threatened to overtake Aspen so she stopped and put a hand to her forehead. What would she say? Would she talk to him for a while first, or just blurt out "I love you"? After so long, she realized she never made a plan for this moment. But it didn't matter. She was going to make sure he knew exactly how much she loved him. How much she regretted not telling him before. How she still needed him and depended on him and couldn't imagine life without him. Those were the things that mattered.

She hurried down another hallway, turned left, then another left, feeling her heartbeat quicken with every step. She rounded one last corner, and stopped cold.

Her breath caught and the pounding of her heart turned audible. Slouched at the entrance of her father's room, looking lost and bewildered, was William.

Aspen clutched at the seconds while they stared at each other, trying not to let them slip by. They were the last moments, Aspen knew, when there was still a glimmer of hope. No one had said the words yet. She couldn't be sure she'd read William's expression correctly. But finally, he shook his head and her hope was crushed.

"He's dead," William said.

Aspen fell to her knees. A physical pressure squeezed her chest, as if crushing her from the inside. The weight of her betrayal pushed her to the floor. Her father was dead and she had never told him she loved him. She had let herself be pulled away from his side, and now he was gone forever. Despite all her efforts, she had missed her only chance.

Aspen felt the comforting hands of nurses, doctors, and Jamison all surrounding her. As they helped her to her feet, the wave passed and she was able to stand on her own. She walked past William, resting a hand on his shoulder for a moment, then entered her father's room.

It was a place as familiar as home. Rufus, predictably, sat at the bedside with his massive head resting on her father's shoulder. Aspen wondered if the dog understood her father was gone. Either way, Rufus had been there for him—faithful to the end. *Devoted*. Aspen couldn't say as much for herself.

She had been in this room countless times, spent hours upon hours with her father here. But it was different then. He had always been alive.

Now, his deceased body lay under the sheets. They had not yet covered his face. His eyes were closed, as if resting peacefully. He still resembled the man she knew, but something was missing. Without his spirit, the body was no longer her father. The man who had shown her so much love throughout her life was no longer there.

Aspen leaned close to his body. "I'm so sorry, daddy," she said. Then, closing her eyes and remembering him as he was, she whispered in his ear. "You wanted my forgiveness. But I know now. There's nothing to forgive. You were the perfect father."

She kissed his cheek for the last time, then turned and left the room.

Aspen

What do you do when your world starts collapsing? If you stay still, if you let the grief and guilt catch up to you, you'll be crushed.

Aspen needed to find a path that would lead to shelter. A highway that could take her to the next destination in life. Or a different avenue leading to family and friends for comfort. A road through the forest might twist and turn, distracting her with destinations yet to be discovered. Maybe a side street could provide relief, a place to hide and ride out the storm.

But Aspen couldn't move. None of the options seemed available to her.

She lived in a place that had no roads at all.

Jamison

The beautiful, enchanted town of Sparkling Pond was a wasteland. Garbage was strewn all over the grassy spaces, covering the wildflowers and blowing in the breeze. Doritos wrappers. Empty cans of Rockstar and Mountain Dew. The remnants of the destruction Jamison had brought upon the town. Word had spread that Pike Collins had died. The ghost was gone. After Jamison's newscast, there was nothing more to see. Nothing to do but move on. It left an eerie calm, like a tornado had just blown through and covered everything in a wave of destruction.

As they walked through the wreckage, Jamison tried to get a grasp on what Aspen was feeling. Somewhere in the back of her eyes, she looked terrified. As if her life was about to resume with a new normal and she would have to find her way without any explanation of how her father had been sending her things.

But what alternative was there? Even if Cornelius' theory had worked and people could somehow see ghosts, even if they could talk to them, Pike Collins was gone. There was nobody left for Aspen to get her answers from. She had missed her chance, and Jamison knew it was his fault.

They headed toward the town square. Whether out of habit or curiosity, Jamison wasn't sure. What would it be like now that the magic was over? Several people were still milling about, hanging onto the last few moments before they left Sparkling Pond for good. In the middle of the playground, gathering his equipment and packing it away, was Cornelius Brown, PhD.

When he saw them, Cornelius came over, his head hung low. Jamison realized he probably wasn't a bad guy. No worse than himself, at least.

"I'm sorry for what happened," Cornelius said. "For what it's worth, sometimes this kind of thing brings people together. Sometimes...well, I'm sorry. The good news is, it's over now."

Judging by Aspen's expression, she didn't consider that good news. Then a breeze blew through the playground and Aspen lifted her chin into it. She smiled for the first time in way too long.

"When I was a girl, I was afraid of the wind," she said. "I thought it would toss a tree branch through my bedroom window and carry our house away. I would be Dorothy. But my dad wrapped me in his arms and I was sure they were at least as powerful as the wind. He explained how wind helped make clouds. He stripped the wind of its mystery and made it safe." She stared at the emptying town square, at the few remaining Team God members, looking around as if they didn't know whether to go or stay. "It's going to be hard, isn't it?" Aspen said. "I'm going to miss him so much."

Jamison squeezed her tightly to his shoulder. "I think that's how it's supposed to be," he said. "If you really love someone, of course you're going to be sad when they're gone. But it's worth it, right?"

"'Tis better to have loved and lost/Than never to have loved at all," Aspen said. "Alfred Lord Tennyson."

"I know. I did a story once on a guy who collects Tennyson memorabilia, if you can believe that. But he told me another of Tennyson's quotes I like even more."

"What's that?"

Jamison brushed her cheek with his thumb. "Who is wise in love, love most, say least." He took her hands and looked at her meaningfully. "It's not all about those three words, Aspen."

Aspen leaned her head against his shoulder. After all they had been through—or maybe because of it—Jamison knew beyond a shadow of a doubt that he would love this woman forever.

Crazy Willie

William St. Vrain sat in his small cottage near the lake, sipping tea and missing his best friend. Now that Pike was gone, he would forever be Crazy Willie. Just Crazy Willie.

It had been hard to handle the identity shift that had happened so long ago. From athletic, handsome, charming William to Crazy Willie in the spark of a second. How does a person make that shift and still remain true to himself? William wasn't sure he had ever figured it out, but what success he'd had was due in large part to Pike Collins. Not only had Pike saved his life, he had also been there any time William had wanted to talk through the emotional chaos that followed the accident—and many times he hadn't wanted to talk, but ended up needing to.

William knew what the townspeople saw in him. Lost potential. Wasted dreams. But he didn't feel that much different than before. The biggest difference he felt after the accident was the loss of function in the cerebellum.

That's what the doctors had called it. The part of the brain that controls balance and movement. In his case, it had affected his ability to unconsciously figure out where to go. He used to be like everyone else—able to walk into a room and make his way through a doorway on the right by taking the perfect diagonal line to it. After the accident, he found himself walking straight, then turning ninety degrees and walking straight again, then through the door. Or he would somehow miscalculate the angle, walk diagonally, and smack his shoulder into the doorframe. He would end up on his butt, staring at the door and wondering what had happened.

Or he would have a place in mind that he was trying to reach, but walk in circles or swerve well out of his route before he would realize he was off track. People would see him and think he was wandering aimlessly. After a while, they barely took notice at all.

But in the end, his ability to not raise suspicion had proven helpful. And William felt grateful that he'd had the chance to help Pike for once.

It had been the other way around for too long.

Because of Pike, he was finally able to accomplish something meaningful. He had been able to feel the power of true love—if only from the periphery. But mostly, he was grateful that he had been able to experience a few glorious moments where once again, he had been more than just Crazy Willie.

Aspen

Aspen couldn't understand why time hadn't stopped. When someone's world changes so dramatically, doesn't time at least pause to pay attention? *Insignificance*, January 1, age 16.

The growing emptiness of the town square made it worse. The excitement and commotion had struck Aspen as ridiculous, but before things turned south, she had begun to associate the festive atmosphere with hope. Now, as the sun went down, darkness blanketed the town square. Only a faint, blue light glowed from inside the giant stadium light bulbs, long since turned off. Silence muffled the last chords of possibility.

She sat with Jamison on the merry-go-round—where it had all started. She closed her eyes and tried to remember the feeling of wonder that had enveloped her each time something from her childhood had appeared. She was able to touch the feelings, but they were like sand, slipping through the fingers of her mind no matter how hard she squeezed. Then all the sand had fallen, leaving only a thin layer of memory she would never wipe clean. It would remain to remind her of the ecstasy of those moments.

Aspen climbed onto the middle of the merry-go-round. Just to touch the spot where her father's magic had started. In that moment, the feeling she had been searching for exploded into her mind. A ray of moonlight shone through a part in the clouds and cast a faint glow on the town square. The pale light shone on the merry-go-round, lighting a small, delicate diamond ring in the center.

"Jamison!" He was next to her in an instant.

"What's wrong? Are you okay?"

With her hand shaking, she held the ring up to the moonlight for him to see. "I found this."

"And you recognize it, I assume," Jamison said, all business. He joined her and placed a calming hand on her shoulder.

Aspen could hardly believe it, despite all that had happened before. "It's my mother's wedding ring," she said.

They stood in silence, both staring at the ring as it shimmered in the moonlight. "I don't understand," Aspen said. "My dad's dead. How can this possibly be happening?"

A deep, gravelly voice came from the growing darkness behind them. "I think it's time we explain."

The voice startled Aspen, and when she saw who it had come from, her mind wheeled uncontrollably. Crazy Willie—William to her—sauntered into the moonlight. His stirrups clicked with each step. Behind him, Claire leaned on the arm of Rad Collie and held Little Holly Torrey's hand.

William approached Aspen and placed his palm on her cheek. His touch was gentle beneath his battered and wrinkled hands. His eyes drooped, bags weighing them down. She could remember this face from her childhood, smooth and vibrant, always a little quirky. Now, his skin hung loosely. She half-expected it to drip like an icicle. He smiled with half of his mouth, as if part of him was still able to put on a strong face while the other had given in to the sorrow.

"What's going on?" Aspen asked. William shifted his weight back and forth, Claire nodded in a maternal way, and Rad looked around the square to avoid eye contact. Holly looked as if she wanted to speak, but restrained herself.

"We came so you could know the truth," William said. "It's what Pike wanted. Even from the beginning, he told me to make sure we told you everything. Afterwards. He said he would love for you to think he was superhuman, but truth and honesty were the right way to go. So when it was over, we should tell you. And now," he said, looking to the ground, "it's over."

Jamison took William by the elbow and guided him to the edge of the merry-go-round. William bumped down onto it and leaned his elbows against his knees. Claire, Holly, and Rad followed as if they were attached. William cleared his throat.

"The things been happening here? The things you been finding? It's true. They came from your father."

Aspen felt dizzy. In her mind, Crazy Willie had as much credibility as anyone. "It's all been real?" she said. "The ghost is real?"

"Oh, he's real alright. He's just not your dad."

Pike

Being told you're dying will change your life in ways you never could have imagined. When Pike Collins heard the news, he was ashamed that his first thought was of all the things he hadn't done in his life. Countries he hadn't visited. Languages he hadn't learned. Books he hadn't read. But finally, he came to what he should have thought of at the very start.

Aspen. His lovely daughter. The one who would be affected by his death more than anyone else. More, even, than himself.

She was a grown woman, more than capable of dealing with the ups and downs of life. But it wasn't that long ago she was a baby, resting in his arms. He had paced the floor of his old house for hours on end when she had been a colicky infant. He had kissed her skinned knees and hugged her hurts away as a child. In his eyes, she would forever be a child. His child. And it was his responsibility to look after her. To care for her—even after he was gone.

His son, Jackson, was also in his thoughts. But Jackson was far away, in Columbia, digging wells for villages with no water. Doing good. Making his father proud. He would be sad, Pike was sure, but the distance would ease the pain. For Aspen, his little girl, his death would be harder.

Lying in bed that night, before he even told Aspen of his diagnosis, he began to hatch the plan that would be his final act of love. He called his oldest friend over to his house the next day, when Aspen was away at the farmer's market.

"I have an idea, Will," he said. "But I can't do it alone. I need help. But not just anyone's help. You're the only one who can do this."

Crazy Willie was shattered when he heard the words *brain cancer*—maybe even more than Pike. He seemed only able to half-listen. He couldn't look Pike in the eye.

"There will come a time when I'm close to death," Pike said. "I might be put into hospice care, or maybe something will happen and they'll put me in the hospital, and I'll never get out. I need you to recognize that moment. When I won't be getting out of that bed ever again."

"Pike," William said. "I can't do it. You know I can't."

"Please, Will. You're the only one. You're the only one who has known her long enough and well enough to pull this off. It can't be anyone else. It has to be you. Please, my friend, I'm begging you. Please do this for me."

William nodded, as Pike knew he would. So Pike told him what he had in mind, and William agreed.

The first thing they did was travel to North Minneapolis. William peppered Pike with questions the entire drive. Pike realized William cared for Aspen nearly as much as he did, and he didn't want Pike do anything that could accidentally cause her harm.

"How are you so sure this is the right thing to do?" William had asked. "People on TV can't be trusted, I can tell you that much."

"I told you, Will. He did a story on a second-cousin of mine who lost his leg in a manufacturing accident. If you had just seen him. Anyone who takes that much time and shows that much compassion for someone who can't do a thing to repay him...well, anyone like that is okay in my book."

But he had to be sure. Before he brought his daughter in contact with someone he didn't know, Pike had to hear what the man was like from his own mother. So they went to the home of Caroline Smith and asked her about her son. She hadn't seen nor talked to him in years, but the only time the darkness in her eyes brightened was when she spoke of him. And that told Pike all he needed to know.

They returned to Sparkling Pond and Pike gave William his instructions. "When it's obvious that I'm on my deathbed, start following Aspen very closely. Find things that happen in her life that relate to things I've taught her in the past. This is why it has to be you, Will. No one else. When something happens, place an object from our past in the town square, right there in the playground—it has to be in the playground. And include a note."

"A note? What note?"

"That's what we're going to do now," Pike said.

For the next several weeks, he and William brainstormed every possible situation that might occur, and what lesson Pike could remind her of. The excitement sustained Pike like he never could have imagined. He stayed up all night, writing notes to his daughter—some notes for if William was successful in getting Jamison Hightower to come cover the story, some for if he wasn't.

He wrote notes for if she had a fight with a close friend. If she was second guessing going to back medical school. If she was feeling sad for no reason at all. And for every note he wrote, he thought of something from her childhood to go with it. An encouraging note from a teacher. An old drawing she had made in third grade. A princess figurine.

"What about this Hightower character?" William said. "I don't trust him. Something bad will happen with him, I'm sure of it."

Pike smiled at his friend and wrote Jamison into a letter about forgiveness. Then, just to cover all the bases in case things really turned south, he scribbled one more.

Jamison is in danger. Don't let him go.

He patted William on the shoulder. "Sometimes, my friend, you just have to have faith in the goodness of human beings."

After a few weeks, Pike had another idea. He would show Aspen, through the entire process, that it was okay for her to move on. Not just okay, but necessary. Knowing her as he did, he knew she would need a catalyst to continue living her life while he was dying. And the most painful thought he had was that she would give up too much to be with him when being there for him would do neither of them any good.

So he thought of the most enjoyable things he could. Things he had done, things he wished he could do. And he scribbled one on the back of each note. He hoped that finding the instructions, and carrying them out, would give her a sense of enjoyment she would otherwise neglect, and maybe give the whole experience an element of mystery. Just for fun.

When he had covered every situation he could think of, Pike sent William home. He had one more letter to write. One he had been putting off since the beginning. It would be the last letter. The only one he knew with absolute certainty Aspen would read. It was important that he get it right. More than that, it was important that he get it perfect.

One moonlit night, as the pain made him wonder if he had waited too long, he brought out a pen and paper, and began writing his final note.

Dear Aspen,

It's a strange truth that the depth of our love for someone is never fully realized until they're gone...

Aspen

Aspen listened to William's story, picturing her father as he stayed up late, writing the notes she had found in the town square. "So you're the ghost?" she said to William.

"I guess, technically, I was only one of the ghosts," he said.

A dozen questions bombarded Aspen's mind at once, but she couldn't put any into words.

Claire lifted her head and spoke for the first time. "It was mostly William. We just helped when we could."

William nodded. "You see, it was all about trying to show you how much he loved you. He wanted to guide you and to help you move on with your life once he was gone. 'Cause he knew he wouldn't last forever."

"I still don't understand," Aspen said. "I mean, you'd have to be able to read my mind. The figurine—"

"Was one of the first things on Pike's list. 'Under the mattress in her old bedroom. You know the one.' And I was at the Squinting Café when you complained about that boy not thinking you're pretty. I have to admit, I been following you around pretty close lately."

The words sounded strange, and in a different situation, could have been creepy. But coming from William, they gave her a sense of calm. As if his presence had been protecting her. Her own guardian angel.

"The running shoes."

"Pike thought your old pair got thrown out at some point, but he knew what kind they were. He knew I'd have a chance to use that one, circled it real big with a red marker and everything. I guess he knew you'd make too many sacrifices to spend time with him."

Aspen mentally continued down the list. "The jeans."

"An unlikely one." William had perked up some, as though the project had sustained him during a difficult time. "But Pike had plenty of time to think of everything. When I saw what you wore for your date," he nodded toward Jamison. "I knew what to do."

"The Lake Superior Agate?" Aspen said.

"Wherever he is, if your daddy knows you forgave him, and that schmuck too," he said, nodding at Jamison, "then he's a happy man. I guarantee it. Specially if he can see how happy you look with the schmuck."

Aspen felt her cheeks warm as she caught Jamison's eye. Behind Jamison, Rad still stared at the moon, like a teenager avoiding a teacher. "You were in on it too?" Aspen asked him.

"The old lady just told me to make sure you thought it could all be magic, dude. Pretty easy, it turns out. You're one gullible chick."

"So you never were a private investigator?" Aspen asked. The pieces were coming together now. Her gut had been telling her that since the beginning.

Rad swore under his breath. "Too close to being a cop for my taste."

Aspen faced Claire. "Then why in the world would you pick Rad Collie to pretend to be an old detective? No offense, Rad."

Rad shrugged as if he had no idea why he should be offended. A small smile creased the lines of Claire's face for the first time.

"You two were about to go find a real one, so I had to think quick. Who else has nothing to do and plenty of time to waste?"

Holly pulled on Aspen's hand. "They even told me about it yesterday because they said they knew they could trust me to keep a secret because I'm trustworthy."

"You sure are," Aspen said.

She felt a moment of disappointment at the realization that her father hadn't been magically sending her things. But it passed quickly, replaced by the warmth of how much he loved her.

"So the notes?" Aspen asked. "You guys planted them, too?"

Claire's eyes bulged. "It was easier before all the crazies came to town. I don't know how we made it without anyone seeing us. So many people around. Or maybe that's why no one saw us. With so many people, we just kind of blended in. Plus, ghosts are invisible, right? Although one boy from the National Guard did look at me funny once while I was sneaking around." She laughed at the memory. "It's a wonder he didn't throw me in the clink. Probably would have, if it hadn't been so full."

Claire and William sneaked a glance at each other, conspirators bound together by a shared adventure. *Antidote*, Aspen thought.

She felt her mother's small diamond ring and spun it in her fingers. The edges of the Princess Cut pressed into her fingertip. She recalled seeing it on her mother's hand and being filled with envy.

"The ring," she said.

"Diane's wedding ring," William said. His voice became subdued. All of his excitement vanished. "Pike said this was the one I should be sure to use. After all, we knew we would have the opportunity."

"He wanted you to give this to me when he died?"

William nodded, looked at his hands.

"Why?" Aspen asked.

"Why? Didn't think you'd have to ask. Pike was sure the memories of this ring would be strong for you."

Aspen thought back to a time she had tried to block out of her consciousness. A time of pain and sorrow. But also of learning, growing, and understanding. It was just three short years before.

"Mom was in a car accident," her father said through the static of her cell phone. "She died, Aspen."

Aspen left Mayo Medical School without speaking to anyone. How can a person from Sparkling Pond die in a car accident? The irony would be funny if it weren't so cruel.

"He was wearing her ring on a necklace when I got home," Aspen said. She looked from Jamison to William, then Claire, Holly, and Rad. William nodded at her, encouraging her to go on.

When a week had passed, Aspen woke to the sound of commotion downstairs. On the way down the steps, she saw her father packing her bags.

"What are you doing?" she asked.

"It's time for you to go back to school."

"I'm not going back! It's only been a week. Mom just died, don't you care about that?"

"Of course, I care. But what are you accomplishing by throwing away your future? If you don't finish medical school because mom died, how do you think she'd feel about that? Do you think she's in some place where her family's misery translates into happiness for her?"

"What about you? You haven't moved on. You still wear that ring around your neck, like you're afraid you won't remember her without it."

"He laughed at that," Aspen said. "Said he couldn't forget a moment they had together if he tried. That he didn't wear the ring to remind him of my mother, but to remind him that she would want him to move on and continue to live. And he wanted the same for me. He thought going back to medical school was the best way for me to do that."

"But you never did," Jamison said.

Aspen shook her head. "No."

Two weeks after her mother's death, Aspen began to see her father's point. She packed her own bags, ate a long dinner with her father, and made plans to leave the next morning.

A noise woke her at 3am. She went to her father's room, where he was writhing in pain, struggling to remain silent.

She rushed him to the emergency room. The hours she waited by herself were excruciating. But not nearly as bad as the doctor's words. Brain cancer.

"So you stayed," Jamison said.

Aspen was jarred from her memory of that day. The professional, orderly admission into the hospital. The terror they both felt.

"Yes," Aspen said. "There was never a question after that."

Translucent clouds swept over the moon, then passed by. The square was thrown into a cycle of darkness and pale gray light.

"You gave up so much to stay with him," Jamison said.

"Maybe. But not nearly as much as I gained. I just hope my father realized that."

"He knew," William said. "You meant everything to him. Always have, since the day you were born. Got downright annoying sometimes, the way he carried on. Couple times I told him to shut his trap about it for once."

Aspen felt a bit awkward until she saw that old gleam in William's eye.

"Nah," William said. "That old codger loved you more than life itself. He loved you in a way that you and I will never comprehend. That special way a father loves his daughter."

William pulled a crinkled envelope from an inside pocket of his jacket and lifted it toward Aspen. "I'm guessing he told you something mushy like that in this last letter."

Aspen stared at it for a moment, but couldn't reach for it. *Trepidation.* "This last letter," William had said. As soon as she read this, it was over. Her father would truly be gone.

Claire placed a soft hand on her shoulder, then shuffled toward her home with Holly at her side. William avoided eye contact, barely holding back his tears. Rad melted into the darkness and slipped away. Jamison half-smiled and began to follow the others. Aspen grabbed his hand and held it firmly.

"Stay," she said.

They sat on the edge of the merry-go-round and stared at the letter for several minutes. Finally, she slipped her finger into the envelope, eased it open, and unfolded the letter.

Dear Aspen,

It's a strange truth that the depth of our love for someone is never fully realized until they're gone. So I imagine right now, you're remembering me pretty fondly. I know I'm enjoying that fact, wherever I am.

By now you understand what has been happening. You know that I'm not any more capable of miracles than anyone else. But I hope you also understand how deeply I love you, and what I want for you now.

I want for you to live. In every sense of the word. Do not let your life pass you by.

Don't just understand how much you love those who are close to you—feel it every day. Don't waste a single minute of your precious life mourning for someone who won't benefit from your pain. If you've found and followed my ideas on the back of these notes, you've begun to remember how exciting, rewarding, and peaceful life can be. You've seen a small glimpse of the possibilities that exist for a soul lucky enough to be given a life on earth.

I know you're still holding onto me. I know it's my fault—I've allowed you to. Even forced you to. It was selfish of me. After all, I did want you to remember me, to honor me. But the best way to do that now is to let go and live your life. That's what I've been trying to say to you over the past few weeks. If my plan worked, you haven't spoken to me since before they put me in the hospital, because you've had better things to do. If that's true, I want you to know that I know. Those three words were never necessary.

You'll find no scribbles on the backside of this note. Instead, I'll write it here in the form of a final request.

On August 13th, when I join your mother, find the most peaceful spot you know, surrounded by those who have loved you the most, and gaze upon the beauty not only of this world, but of all that God has created.

Aspen, my daughter, the true, unconditional love of my life. I believe I'll see you again. Until then, live well.
Love always,
Daddy.

Aspen couldn't stop staring at the words. With the knowledge of how her father had been sending her messages came a release of sorts. She was no longer burdened by the need to find the truth.

But also, a sense of loss.

In that way, she was grateful for one last mystery. According to the note, her father wanted his memorial to be August 13th. Aspen thought for a moment that he had expected to live much longer than he had. After all, August was still eleven months away.

But he wouldn't presume to know when he was going to die. And that meant there had to be a reason why he wanted her to wait eleven months before holding a service for him.

And that meant eleven more months in which she would feel as if her father was still with her as she continued with her life.

She thought back on the final words her father had written and realized he had left her with a responsibility. It wasn't in the form of a weight, but a freedom. A freedom to live life to the fullest. With no instructions for how to do it. No list of things to do or learn or see. Just the reassurance that he wanted her to have a full, meaningful, intentional life.

Aspen set the envelope by her side, squeezed Jamison's hand, and began the lifelong process of figuring out what that meant.

Eleven Months Later

Jamison

When Aspen burst into Claire's kitchen, it had been two days since Jamison had seen her. She had been at Sparkling Pond Hospital for forty-eight hours straight—medical residencies are like that, or so Jamison had heard. But their trip to the Boundary Waters was only a few weeks away, and when Aspen finished residency, they would be able to see a lot more of each other.

That much was certain—because Jamison wasn't going anywhere.

The second he saw Aspen, his heart and his legs sprang to life. He hopped up, wrapped her in a hug, and breathed the scent of the hospital. Somehow, it had become a smell he enjoyed. Probably because it reminded Jamison of the day she first took him to see her father. She had looked at Jamison and said, "I think I kind of like him." It was amazing how far they had come.

"You're both here?" Aspen asked Jamison and Claire. "Who's at *The Bonne Bouffe*?"

The Bonne Bouffe. Who would have guessed Jamison would be a partner in the restaurant business? But when Claire had offered part ownership in exchange for helping her get it up and running, Jamison had jumped all over it. His name even shared the small sign on the door—"Claire Lyons and James Smith, Owners."

For the past six months it had been the hottest eatery in Sparkling Pond. Claire said she couldn't have been happier if Amelia Earhart dropped her plane down right in the middle of Sparkling Pond. And Jamison couldn't possibly have been more proud of her. After all these years, she had finally become a chef.

"Closed," said Rad Collie, in answer to Aspen's question. "Solar storm." It wasn't uncommon for Rad to drop by and share a cup of coffee. Turned out he was a little short on friends, and the rest of them tended to enjoy his unique style of wisdom.

What started that morning with just Claire and Jamison started to feel like a party. Rufus was even in the corner, wagging his tail at Aspen, even though he wasn't strong enough to greet her anymore. So she went over and scratched his head.

"Solar storm?" Aspen said.

"It's been all over the newspapers," Claire said. "The biggest solar flare storm on record. Since we opened, the entire town's been coming to our restaurant. Poor Crystal Lux hasn't had much business since then—not that she realizes it, as batty as she is for that Cornelius boy. But *The Bonne Bouffe* is closed until the solar storm is over, except for a couple people preparing food for the party. We're encouraging everyone to visit the Squinting Café instead."

"Actually," Jamison said. "Most of the town's closed today for your dad's service."

Aspen went to the cupboard, pulled out a mug, and filled it with steaming coffee. "Where's William?" she asked.

William hadn't been around much, and it was one of two things that always seemed to be on Aspen's mind. Jamison could see how much it pained her. He had been able to get William to open his door a few days earlier. Enough to see that he wasn't physically ill or anything—at least nothing more than too much whiskey. Unfortunately, The Ghost hadn't been able to get over the passing of his best friend.

"And you?" Aspen jabbed Jamison in the ribs with her elbow. "Have you seen your mom yet?"

That was the second thing that was always on her mind. Jamison had tried to explain that he wanted to see his mom—he really did. But he was terrified for reasons he couldn't quite explain. Talking to his mother on the phone was one thing—they had spoken several times. But actually seeing her after all these years?

"I'll be ready soon," Jamison said. "Really."

Claire gave Aspen a conspiratorial wink that Jamison was pretty sure he wasn't supposed to see. He wondered what his friend and business partner had up their sleeves.

"Well, now that everyone's here," Claire said, "it's time to bring out the surprise."

She walked silently out of the kitchen and shuffled back a minute later with an enormous machine on a rolling dolly. Jamison bounced up to help her, taking the handles of the dolly and rolling it near the table. His first thought was that it looked like she'd swiped something from Cornelius, but as he looked more closely, his heart started to race. Claire put her hand on it and grinned across her entire face.

"What is that?" Aspen asked.

"A printing press," Claire said. "For my friend and business partner, James Smith."

She was beaming at Jamison, who tried to say something. To give her the faintest idea of the depth of his gratitude. But when he tried to speak, nothing came out.

"Things at the restaurant will calm down soon enough," Claire said. "And this town has always been in need of a proper newspaper. I just thought you might want to dabble with it a bit."

Since his voice wouldn't work, Jamison leaned over, wrapped Claire in his arms, and squeezed. After several moments, he realized he was probably squishing her, but when he let go, Claire's face was beaming like a schoolgirl.

We all have a story to tell. And telling people's stories was what Jamison did. Now, he would be able to tell their stories, and share them not with the world, but with each other. With his fellow residents of Sparkling Pond.

"I can't possibly thank…" It was the best Jamison could do. He covered his mouth with his fist.

There was a small knock at the front door, saving Jamison the discomfort of breaking down in front of everyone. Seconds later, Little Holly Torrey wandered into the kitchen. She grabbed Jamison's hand and started yanking. "Come with me," she said in that sweet voice of hers. "There's a car trying to get in."

"A car?" Jamison asked.

Holly nodded hard. "With letters on the side. It keeps going back and forth. I think the driver's mad."

Jamison only needed one guess who that was.

Since Sparkling Pond was mostly shut down for the day and no one had anywhere they needed to be until the memorial service, they all walked across the grassy open spaces of Sparkling Pond, which had finally returned to their former wildflower-covered glory. They neared the fountain at the entrance to town and sure enough, there was a KTRP news car. Inside, John Hammerstein, co-anchor of the KTRP News at Noon, pounded the steering wheel and scanned every direction. Jamison couldn't help but chuckle.

This was going to be fun.

"He's been doing it forever," Holly said.

The car stopped in the middle of the road and the window slid down. John Hammerstein stuck his head out. "Hightower, is that you? How do we get in there?"

Jamison smothered a grin and yelled back. "What do you think, John? Just follow the road."

"That's what I've been doing!" He cursed, rolled the window up, and turned around. He passed by four more times, getting more frustrated with each passing, until he finally pulled the car to a stop in the middle of the road. It looked as if he had intentionally blocked both lanes. John marched toward them while a photographer Jamison didn't recognize got out of the car and retrieved a camera from the back.

"Who wants the media circus back in town?" Jamison asked quietly as John Hammerstein made his way toward them.

After a cluster of "Not me" and "No way," Jamison said, "Then just follow my lead."

He stepped forward and extended his hand. "John, great to see you. How are things at the station?"

Hammerstein ignored the question, and Jamison's handshake attempt.

"It's sweeps again, Hightower--"

"Actually, I go by James Smith now. It's my real name, after all."

"Whatever. Harris is still pissed that you didn't finish this story, so now with the anniversary coming up, I have to, thanks a lot. So who can I interview about it?"

"You can interview me," Jamison said. "Guess what? I see dead people."

Hammerstein whipped out a notepad and scribbled something. "Dead people? Really? So it's still going on?"

"Oh, yeah," Jamison said. "And there are huge machines here that transform and fight for good and evil. One of them has the coolest name—Optimus Prime."

Hammerstein started scribbling again, but stopped abruptly. "What?"

"Excuse me, sir." It was Holly. Jamison should have known she'd pick up on it. "There's actually a whole other race of people that live here. They have blue skin and they live in a giant tree. *Don't* cut it down."

As Hammerstein caught on to the joke, he glared at them, not amused.

And then came the icing on the cake. Claire stepped forward, all innocence. "There's the cutest little extraterrestrial living in my closet that just loves to eat Reese's Pieces."

"Oh, for Christ sake," Hammerstein said. He threw his hands in the air and stomped off, pulling his camera man with him. They slammed the doors to their car and sped back toward Rock Prairie, where they would have to deal with the wrath of Harris.

Jamison, Aspen, Claire, and Holly giggled hysterically. Rad just looked confused. Claire wiped a tear from her eye and bounced with laughter. "Sorry," she said. "I haven't seen a movie in ages. It's the only thing I could come up with."

"It was perfect," Aspen said. They watched the trail of dust speed up the hill and out of sight. Jamison was pretty sure Sparkling Pond wouldn't make it into the news again for quite some time.

"Absolutely perfect."

Aspen

With one hand, Aspen felt the strong grip of the man she found herself falling more deeply for each and every day. In the other, she held her father's ashes in a hollow, ceramic piece of pottery. It was dark green, heavy, and had six "leaves" that sprouted from the center, each of them with sharp, porcelain points protruding out. Aspen was reminded that she needed to thank the girls at the Ubaid Potter's Wheel for their craftsmanship. The urn was the perfect representation of a thistle. *Butt cheek*, Aspen thought, but knew there would be a more powerful word for this day.

When she and Jamison approached the gates to the Sparkling Pond Cemetery, the music was already blaring from the sound system. They walked into the garden and up the hillside, where the dance was already in full swing.

People Aspen had known her entire life, as well as many she had only seen in passing, had come to celebrate the life of her father. It was a Sparkling Pond tradition: don't mourn the death, celebrate the life. Throw a party for the transition from a flesh and blood human to a flowering plant—and whatever else God has in store.

Aspen strode up the grassy hill to the base of her mother's cherry tree and set the urn behind it. A Grey Nightjar sailed by and Aspen watched it glide to a Pink Lady Slipper, where it settled contently. Almost never seen in North America, the Nightjar had been attracted to the garden—drawn to it by instinct. Something deep inside it knew what it needed to survive, and where to find it. Without the sustenance it found in the variety of plants here, it would starve. Without this place, it wouldn't survive.

Aspen could relate.

She took Jamison's hand and led him down the slope. She pulled him close and they danced to REM's "Shiny, Happy People" as the sun's evening rays slanted through the leaves.

Crystal Lux swayed over, looking as if she had a near overdose of caffeine in her system. She clung to Cornelius as if afraid he might run away. Despite being wired open, her eyes looked sad. Aspen wondered if she had known her father well. Shouldn't she be ecstatic about the solar flare storm and all the patrons at her café? And the fact that Cornelius Brown, PhD. had decided to stay in Sparkling Pond and conduct online Ghost Hunting classes from her home?

"Hi Aspen," she said. "Did you hear the news? A new coffee shop is moving to town."

So that's where the sadness came from, Aspen realized. "Want to know the worst part?" Crystal said. "It's called the Barking Dog Café. And guess what its slogan is, painted right on the window? 'Come. Sit. Stay.' Brilliant, isn't it? How can I compete with that?"

Aspen smiled. She had no idea how to answer.

"I was wrong. The worst part is that they have a five-dollar Vitamin D Recliner." Crystal's eyes suddenly brightened. "Hey Aspen, this would be the perfect time for 'Dark Star' by the Grateful Dead, don't you think? Day two, fifth band, third song of the set. I can go home and grab it if you'd like."

"Thanks, Crystal, but I'd hate to have you miss any of the party," Aspen said. "I'm sure we'll manage without."

"Okay," Crystal said. Cornelius began to dance her away. "If you're sure."

Aspen and Jamison danced until their feet ached. Then they sauntered under the tent, where Claire slaved over the crepes with a giant smile. They ate their fill of food catered from *The Bonne Bouffe*—honey and crushed walnut crepes and the most savory *cocottes brioches* Aspen had ever tasted.

At one point, Aspen set her fork down and looked all around her. She realized that Sparkling Pond had changed as a result of the miracles. No longer was it a place where people took for granted the enchantment on every corner. Sometimes, she thought, it's impossible to see how wonderful something is until it's threatened.

When neither she nor Jamison could force down another bite, they found a spot on the hillside and listened as friends approached a microphone to tell stories and relive memories of Pike Collins.

It was as if stories could bring a piece of him back for a moment. But when the story ended, that part of him drifted away. To Aspen, the rollercoaster was painful. But she realized it also provided much needed closure.

Claire was at the microphone, telling her third story about Pike Collins. The crowd roared in laughter at all the right places. But just before the punch line, Claire stopped. Her gaze focused on the edges of the cemetery and she shielded her eyes from the setting sun with her hand. Aspen looked with everyone else to see what had distracted Claire so thoroughly.

There, passing under the arching gates of the cemetery, was Little Holly Torrey with her hand entwined with that of Crazy Willie. Holly led William through the crowd of people and to the microphone. Aspen heard Holly's small voice, the microphone barely amplifying it.

"Go ahead, William. Tell them."

William rubbed his eyes and took a deep breath. His exhale sounded like a tornado through the amplifier and feedback screeched through the air, but William didn't seem to notice. He leaned in so his lips pressed against the microphone and his voice came out distorted.

"Pike Collins was the best friend I ever had."

He looked around at the crowd, then nodded hard and walked away. As they left, Aspen barely caught Holly's voice through the microphone. "You did great, William. I'm proud of you."

As the sun dipped below the horizon and the string of lights on the tent began to glow, the party started to wind down. Many people approached Aspen, congratulated her on her father's life, and wandered home. Aspen was happy to see Tammy Wellington— basketball team manager, nurse, and one of the best at message-delivery since the Pony Express. They embraced and Aspen thanked her again for her efforts before Tammy wandered away. Soon, only a small circle of close friends remained.

Aspen stood from her blanket and prepared her mind for the final act of the ceremony. But out of the corner of her eye, she noticed a figure walking up the slope toward them. When no one else reacted, Aspen assumed it was someone who had drunk one too many glasses of punch and was wandering aimlessly. But then she noticed that Jamison hadn't moved and his eyes were as wide as half-dollars.

He started to stand, only to stop and sit back down on the blanket. His head cocked sideways and he stood again. Soon, his long strides were covering the distance to the figure, now apparent to Aspen as a woman.

Jamison and the woman spoke for several minutes—two silhouetted heads close together while Aspen, Claire, and Rad watched from a distance. Aspen noticed a gentle smile on Claire's face, as if she knew exactly what was happening. Then the figures hugged. A firm, lasting hug. Finally, Jamison and the woman walked up the slope— holding hands.

As they got close enough that Aspen could make out their features in the fading light, she noticed that the woman was older.

"Aspen," Jamison said when they arrived. "I'd like you to meet my mom."

"Caroline Smith," the woman said in a shaky voice.

Aspen extended her hand. "It's a pleasure to meet you. I'm—"

But the woman ignored her hand, stepped close, and wrapped her arms around Aspen's neck. Her breath was choppy and her arms frail, but her grasp was strong. "I know who you are," she said. "You're the Aspen who showed my son how to forgive." She pulled away and grasped Aspen's arms as if afraid to let her escape. "You're the reason I have my baby back."

Jamison's mother rested her palm on Aspen's cheek and stared, as if memorizing Aspen's features. "You're a princess," she said with a choked voice. Then she took her son's hand again—this time with both her hands—and leaned her head against his shoulder.

When Aspen caught Jamison's eye, she saw tears shimmering, threatening to break free. He mouthed the words "thank you" and pressed his face into his mother's hair as they embraced.

Aspen could have watched Jamison and his mother hug for hours, but she knew it was time to plant her father's flower. The realization made her hesitate. In their traditions of celebration, this was the only part that felt final. Something about emptying the urn was akin to watching a casket drop into the ground. For the first time all day, Aspen's cheeks relaxed and her smile softened.

As she approached her mother's cherry tree, she pulled the eupatorium seeds from her pocket. They were small and insubstantial. Alone, they would dry out, biodegrade, and become flecks of dirt. But with help—the help of soil, sunlight, water, and her father's ashes— they would become a beautiful, flowering life that could be used to help people in many ways.

Aspen's heart warmed when she saw Holly and William stride up the hill and join them. With Jamison and his mother, Claire, and Rad, all watching in silence, Aspen picked up a spade from near the base of the cherry tree and pressed it into the earth. She dug a neat, six inch by six inch hole. Then she set the seeds in the bottom and covered them with dirt. She took the thistle-urn and opened the top. She kissed the side of the urn, then poured her father's ashes into the earth. She stared at the ashes, gray atop the black soil, and felt a tear roll down her cheek, knowing it would be the last she would shed for her father. It dripped from the line of her jaw and landed atop the ashes.

There. Now part of her would be a part of him forever.

She piled the rest of the soil on top and smoothed it with the spade. Nearby, her friends watched with small smiles of understanding.

Rad strutted toward her. He stumbled a bit and his eyes were red. "You're a good climber," he said, and then walked away.

Claire stepped forward and embraced Aspen. Her frailty reminded Aspen how old her friend was. "Free crepes all week at the restaurant," she said.

As Claire waddled down the hillside, Aspen saw Holly tug at Jamison's hand. Jamison bent down and wrapped her in a hug. Then Holly's eyes became very serious.

"Is it okay if I'm best friends with William now?" she asked. "He just lost his and he needs someone to take care of him."

Jamison knelt next to her. "I would literally love for you to be William's best friend."

As Holly took William's hand again and led him down the hill, Aspen heard her tiny voice. "So get this William. A man wakes up in the hospital after having a serious accident and says, 'Doctor, I can't feel my legs…'"

Aspen covered her lips with her fingers and thanked God for eight year-old girls.

Jamison's mother stayed back as Jamison walked up to Aspen and took her hand. She looked into his chestnut eyes and saw such compassion, such love. Of all the things for which she had her father to thank, bringing this man into her life was surely high on the list. Jamison squeezed her hand and Aspen sensed that there were no words that could articulate the spectrum of emotions they both felt. So she motioned for his mother to join them and put her arms around them both.

They sat on the grass beneath the cherry tree, next to the newly planted eupatorium seeds. Aspen breathed the scent of butterscotch. She listened to the fluttering of birds in the trees and the lonely hooting of an owl. The sun was gone now, its last rays of light coloring the western horizon.

Near a wisp of purple cloud, Aspen saw the first two stars of the night. They twinkled in the sky and she wondered where her parents were now. Somewhere in the cosmos, or heaven, or even here in the garden? Could they have somehow put those two stars in the sky for her to see?

Probably, it was the time of year those two stars happen to be in that position. Probably, there were others in this world of billions who were staring at the same stars, thinking the same thoughts. Probably, they were all wrong.

But Aspen wasn't concerned with what was probable. She had seen enough magic to know that anything was possible. And then, as if in response to her thoughts, a light streaked through the sky. It was gone as quickly as it had come, but Aspen was surprised by its brightness. She had never seen a shooting star so vividly.

Another star shot through the sky, lower on the horizon. Then two more out of the corner of her eye. Suddenly, the sky was awash with meteors. Aspen basked in the beauty of it, amazed that it could be real. What happened next made her stand and stare in awe.

A giant wave of deep purple, glowing yellow, and crimson red danced through the sky, then disappeared. Then a blanket of emerald green skimmed along the clouds and was gone.

Realization slowly came to Aspen, but it only enhanced her awe. She thought back on her father's final letter.

On August 13th, when I join your mother, find the most peaceful spot you know, surrounded by those who have loved you the most, and gaze upon the beauty not only of this world, but of all that God has created.

August 13th. The annual Persieds meteor shower. That's why her father wanted her to wait eleven months. But the solar flares that caused the Northern Lights, could that have been her father too?

Aspen stared at the sky and knew she was watching a miracle. And suddenly she was certain of the perfect word for the day—*Content*. She felt the presence of her parents. She smiled at the stars, the meteors, and the Northern Lights. "I love you, mom," she said.

And then, finally, she said the words she felt sure her father could hear. "I love you, daddy."

She thought about what else to add. After everything they had done for her, after everything they had been through together, there were so many things she should say. And then she decided that what she had already said was exactly enough.

Jamison

It was true, Jamison had reached the end. But a different end than he had anticipated. The end of selfishness. The end of holding grudges. The end of pretending to be someone he wasn't.

But he had also reached the beginning. The beginning of a new life. A new love. And a new understanding of what it truly meant to live and love well. He had reached the beginning of a new story, still waiting to be told.

Amazing, isn't it? Who would have guessed that the end and the beginning could be the exact same thing? That was why Jamison felt such satisfaction, such excitement and such hope, to say that it was, indeed…

The End.

Author's Note

In the summer of 2011, a small bump appeared on the left side of my forehead. It started as an inconvenience. I began growing my hair out, hoping to cover it up. I wore hats. I assumed, given time, it would just go away. But three months later, it had only grown.

Although I had no medical knowledge to back it up, I began to wonder if the bump could be a tumor, possibly caused by brain cancer. My thoughts turned existential. I had lived a full, although short, life. I wasn't afraid of death. In fact, I could have faced it with complete bravery and grace had it not been for two things—my 4 year-old and 6 year-old daughters.

My first thought was, would they remember me? If I died, would they be able to picture my face, or hear my voice telling them how much I loved them?

At that point, I realized I was being selfish. My death would have very little to do with me, and very much to do with those I left behind. Rather than focusing on egocentric things like how I would be remembered, I had more important work to do.

I had heard enough stories about lives gone astray to know that the presence of a father has a tremendous effect on children as they grow. The absence of a father, equally so. From that day forward my life's work—for however long that might be—was to find a way to guide my little girls after I was gone. To help them when they needed a father who wasn't there.

So I began to write…

The story you just read has changed since the first draft, as does any work of fiction. But at its core, this story is my attempt to guide my daughters after my death. When they face difficulties, they can read this book and consider some things I've learned in my life.

That people have the power to change. That empathy is the most human of emotions, and forgiveness the most human of actions. The importance of caring for others, and for yourself. And of living a life true to yourself.

But more than anything else, this story is my attempt to tell my daughters how much I will always love them. Unconditionally.

Joe Siple
August, 2018

About the Author

Joe Siple is a television sportscaster turned novelist and speaker. His debut novel, *The Five Wishes of Mr. Murray McBride*, was named 2018 "Book of the Year" by the Maxy Awards and "Award Finalist" by the American Fiction Awards. Learn more about him by visiting www.joesiple.com.

Thank you so much for reading one of our **Literary Fiction** novels.
If you enjoyed our book, please check out our recommended title for your
next great read!

The Five Wishes by Mr. Murray McBride by Joe Siple

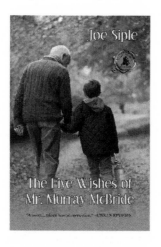

2018 Maxy Award "Book of the Year"

"A sweet...tale of human connection...will feel familiar to fans of Hallmark

movies." *–KIRKUS REVIEWS*

"An emotional story that will leave readers meditating on the life-saving

magic of kindness." *–Indie Reader*